Scheduled to Death

The Maggie McDonald Mystery series by Mary Feliz

Address to Die for

Scheduled to Death

Scheduled to Death

A Maggie McDonald Mystery

Mary Feliz

LYRICAL UNDERGROUND
Kensington Publishing Corp.
www.kensingtonbooks.com

LYRICAL UNDERGROUND BOOKS are published by

Kensington Publishing Corp.
119 West 40th Street
New York, NY 10018

All Kensington titles, imprints, and distributed lines are available at special quantity discounts for bulk purchases for sales promotion, premiums, fund-raising, educational, or institutional use.

Special book excerpts or customized printings can also be created to fit specific needs. For details, write or phone the office of the Kensington Sales Manager: Kensington Publishing Corp., 119 West 40th Street, New York, NY 10018. Attn. Sales Department. Phone: 1-800-221-2647.

Lyrical Underground and Lyrical Underground logo Reg. US Pat. & TM Off.

First Electronic Edition: January 2017
eISBN-13: 978-1-60183-665-6
eISBN-10: 1-60183-665-1

First Print Edition: January 2017
ISBN-13: 978-1-60183-666-3
ISBN-10: 1-60183-666-X

Printed in the United States of America

For my dad, who launched my love of community gardens and all growing things.

ACKNOWLEDGMENTS

Acknowledging the help of anyone is terrifying, because I'm so afraid I will leave out several essential and important people or accidentally include those who wished to remain anonymous. With that in mind, I want to give a nod to all my editors who work so hard to make Maggie and me look our best and who answer every question with great patience and expertise. And to everyone at Kensington and Lyrical, including those I've not yet met, who have worked to get Maggie's stories into the hands of readers. And to everyone in Sisters in Crime, my friends, and my family. The transition from writer to author is tricky and full of opportunities for new authors to become completely flummoxed. Thanks to all of you for having my back, holding my hand, and helping me up.

Chapter 1

We don't use the word *hoarder* in my business. It holds negative connotations, few of which are true of the chronically disorganized.

From the Notebook of Maggie McDonald,
Simplicity Itself Organizing Services

Monday, November 3, 9:00 a.m.

I couldn't be sure where the line was between a mansion and a really big house, but I knew that I was straddling it, standing on the front porch of the gracious Victorian home of Stanford Professor Lincoln "Linc" Sinclair. The future of my career here in Orchard View straddled a similar line—the one between success and failure.

I rang the doorbell a second time and glanced at my best friend, Tess Olmos. She was dressed in what I called her dominatrix outfit— red and black designer business clothes and expensive black stilettos with red soles. I wore jeans, sneakers, and a long-sleeved white T-shirt, over which I wore a canvas fisherman's vest filled with the tools of my trade. I'm a Certified Professional Organizer and my job today was to finish helping the professor sort through three generations of furniture and a lifetime's collection of "stuff" he was emotionally attached to.

The professor was a brilliant man on the short list for the Nobel Prize in a field I didn't understand, but his brain wasn't programmed for organization and never would be.

And that's where I came in. Organization is my superpower.

I glanced at my watch. It was 9:10 a.m. We had arrived promptly for our appointment at nine. Tess had arranged to use the house for her annual holiday showcase to thank her clients and promote her business, but she wanted to double-check our progress on clearing things out before she finalized her own schedule. All but one of the rooms was empty, but Tess had a sharp eye and might well spot something I'd missed. If she had questions about anything Linc and I had done, I wanted to be on hand to answer them immediately.

Participating in Tess's holiday event would give my fledgling business a huge boost. Endorsements from Tess Olmos and Linc Sinclair were likely to bring me as much—if not more—business than I could handle.

"We did say nine o'clock, didn't we?" I asked Tess. "I wonder if he overslept after that storm last night?" A rare electrical storm had coursed across the San Francisco Bay Area the previous evening, bringing buckets of much-needed rain. With it came winds that downed trees and power lines. Thunder shook my house to its foundation.

"What did the weather folks predict? *Isolated storm cells with a chance of lightning.* The morning news was showing footage of funnel clouds in Palo Alto. My dog whined all night." Tess bent to peek through one of the front windows. "Wow, you've really made a lot of progress in there," she said. "I can see clear through to the dining room."

I smiled as I stepped off the porch and onto the fieldstone path running across the grass and past the chrysanthemums and snapdragons that edged the front garden.

"Linc's been working hard," I said. "All that's left, beyond a few boxes, is his upstairs workroom with all that electronic equipment and research papers. I'm hoping to organize most of that today and take it to his freshly cleaned and cataloged storage unit. If it goes well, we'll tackle his office at Stanford."

I looked up and down the street. No professor.

"Where is he?" asked Tess, echoing the question I'd already asked myself.

"I'll take a look 'round back," I said. "He may be working in the garden or kitchen with his headphones on and can't hear the bell."

I followed the flagstone walk around to the side of the house and let out a yelp. My hand flew to my throat and my heart rate soared.

"Oh my! Sorry—I'm so sorry," I said to the woman blocking my way. I fought to regain my balance after my abrupt stop. "You startled me. Can I help you?"

"Humph!" said the woman, straightening as if to maximize her height. "I could ask you the same question. Does Professor Sinclair know you're here? He appreciates neither visitors nor interruptions." Her face was overshadowed by a gardening hat the size of a small umbrella. Green rubber boots with white polka dots swallowed her feet and lower legs, which vanished beneath a voluminous fuchsia skirt splattered with potting soil. A purple flannel shirt completed her outfit.

Tess's stilettos clicked on the path behind me. With one hand on my shoulder, she reached in front of me, holding out her hand to greet the woman.

"Tess Olmos," she said. "I'm Linc's Realtor and this is Maggie McDonald, his professional organizer. We're here for an appointment."

I scrambled in my cargo vest for a business card as the woman picked up the business end of a coiled garden hose. I had the distinct impression she was waiting for an excuse to turn the nozzle on us. I found a card, plucked it from my pocket, and handed it to her.

"I was checking the professor's house for damage after that storm last night," the woman said as she took my card and put it in her pocket without looking at it. "My nana would have called it a *gully-womper*. Nice to meet you ladies, but I need to get to work. For twenty years, the Sinclairs have allowed me to use their water in my community garden." She waved her arm toward an overgrown hedge at the back of the half-acre property. "In exchange, I provide them with fresh vegetables."

"Of course," Tess said as if she knew all about the arrangement. "And you are?"

"Oh, sorry." The woman wiped her grubby hands on her pink skirt before shaking Tess's outstretched hand. "I'm Claire Domingo, but I go by Boots. I'm the president of the Orchard View Plotters Garden Club. We run the community garden in back of the house."

Before any of us could say anything more, I heard the screeching of bicycle brakes. Linc careened around the corner with his legs outstretched and his jacket flapping behind him. His Irish wolfhound, Newton, loped beside him and made the turn easily.

Out of breath, the professor jumped from the bike and let it fall to the ground beside him as if he were an eight-year-old who was late for lunch.

"Sorry. Sorry. Sorry," he said, scurrying toward us. "I had an idea for a new project in the middle of the night and I rode over to the university. Time got away from me. Sorry to keep you waiting."

Newton barked in greeting and lunged toward me.

Linc unhooked the dog from the bicycle leash he'd invented ten years earlier but had never sought a patent for. Once he'd created it and proved it worked, he'd lost interest.

Newton barreled in my direction. I stepped back and knelt to give him more room to slow down before he plowed into me. Linc had trained him well, but his exuberance sometimes got the better of him. I scratched him behind the ears in a proper doggy greeting before turning my attention to Linc, who picked up the bicycle and leaned it against the fence.

"No problem, Linc," I said. "You're here now. Shall we get started?"

Linc patted the pockets of his jacket, his jeans, and his sweatshirt and looked up, chagrined. "I'm afraid I've forgotten my key again."

Tess, Boots, and I each reached into our own pockets and plucked out keys labeled with varying shades of fluorescent tags. I laughed awkwardly and headed toward the back porch, knowing that the lock on the kitchen door was less fussy than some of the other old locks on the house.

"Let's add installing new locks to the list of jobs," I told Tess.

Boots followed us. We stepped carefully around some of the boxes of discarded clothing and housewares that awaited pickup by a local charity resale shop. I unlocked the door and we trooped in.

Linc shifted from one foot to another, took off his glasses, and cleaned them with his shirttail. He looked around the room, blinking as if surprised to find he was no longer in his Stanford University lab. I flicked the light switch, but the room remained dim. Last week I'd brought over a supply of bulbs to replace several that I'd found burned out. I must have missed this one.

"Did you lose power in the storm?" I asked Linc.

He answered with a shrug. "I'm not sure. Maybe? I was at my lab working on my project."

Boots pulled open the refrigerator door and plucked a bag of lettuce from the darkness within. It had turned soggy in the bag.

"I'll take this for compost and bring you back some fresh spinach this afternoon," she said. "The kale's coming along nicely too."

"Can I get you all a cup of tea?" Linc asked. It was a delaying tactic I recognized from experience. Sorting and organizing were nearly painful for this man, who was said to have several ideas that could reverse the effects of climate change.

"Let's get started upstairs," I said. "I want to show Tess how much progress you've made."

Boots rummaged in the refrigerator. "I'll see what else needs to be tossed, Linc. Go on. I'll let myself out."

"I can't withstand pressure from all three of you." Linc shrugged and turned toward the staircase that divided the kitchen and living room. I started up the steps behind him, then stopped and called over my shoulder. "Tess, I'm going to show you Linc's workroom first. He's been working in there while I've been tackling the other rooms." I mouthed the words *praise him* to her. Linc hadn't, actually, made all that much progress, but he *had* agreed on broad-based guidelines for culling the equipment and organizing some of his papers.

Newton nudged past us to lead the way up the stairs. When I reached the hall landing, it was dark. *Right,* I thought. *The storm. No electricity.*

Newton growled, low in his throat, then whimpered. Linc moved down the hall toward his office and workroom. In the doorway, he gasped and froze. His mouth dropped open. His eyes grew wide. He stepped back, but leaned forward with his arm outstretched.

"Whatever it is, we can fix it," I said, rushing toward him, terrified I'd tossed out something of great value. "Everything we moved out of here is still in the garage."

Peering over Linc's shaking shoulders, I bit my lip, swallowed hard, and grasped his arm as he tried to move forward into the room. We couldn't fix it. Not this.

"No, don't," I said, pulling him back. "Tess, get the police. An ambulance."

Tess moved forward in the narrow hall, apparently trying to get a look at whatever had shocked Linc and me. I shook my head and whispered, "It's Sarah. Just dial. Quickly."

I hoped my voice would carry to the kitchen. "Boots, do you know where there's a fuse box or electrical panel? Can you make triple sure the power is out all through the house?"

"What's going on?" shouted Boots.

I couldn't think of an appropriate answer, but I gave it a shot. "We've got a problem up here, Boots. Can you make sure the power is off, *now*? Please? Right now?"

"'Kay," said Boots, though I could hear her grumbling that she wasn't our servant to command. Her voice was followed by the creak of old door hinges and the sound of her rubber boots galumphing down the basement stairs.

I forced myself to look at Linc's workroom again. Nothing had changed. Sarah Palmer, Linc's fiancée, lay sprawled on the floor in a puddle of water. Sarah, one of my dearest friends, whose caramel-colored skin normally shone with warmth and health, lay facedown with her hand outstretched, clutching a frayed electrical cord.

Worst of all, the body that had once been Sarah's looked very, very dead.

Chapter 2

Whenever you're working with electrical appliances or systems, check at least twice to assure the power is off.

From the Notebook of Maggie McDonald,
Simplicity Itself Organizing Services

Monday morning, November 3, 9:45 a.m.

I'd always admired Sarah's smooth and beautiful skin, but today her face and arms were tinged a bluish gray that left no question the ambulance would transport her to the morgue instead of to an emergency room.

The smell of burned metal and singed flesh hinted that Sarah had been electrocuted. I yearned to rush to her side, to comfort her, but some part of me knew the wiser course was to avoid going anywhere near her.

Newton leaned against Linc's leg and nudged his master's palm with his nose, offering comfort and asking for reassurance in return.

"All clear," Boots shouted up from the kitchen. The stairs between the first floor and the second creaked as she trudged up them to join us.

"Everything okay up here?" she asked. "I'm heading back over to the garden, unless you need more help?"

"Thanks, Boots," I said, turning to speak to her as she crested the top of the stairs.

Her forehead creased as she looked from Tess to me and then to Linc. "What's wrong?"

Before anyone could answer, Boots shoved past Tess, moved toward Linc, and gasped. "Oh, no. Oh dear God, no. That's not Sarah."

Her hands flew to her throat. She took a step back and leaned against the wall. "It can't be."

I reached around the doorway to the light switch inside the door of Linc's workroom. I flicked the switch. No lights came on. The power was definitely off, but I kept flicking nervously, as if that could somehow revitalize Sarah.

"Emergency is on its way," Tess said, putting her phone back in her tidy red leather business tote. She pulled it out again immediately. Touching Linc's back, she asked, "Is there someone I can call for you?"

Linc looked at Tess, then at me, and took a half step forward. "I have to go to her," he said, gulping and wiping tears from his eyes.

Both Tess and I had a little experience with the police and sudden deaths. We looked at each other and then at the distraught man who reached toward his fiancée, looking desperate to touch her.

In my heart, I felt Linc's need for comfort probably outweighed any damage he might do to the evidence. But my head said the police would need the room to remain undisturbed and I feared nothing would bring Linc comfort. Not for a long time.

"Linc," I said softly. "You can't. The police. They need to examine everything first. To find out what happened."

"What happened?" asked Linc, staring through me and speaking in a voice that sounded nothing like his own. "It's Sarah. Sarah's gone, that's what happened. I can't leave her here like this. I can't."

"You don't have to. You and Newton can stay here until the police come, but you must keep out of the room."

I put both hands on Linc's chest, pressing him gently backwards at the same time he leaned forward with an atavistic need to protect and comfort the woman he loved. His shoulders slumped. He stumbled backward and sank to the floor, leaning heavily on the wall behind him.

I left Tess upstairs with Linc and went downstairs to await the police and flag them down if they had any trouble finding the house. That's what I'd told Tess, anyway. But once outside I bent over, put my hands on my knees, and sucked in deep, cool breaths of the rain-freshened air. I shook my head. How on earth could any of us live in a world without Sarah? She was one of those people who provided the glue that held a group of friends together. The elastic that kept anyone from straying too far from the center or from feeling like an outsider, lost and alone.

I looked up and down the street, which was empty now that the kids were in school and the adults had headed off to work. Everything looked just as it had a few minutes earlier, before we knew Sarah was dead. *How on earth could it look so much the same when so many things had changed?*

I stood and paced back and forth on the sidewalk in front of the house, mentally listing all the things that Linc would need to do. Who would need to be notified? Did Sarah have other family? I couldn't remember, which made me feel like a terrible friend. I knelt and retied my already neatly tied sneakers, which made me feel like an idiot.

It seemed as though hours had passed, but I'd probably been waiting only a few minutes when a green Subaru pulled into the driveway. The car sported a mountain bike on the roof and I wondered if the driver, Paolo Bianchi, had been hitting the trails before work. Paolo climbed out of the driver's seat. He wore khakis with a button-down shirt and tie, and a gold detective's badge clipped to his belt. Detectives in many local police departments still wore suits and ties, but Orchard View was a small force and the old chief had mandated a more casual look to help detectives seem more approachable.

"Morning, Paolo," I called, crossing the front lawn. Paolo waved while rummaging in his overstuffed messenger bag. He triumphantly pulled out the tablet he used for taking case notes and nearly tripped as he stepped from the driveway onto the grass.

"Morning, Paolo," I tried again, reaching out my hand to shake his. He enveloped me in a hug.

"Hey, Maggie," he said, releasing me and smiling. "How can I help? Who is hurt?" Paolo spoke a tad too loudly and stopped as if he'd heard his own voice and realized it wasn't quite appropriate to the situation. The youngest detective on the force, his manners were a little rough around the edges and he lacked confidence in unscripted situations—especially in the absence of his mentor, Detective Jason Mueller.

"It's Sarah Palmer." I turned and waved my hand toward the house. "She's d—dead, I'm afraid. It must have happened sometime—er, sometime last night."

Paolo sighed, gestured toward the house, and said. "Let's take a look."

I thought I'd followed him immediately, but he must have detected some hesitation on my part because he turned around and smiled. "It will be okay, Maggie. We'll take care of it, whatever it is. If you don't want to come inside, just tell me where she is."

I trudged forward and tried to pull myself together. Before we reached the porch, a black Orchard View police SUV came screaming around the corner with the siren on and lights flashing. My eyebrows drew together and I frowned.

The noise clashed with my need for a somber, respectful atmosphere in which to grieve the death of my friend.

The SUV screeched to a stop at the curb, facing the wrong way on the street. I sighed, knowing that the investigation of a death—any death—seldom considered the needs of grieving relatives and friends. I watched as an older man I'd never met opened the car door and leveraged his considerable bulk from the front seat. Standing, he smoothed his shirt over his belly and adjusted his tie, his ill-fitting suit, and his sunglasses before scowling and approaching the house.

"Who's that?" I whispered to Paolo. "Where's Jason?" Detective Jason Mueller was a friend of my family and he'd gone above and beyond to help us out. While Orchard View detectives theoretically investigated all cases, with no specialized robbery or homicide teams, I'd understood that Jason was typically dispatched to the scene of violent or unexpected deaths.

"I'll fill you in later," Paolo said. "Follow my lead for now."

I'd expected Paolo to tell me Jason would arrive shortly. His cryptic answer made me turn to look at him, my eyebrows raised in question.

"Later," he said through a clenched jaw. "Not now."

Paolo descended the porch steps to greet the detective.

"What we got?" the detective asked.

"I just arrived a moment ago myself, sir," Paolo said. "I'd like to introduce you to Mrs. Maggie McDonald, a friend of Detective Mueller. Maggie, this is Acting Detective Lieutenant Gordon Apfel."

I shook the man's damp hand.

"Are you the homeowner, Mrs. McDonald?" he asked.

I shook my head. "No, I'm employed by Professor Lincoln Sinclair, who owns the house. Sarah Palmer is his fiancé. Sarah *was* Linc's fiancé. She's dead. We found her this morning."

"Yes, yes." said the detective, dismissing me. "Wait here, please. We'll have questions for you shortly." He cleared phlegm from his throat and brushed dandruff from the shoulders of his worn and too-small suit jacket.

I felt that I should escort the police inside and introduce them to Linc. Or perhaps we'd do better waiting for Jason Mueller. I wasn't sure where Gordon Apfel fit into the hierarchy of the Orchard View police force, but I was certain Paolo Bianchi wouldn't want to start an investigation without Jason's keen and experienced eye.

"Should we—" I began.

The detective cut me off, bringing his hand up like a crossing guard ordering me to stop.

"Ma'am. Please. I'm the detective in charge. Have a seat here on the porch." He hooked his foot around the leg of one of the wicker porch chairs and pulled it forward a full inch.

I spoke directly to Paolo, ignoring the older detective. "Paolo, we've turned off the electricity. Tess, Linc, and someone named Boots are upstairs. Tess may need help moving Linc away from Sarah. He's understandably very upset."

"You let him touch the body?" The detective I was now referring to in my head as "Detective Awful" looked from Paolo to me and back again, as if he were unsure which of us he should arrest first. "That's a misdemeanor."

I stared back, unsure how to respond. I didn't think I'd done anything wrong. Linc had been outside the room when I'd left him, and Tess would know to keep Linc from touching Sarah. Paolo said nothing. He just stood aside, inviting Detective Awful to precede him into the house.

Making an effort to shake off the discomfort Detective Awful had left with me, I sat down, choosing the couch instead of the chair the detective had touched. I pulled out my phone and stared at it. I scrolled through emails, too distracted to absorb what I was reading. I was relieved when Tess, Linc, Boots, and Newton emerged from the house.

"We've been dismissed," Tess said. "But asked not to leave the scene."

Boots looked uncomfortable. "I need to get over to the garden." She looked around as if in search of an escape route.

"I can't leave Sarah," Linc said, staring over his shoulder into the house.

I patted the cushion next to me on the couch. "Sit down, Linc.

Paolo Bianchi is a friend and a great police officer. Sarah is in good hands."

"I'll go make tea," Tess said, "for while we're waiting." I'd known Tess long enough to be able to see that underneath her warm words and demeanor, she was bristling with anger. I could only assume that her first encounter with Detective Awful had gone no better than mine.

Linc leaned forward with his head down. His hands gripped his thighs. He sighed heavily, then looked beyond the porch at the quiet street. If I'd had to guess, I'd have said he was hoping to see Sarah walking toward the house. Newton scrunched his large body in between Linc's feet and the round coffee table. He sighed, squirmed to get comfortable, and dropped his chin on top of Linc's shoe.

"What time is it?" Linc asked.

I glanced at my phone to make sure I got it right. While Linc was arguably in much greater distress than I was, I had a sense that hours, days, or even decades had passed since we'd arrived at the house.

"Ten o'clock," I said. "It feels like we've landed in another time and another world, doesn't it?"

"I don't know about that," said Boots. "But I don't have time for that detective's nonsense. I hadn't planned on a delay like this today. He really can't keep us here, you know."

Linc sighed and shifted in his chair, then reached down to pat Newton. He pushed his hair back with his hands and leaned against the chair cushion. "This can't be happening. I'm a scientist. A trained observer. How can Sarah be dead? I want to click my heels together and go back to the world that makes sense. The one where Sarah is still alive."

"What did you see up there, Linc?" I thought it might help him to focus on something analytical. "Was there anything that might explain what happened or when? Why was Sarah here at the house in the middle of last night's storm?"

Oh my God, I thought. *Sarah didn't show up for work. They're going to panic, wondering what happened.* I reached for my phone to call the principal of the middle school where Sarah served as librarian. I pulled my hand back before I dialed the number. I guessed the police might appreciate postponing the explosion of gossip that would accompany the news of Sarah's death. They'd want to control the release of information as much as possible.

I didn't want to wait. I wanted to lessen the pain I'd felt upon seeing the evidence of Sarah's death. I had a sense that sharing the story would take some of the crushing weight off my chest.

Linc stared at a cobweb in the corner of the porch ceiling. His forehead creased as though he was rebuilding the scene in his head and painstakingly examining each portion of the room.

"The window was open," Linc said. "And the floor was wet. I don't think any of my equipment was disturbed. And none of my books or papers seemed damaged by the water." He looked out to the front walkway, where small puddles of water evaporated in the sun, giving the air a touch of humidity that was rare in the drought-besieged San Francisco Bay Area.

"What was she doing here, Maggie? Wasn't she supposed to be at work? She wasn't planning on meeting us here, was she?"

I shook my head. "I don't know, Linc. Your workroom was the last step of our project here. Was she trying to help out or hurry things up? Were you at her house last night or here?"

"Sunday nights, she likes to stay at her house by herself. She gets all her materials ready for school, gets her laundry up to date, and goes to bed super-early. I was here in the evening, but like I said, I had an idea and took off for my lab in the middle of the night."

Something was bugging me about Linc's story, but I wasn't sure what. It wasn't unusual for me to have trouble following his train of thought. His train was an express, whereas most people's minds needed to stop at every station.

Before I could figure out what was bothering me or ask another question, Tess stepped through the front doorway carrying a tray with a teapot, mugs, and a tin of shortbread cookies. She cocked a hip and stared at the low coffee table.

"Give me a hand here, Maggie. I don't think I can put the tray down without spilling everything into Linc's lap."

I jumped up to help and we spent a few minutes pouring tea, stirring plenty of sugar into Linc's cup, and encouraging him to drink and to eat. I couldn't remember where I'd read that sugar and carbs helped calm people in shock, but that was the prescription we were applying. Newton raised his head just enough so that his nose was visible over the edge of the table, sniffing.

I took three cookies and put them next to my own mug. Tess must have spotted my slightly guilty look, because she smiled sheepishly and grabbed a handful herself. "We've all had a shock," she said, as Linc nudged a cookie toward the dog's nose. Newton lapped it up with his tongue.

I took a sip of tea and felt the comforting warmth seep into limbs I hadn't known were chilled. "Thanks, Tess, this is great. Linc and I were trying to piece together what might have happened and what Sarah was doing at the house. Any ideas?" I cringed at the sound of my falsely cheerful voice.

Tess shook her head. "We had that electrician out a couple of weeks ago. His job was to check out the system and make sure everything was safe. I can't believe he made a mistake that would have killed Sarah."

Linc put down his tea mug. "Sarah wasn't an idiot. She knew about basic electrical safety. Yet she was lying facedown in a puddle of water with an electrical cord in her hand. She knew better than to touch an exposed wire while standing in water. Who does that? Definitely not Sarah." His eyes glistened with unshed tears.

I grasped his hand.

Detective Awful burst through the front door before I could think of anything to say that might comfort Linc. None of us rose respectfully, although I briefly wondered if I should. The detective sank into the last remaining chair without being invited and Paolo leaned against the porch railing with his tablet poised, ready to take notes. He looked to Detective Awful as if expecting him to take control of this impromptu meeting. Detective Awful cleared his throat and flapped his hand at Paolo.

Paolo looked at each of us. "I know you've had a rough morning, but we have a few quick questions."

Detective Awful interrupted. "We've got *plenty* of questions and will need to interview you each separately. Our crime-scene team will be here shortly."

"Crime-scene team?" I said. "Surely it was an accident?"

Detective Awful made a noise of disgust. Paolo jumped in to answer me.

"In any case of violent, sudden, or unattended death, the scene falls under the control of the Santa Clara County Medical Examiner/Coroner." Paolo spoke slowly and gently, which was giving us the time we needed to hear what he had to say. "We've called Dr. Pravadi, the MEC, and he's sending one of his investigators. He's also given us permission to call in some of the Orchard View officers to help us gather evidence."

"You mean you think it's mur–" I began, but Detective Awful interrupted, flapping his hand toward Paolo.

"Call again, Bianchi, they're late. For now." He turned toward Linc. "I understand you were the deceased's fiancé? This is your home? Not her primary residence?"

Linc winced when the detective referred to Sarah as the *deceased*, but nodded in answer to his questions.

"So where were you last night? Your girlfriend was here and you weren't?"

Tess gasped. There was a hint of something ghastly in the dreadful man's tone that we all reacted to. Newton growled, Boots made a tsking sound, and I leaned back in my chair to get as far away from Detective Awful as I could. Linc stared as though he hadn't understood.

I couldn't put my finger on what the detective was implying. Did he think that Linc set a deadly trap and protected himself by making sure he was elsewhere? Or was the detective saying that Sarah would be alive if Linc had been at the house to protect her? I wasn't sure. All I knew was that my hands were fisted, my skin prickled, and I was tempted to run.

Gordon Apfel was a jerk, that much was certain. Detective Mueller would never have been so insensitive to Linc's feelings. Where *was* Jason Mueller? We needed him. If Paolo wasn't going to contact him, I would. I reached for my phone, but before I could begin to type a message, Paolo leaned forward, putting himself between us and Detective Awful, almost as if he were trying to protect us.

"Linc, we're going to need to look at Sarah's house," Paolo said. "Do you have a key?"

Linc patted his pockets and shook his head. He looked at me.

I opened my bag, pulled out my key ring, and removed the key with the pink bumper that would open the front door of Sarah's bungalow. Organizing and clearing out Linc's house was only part of the job I'd undertaken with the couple. They wanted to maximize space in Sarah's smaller house, making room for Linc's things and weeding out duplicate belongings. Sarah was particularly interested in developing organizational systems that would keep them from driving each other crazy when they combined their households.

I handed the key to Paolo.

"I'd like this back, please, when you're done," I told him. "Do you need us on site when you're there?"

"I'll give the orders around here," said Detective Awful. "We're not in the habit of requiring civilians to help our investigations. You will all stay here until we get a few things straight. Bianchi, get the address and send a team to the dead woman's house. We want to learn all we can about her." He looked up and scowled at each one of us. "Before anyone messes things up."

He focused his attention on Tess. "You," he said, pointing his finger. "Inside. I'll interview you first."

Tess stood to her full six feet one inches, a height she achieved with the help of her stilettos. She was my friend and I knew her well enough to know that her dominatrix-like persona was an act. The real Tess was a marshmallow and a slob. But the detective was suitably intimidated. He pushed his chair back a few inches and looked up at Tess's face.

"Sir," she said. "Detective Awful, is it?" I held my hand to my mouth to hide an uncontrolled smirk, delighted that Tess had come up with the same disrespectful nickname that I had for the man.

"*Apfel*. Gordon Apfel."

"I'm happy to answer any questions you might have, but right now, I have a meeting." She handed him her card, staring him down and forcing him to scoot backward.

"You can reach me on my cell phone to make an appointment. Tomorrow afternoon at two o'clock would work well, at my office. The address is on the card."

Tess turned her head toward me and away from the detective. Out of his line of sight, she winked at me and mouthed the words *call you in a minute*. She strode down the steps and walked to her sleek black BMW, heels clicking on the front walk. Before anyone could react, she'd jumped into her car and was gone.

Chapter 3

Organization isn't always about efficiency. A well-organized system gives most people a comforting and workable routine to follow during stressful or busy times.

From the Notebook of Maggie McDonald,
Simplicity Itself Organizing Services

Monday, November 3, 10:30 a.m.

If Detective Awful had been a porcupine, Tess would have been imbedded with sharp quills. But all Tess had done was stand up to him.

And she was right. Detective Awful couldn't hold her there and couldn't force her to talk to him. His response to Tess's assertiveness was that of most puffed-up bullies. He deflated and converted his aggression into anger. Tess had stormed off, leaving me to respond to his red face, clenched teeth, fisted hands, and splayed feet. But she didn't leave me completely alone. Just as the detective opened his mouth to begin grilling me, my phone rang. I looked at the screen. It was Tess, calling just as she'd promised.

I held up one finger. "Hold that thought, Detective," I said. "I need to take this call. And I may have to leave right away." I stood and walked to the corner of the wraparound porch.

"Thanks, Tess," I whispered. "Who is this guy? Why isn't Jason here?"

"I have no idea. We need to get the story from Paolo. Or, even better, as soon as I get off the phone with you, I'm calling Jason directly. Apfel's a caricature, like someone they dug up from an old movie about corrupt and inept police officers."

"Linc's exhausted. I need to get him out of here before he falls on his face."

"Need any help with that?"

I shook my head and whispered into the phone. "I don't think so. Text me again in ten minutes, just in case."

"Will do," Tess said, hanging up without saying good-bye. That was Tess. She had excellent manners and was as warm and caring as anyone I'd known, but she wasted no words on the telephone.

I pocketed my phone and walked back to the grouping of chairs.

Boots stood, eased herself around the coffee table, and handed Paolo her card, ignoring Apfel. "Here's my card too. I really must go. But I'm happy to answer your questions later on." And with that, she walked down the steps of the porch and turned toward the back of the house.

Paolo nodded and put the card in his shirt pocket.

Apfel stood, fuming. "Now wait just a minute," he said.

Paolo took a deep breath. "Let her go," he said. "I know her. She works in the garden behind the house. We'll question her as soon as we're done here. She won't be going far."

I looked to Paolo with my eyebrows raised. "What comes next?" I asked. "Linc is exhausted. Can I take him over to Sarah's for now?"

Apfel bristled and Paolo leaned forward to answer my question. I guessed he was trying not to let the detective alienate us any more than he already had.

"We can catch up with all of you later," Paolo said. He turned to Apfel. "Detective, I know these procedures may seem a little informal to you, but I know these people. They'll cooperate."

Paolo was sweating, though he was an athlete, lean and fit, and the late-fall day was cool. I put it down to nervousness. His jaw muscle bulged as he gritted his teeth, awaiting Apfel's response.

"This is no way to run an investigation," Apfel said. "We'll see what the chief has to say about this."

"Yes, sir," Paolo said. "Would you like me to continue here?"

"By all means." Apfel gestured for Paolo to go on. "You can't mess things up any more than you already have."

Detective Awful's barbed remark was unfair, I thought, as Paolo flinched. Paolo was young but learning fast.

Paolo focused on Linc, not giving Apfel a chance to change his mind. "Linc, if you have a minute, I'd like to fill you in on what's going to happen over the next few days."

"Thank you," Linc sighed heavily and slumped against the cushions with his hands clasped tightly in his lap.

"First, here's my card." Paolo handed one card to Linc and another to me. "Call anytime. If you've got questions, think of something we should know, if you're worried, or for any reason at all, please call. We're here to help."

I smiled at Paolo's remarks to Linc. I'd heard the same words from his supervisor Jason Mueller when the team was investigating a death at my house last August. And yet where was Jason? I couldn't believe Paolo had *asked* to work with the dreadful Detective Awful instead of Jason, one of the most decorated and respected police detectives in the county.

"This process always takes longer than anyone anticipates," said Paolo to Linc. "An ambulance will be here in a few minutes to take Sarah to the doctor, who will care for her from here on out and learn everything he can. That's Dr. Pravadi, the medical examiner. I'll keep you posted on that process and you can let us know if there's a funeral home you'd like us to coordinate with."

Linc looked gray.

"I can help Linc with that, Paolo," I said.

Detective Awful sneered. "You seem to be very close to the professor here, ma'am. What's your name again? And your connection?"

Paolo interrupted before I had a chance to tell the detective exactly what I thought of him.

"Professor Sinclair," Paolo said, "the police will be working here and at Sarah's house for several hours at least. We can't let you have access to either home until our guys are finished collecting evidence and the room here has been professionally cleaned. Do you have another place you can stay? Someone you can stay with? Family maybe . . . or friends?"

"Max and I would love to have you stay with us," I told Linc. "I can offer you our third-floor guest bedroom and bath, if you don't mind stairs."

"What about Newton? And Jelly?" Linc asked.

"Maybe Paolo can bring Jelly over later." I looked at Paolo, whose eyebrows were raised in question.

"Jelly is Sarah's kitten," Linc explained. "It was meant to be Jellicle, based on the cats in T.S. Eliot's book, but that seemed too long for such a tiny cat, so we shortened it." Linc stumbled over the memory, but it seemed important to him to share it and none of us interrupted.

I quickly agreed that Linc, Newton, and Jelly were all welcome at our house for as long as they needed to stay. Paolo promised to bring Jelly over later that afternoon. He said he'd also throw a few clothes and basic toiletries into a duffel for Linc. That kind of service might not be usual for the police in big cities, but Orchard View was a special community, and we did everything a little differently.

We wrapped things up and prepared to leave. Detective Awful huffed and puffed like the Big Bad Wolf. I followed Boots's and Tess's example and handed him one of my own business cards. Then I walked to my car, focused on urging Linc along and ignoring the fuming detective behind us. I suspected Paolo would bear the brunt of the detective's wrath as soon as we pulled away from the curb. I was also certain that the next time we saw Apfel we'd pay the price for outwitting him today.

But I'd worry about that when the time came. For now, my job was to get Linc and Newton back to my house.

Just before I started the engine, Paolo jogged across the lawn and knocked on the passenger window. Linc fumbled with the unfamiliar switches, but managed to lower the window.

"Sorry," Paolo said. "A quick question. Was Sarah ill? Or worried about anything?"

Linc shook his head. "She was managing all the details for our wedding. She could have been worried about that, I guess. But it all seemed to be going smoothly. She said anything that didn't work out would make a great story later, so no, I don't think she was worried." He shook his head again. "No. I would have known. She would have told me if something was bothering her."

"An illness?" Paolo prompted.

"Like I said, I would have known."

Paolo thanked him. Linc pushed the button to raise the window. I put the car in gear and we set off. I didn't think Linc much cared where he was at this point, but I was aching for the security of my home.

I glanced toward Linc at a stoplight. He had deep circles under his eyes. He'd been up half the night in his lab and returned home to a horror he couldn't possibly have imagined. Newton sat in the backseat, but rested his chin on Linc's shoulder, snuffling his ear and whining quietly.

I pulled into our driveway, dislodging Newton as I bounced over the ruts and potholes that were still on our list to repair. Our family—me, my husband, Max, and our two adolescent boys, David and Brian—had moved into the house three months earlier, along with our golden retriever and two cats. We'd whipped the house into shape pretty quickly, but then an arsonist had torched our barn and we'd focused on rebuilding and ignored the driveway. I hoped we'd have time to get it fixed before it turned to a quagmire when the winter rains started in earnest.

"It's a beautiful house, Maggie," Linc said as we climbed the stairs to the front porch. I could tell that his words were the habit of a man who strived to show good manners. Everything Linc said had a stilted, emotionless quality as if he were a puppet being operated remotely.

The three-story, 1920s-era Craftsman home truly was, however, beautiful. It sat on a hill that stretched down to a small creek, beyond which Midpeninsula Regional Open Space land extended into the Coast Range and all the way to the Pacific Ocean. It had belonged to my husband's great-aunt and we were thrilled she'd left it to us, along with funds sufficient to manage the taxes and upkeep. Otherwise, there's no way we could have afforded it. We were lucky and every member of my family knew it.

I unlocked the front door and was greeted at once by our exuberant golden retriever, Belle. Wagging her tail, she made little hops toward me and away, head-butting my knees in greeting. We'd trained her not to jump and she didn't, but every muscle in her body tensed as she fought the urge to leap up and lick my face to welcome me home. Then she spotted Newton. Both dogs barked in greeting and performed as doggy etiquette required, sniffing each other's rears and circling with tails wagging. I knelt and grabbed hold of both collars. "Belle," I said, "This is Linc and Newton. They will be our guests for a few days." I ruffled Newton's ears to give Linc a chance to get to know Belle.

Linc knew how to properly greet a dog in her own home. He sank to his knees, patted her head and rubbed her chest. "Hello, Belle," he said in a strained voice. "I've had a rough morning." Belle smiled as only a golden retriever can, leaned against him and raised her brown eyes to his, adoringly. Linc buried his head in her fur and hugged her.

"I'm bringing in an interloper later," he said. "A very small kitten not worth noticing at all."

I left them to their bonding moment and dropped my purse and file bag on the dining-room table—a disastrous jumble of homework projects, bills waiting to be paid, marketing materials, and other papers relating to my business. As a professional organizer, I advised my clients how to avoid creating disaster zones like this one. Long-term, Max and I planned to install a home office to better organize my business and all of its associated paperwork, samples, and other paraphernalia.

Max needed some space of his own too. He worked for Influx as a software manager and could work from home as easily as he could from his office in Santa Clara. The problem was that neither Max nor I could decide whether the newly rebuilt barn or the attic was the best place for our offices. For now, my husband and I shared the long dining table with Brian, our twelve-year-old, and David, his fourteen-year-old brother.

"Belle, let's show our guests to their room," I said, and the four of us trooped up the two flights of stairs to the attic. Belle was an attentive hostess.

"The bed's all made up with fresh sheets," I said. Newton pushed past me and leapt onto the bed, sniffing and turning in circles to create a comfortable nest.

I nodded to Linc that we were okay with dogs on beds. Even if we weren't, I'd have made an exception in this case. Linc was in great need of the unconditional comfort that only a dog could provide.

"I'll bring you some sweats and a T-shirt of Max's for now. Are you hungry? Would you like some soup? A sandwich?" Linc looked dead on his feet. While I peppered him with questions, his shoulders scrunched up and he looked away.

"I'll make you a sandwich and bring it up in a moment with the clothes. You can eat it if it looks good to you. Or not. No pressure. I have to run a few errands, but feel free to explore the house. Sleep as long as you want. Take a shower. Whatever you need."

Linc nodded and sat on the bed. Belle and I clattered down the stairs.

When I got back with the sandwich and sweats, Linc was fast asleep.

Newton snored with his head on Linc's chest. I removed Linc's shoes without disturbing either one of them and covered him with a blanket, hoping he'd sleep for many hours, untroubled. Belle and I tiptoed back down the stairs.

I needed to tell Max and the boys that we had a houseguest. I sent a group text and then phoned Paolo Bianchi. It was time for him to tell me what had happened to Jason and how long we'd need to put up with Detective Awful.

While the phone rang, I told myself I should stop using that nickname. If I wasn't careful, I'd call him that to his face.

"Paolo? It's Maggie. Do you have a minute?"

"Sure. Did you get the professor settled?"

I briefly sketched out the plan for housing Linc with us and reminded Paolo that he'd promised to bring the kitten, a change of clothes for Linc, and basic toiletries for both of them.

"That kitten is madly in love with one of our techs," Paolo said. "I had to put her in the crate so she'd stop getting in the way of the investigation. You know how we wear those puffy booties? Like shower caps for shoes? Jelly thinks they're cat toys."

I laughed. "I look forward to meeting her. In the meantime, what's with Gordon Apfel? What happened to Jason? Did he get a promotion or something?"

Through the phone came a sound I could only describe as an anguished, snorting growl. And then silence.

"Paolo?"

"Argrh," Paolo said. "It's just that I don't know where to start and I don't want anyone to overhear me."

"Just tell me what happened to Jason, then."

"He broke his femur heading up SWAT training. He may still be in the hospital—" I could hear someone in the background talking to Paolo. "Hang on, Maggie."

I sat down, feeling a little dizzy as I imagined the horror of pain, infection, and inactivity that a broken femur could inflict on an action-oriented alpha male like Jason. I was only half-aware of the muffled conversation that came from the phone.

"Look, Maggie, I gotta go. Call Stephen. He'll tell you what's up with Jason. Or I can stop by and fill you in this afternoon. We're going to wrap things up quickly. It's not a crime scene here at Sarah's. We're just looking for clues and background on Sarah and Linc."

"Stopping by as a cop or a friend?"

"Friend," Paolo said. "As long as I can ditch Gordon Apfel."

"Later, then," I said. "I've got chili on the stove."

Chili wasn't, in fact, on the stove, or even near the stove, but I started to write the ingredients I'd need on my grocery list while I dialed Stephen Laird.

Stephen was Jason's husband and one of the kindest men I'd ever met. A disabled veteran, he suffered from post-traumatic stress disorder and was missing about half of his right foot following an explosion in Afghanistan. He was an enormous man and was always in the company of an enormous dog—a mastiff named Munchkin.

"Stephen?" I said when the phone stopped ringing. "It's Maggie. I heard Jason was hurt. How are you both?"

Stephen sighed. "He got out of the hospital yesterday."

"What happened?"

"It was a SWAT workshop. He signs up every time they need instructors. He gets paid, but mostly it's a fun thing for him to do."

"Okay," I said, to let Stephen know I was listening.

"Right . . . well, whatever idiot arranged the training location, or secured the scene, or whatever they call it, missed the fact that the roof was rotten. Jason should have checked too, but he didn't. He was chasing one of the bad guys and fell through the roof. He's got a broken femur and a whole mess of lacerations from the sharp edges of God-knows-what sort of building crap that scraped him as he fell. But he's lucky—I'm lucky—he's not dead." Stephen stopped speaking with an audible catch in his voice.

"Do you need anything? I'm about to head to the store and I could bring you dinner—or eggs and milk and coffee—or give you a chance to get out if you're going stir-crazy. Is he up to visitors?" Jason had saved my life a few months ago and protected my entire family. Whatever he needed I would do my damnedest to provide.

"Some of the squad members and the guys from the VA have been bringing us food. His leg looks like something out of a *Terminator* movie—metal rods inside and out. He's on painkillers but he's still pretty darn cranky."

Stephen was the only Marine veteran I knew who used words like *darn* and *cranky*.

"Do you want me to bring you dinner?"

"Actually? We'd love dinner. But would it work for us to come to you? He needs to get out of the house."

"That's great. I know Paolo would love to talk to Jason about the case."

"Case?"

I paused, but I trusted Stephen to handle the news and treat it with the appropriate deference. He was no gossip. Living with Jason, he was privy to any number of police secrets and the need to keep them from the general public.

"You haven't heard? We found Linc's fiancée dead at his house. Sarah Palmer from the middle school? You met her, I think, at the potluck at our house in September."

"Slender? Deep brown eyes? An infectious laugh and an offbeat sense of style with sensible shoes?"

I burst out laughing. Stephen had nailed the description. Then my voice caught as I realized I'd never hear her laugh again. Nor be able to help her plan one of her teen-friendly events to draw more kids into the library.

"I didn't want to say anything until I was sure the police had notified everyone they needed to," I said.

"I'm sure it's only a matter of minutes until our boy Bianchi calls Jason for advice. He's been calling frequently, the past few days. Jason's been trying to help him develop strategies for dealing with Gordon Apfel, the guy they brought in while Jason's on sick leave." I heard in the chill of Stephen's voice exactly how he felt about the other detective. He coughed quietly.

"Sorry. Have you met him?" he asked.

"Oh . . . we've met," I said, knowing that my tone of voice must be nearly as revealing as Stephen's had been.

He made a harrumphing noise, but didn't say anything more.

"Look, come to dinner and you can fill us all in on Apfel, as long as we keep the conversation clean enough for the boys to overhear. I'll get Tess and Teddy to come too."

"Thanks, Maggie, you're saving my life."

"Hardly, but that would make us even."

"I don't know how long we'll be able to stay. This will be our first trip, if you don't count coming home from the hospital, . . ." Stephen's voice trailed off and I guessed he was second-guessing his decision to eat with all of us.

"Look, I get it. How 'bout this," I suggested. "We'll eat at the dining-room table. There's that big archway between the table and the living room. We'll fix Jason up on the sofa and he can listen in. We can even turn the couch around so it's facing the dining room. If he needs to snooze, he can. And if it seems like too much to take him back home tonight, you can both stay or leave early—whatever you want."

"Perfect—or as perfect as things are going to get around here for a while yet. But if he gets so cranky I want to kill him, will you either stop me or help me get away with it?"

"Of course! What are friends for?"

We covered a few other details and hung up, but not before Stephen had a chance to ask me to convey his sympathies to Linc. I phoned Tess and we chatted quickly. I told her we'd evaded Detective Apfel, but couldn't expect it to be so easy next time. I filled her in on Jason's status and invited her and her son Teddy to dinner.

I texted Max to let him know the hordes were descending. I knew he'd either join us or take the opportunity to get caught up on some work at his office. I also texted Paolo to let him know who all was joining us for dinner.

Ten people. An easy fit around the big oak table. Chili, a fruit and cheese plate, and a few loaves of sourdough bread would round things out nicely. I had plenty of milk, beer, and wine. We were in good shape.

I was headed out the door to get the chili fixings when my phone rang again. It was April, the principal at Brian's school.

"Hey, April," I said. "Is Brian okay?" April and I had worked together on a number of projects, but, like any other parent, when the school called my first concern was the health of my kid.

"Hey, Maggie. Brian's fine. I guess you've heard about Sarah?"

"It's dreadful. I can't believe she's gone." I didn't tell April I'd found her body. The longer it took for that news to get out, the better, as far as I was concerned.

"It's horrible," April said. "She was the healthiest person I know. And so looking forward to her wedding and moving in with Linc."

A silence grew between us as we both took a moment to think about Sarah. But April couldn't remain quiet for long.

"Look, Maggie, I've got a few things I need to go over with you, since you were Sarah's chief volunteer. Do you have a minute?"

"Actually, I was on my way out the door. I've got a gang of folks coming for chili tonight and I need to get it simmering soon. Do you want to come? We can talk then. Linc's staying here for a bit and Jason's coming over."

"Jason? That's great. I thought he was still in the hospital. I'd love to come, but library funding is on the agenda at the school-board meeting tonight. Can you swing by my office when you drop Brian off at school in the morning?"

I agreed and wished April luck at the meeting. In Orchard View, school administrators spent an enormous amount of time campaigning to keep essential programs alive.

On a whim, I texted Elaine Cumberfield, a retired principal who lived across from the middle school. I hadn't seen her since we'd worked together trying to tackle a spate of vandalism at the start of the school year. She knew everyone else who would be here tonight and it would be fun to catch up with her.

I hung up and texted Brian and David to warn them that we were having folks over for an informal dinner. I told the kids that if they had homework they could bow out early. Our guests wouldn't stay late. Everyone needed to work the next day.

I hesitated a moment, wondering if I should let them know about Sarah. Brian probably already knew, since Sarah was the librarian at his school. Knowing the remarkable power of the teenaged grapevine, every high school student, including David, had probably also heard. Either way, there was time to fill them in before our friends arrived for dinner.

I decided Max also needed to know. I sent him a text to call me if he got a chance. No one wants to get news of a friend's death via a text.

David responded quickly in teen text-speak—a language in which I was barely literate: *Great. Got ride. See you.*

I didn't hear from Brian, but that didn't mean anything. He tended to check his phone frequently, but seldom responded to anything other than a direct question.

The phone pinged again, alerting me to Max's text. I wondered if I'd ever get out of my driveway, let alone to the store and back. He wrote:

If I can't get home in time I'll call so you can fill me in. Sounds like something's brewing.

He knew me too well.

Tess also texted her RSVP: *As long as Detective Awful won't be there, Teddy and I will* she typed, followed quickly by *I'll bring dessert.*

Dinner would be fun, I thought as I dashed out the door. Or at least as much fun as anything could be with Sarah gone. But that's what friends are for: sharing both joys and grief. We were a tight group with bonds formed during the disastrous weeks following our arrival in Orchard View. But we were clearly out of touch. We needed to comfort each other following Sarah's death and catch up on the other minutiae that strengthened community ties.

Chapter 4

For casual entertaining, it pays to develop a signature dish you can throw together in a flash. One so easy, reliable, and great-tasting that even your best friends won't care that you served it the last three times they visited.

From the Notebook of Maggie McDonald,
Simplicity Itself Organizing Services

Monday, November 3, 6:00 p.m.

Linc was still asleep when most of our dinner guests arrived. As usual, when we had a large group with a whole lot to discuss, Stephen took the reins. After everyone had filled a plate with food, Stephen summarized Jason's story and prognosis, then asked Jason to tell everyone what he knew about Detective Gordon Apfel.

"Oh, man," said Tess. "I couldn't stand to see him adjust his pants or wipe his nose one more time. Please tell me he's a better detective than he seems."

Jason, looking like he was having a little trouble focusing, probably because of the painkillers, shifted himself on the sofa. "'Fraid not. He's had a long career of screwups. Started on patrol back in the late seventies. His grandfather and great-grandfather were cops and his father was a local politician." Jason took a deep breath, winced, and adjusted his pillows. "Word was, his mom came from money—the kind of money that gets you a board seat on a foundation that writes hefty grants to small-town police departments."

"Surely, over a forty-year career, *someone* must have noticed his incompetence," Tess said, pouring herself a second glass of red wine.

Jason nodded. "His family pulled strings to get him on the force and keep him there. Rumor has it he collects secrets that others would prefer to keep quiet. He had problems settling into the job, though. He started as a canine officer who couldn't bond with his dog. He worked with schools and youth groups until complaints about foul language and inappropriate jokes piled up and they moved him to night patrol. No one wanted to work with him because he wasn't reliable backup." Jason leaned back against the cushions. Munchkin whined and nudged Jason's hand with his nose.

"Don't worry, boy, I'll live," Jason said, patting Munchkin until the overprotective mastiff settled by his side. "During a downsizing effort following the dot-com bust, administration offered him a severance package that he couldn't turn down and we were rid of him.

"Unfortunately, that put him on reserve in a position to be reactivated when we needed extra staffing. Like now." Jason nodded at his leg, which was sporting an uncomfortable-looking steampunk array of rods and steel rings. According to Stephen, the break had required complicated surgery and more than the usual amount of support from internal rods, plates, nails, and screws, in addition to the external stabilizers.

"But why bring this Gordon guy back, if everyone knew he was no good?" Tess asked. "Surely there's someone to promote or borrow from a neighboring force?"

"You heard we have a new chief?" Jason asked. "He came up from San Jose and doesn't yet know who he can trust and who he can't. He's going by the book and the book says we rehire Detective Awful. Love the name, by the way."

Tess raised her glass to him and smirked. "Anything to help the team."

"So what does that mean for us?" I said. "Linc wants to get back in his house and find out how Sarah died."

"And I don't want Maggie involved in another homicide investigation." Max's deep voice rumbled across the front room and made my stomach do that little fluttery thing it always did at the sound of Max's voice. I was glad he'd found time to phone me earlier. I'd already told him about Sarah's death and about the friends who'd be at the table when he walked in the door.

He dropped his backpack on the coffee table and loped into the dining room with nods of greeting to his friends, a kiss for me, and a pat on the back for each of the boys. Belle stood to greet him and he rumpled her ears. "Let me grab another bowl and I'll join you. Does anyone need a beer? Should I open another bottle of wine? Turn on the coffee?"

Drink orders taken, Max disappeared through the pantry into the kitchen. While he made trips back and forth, Jason added a few more key points.

"The chief asked me to advise the team, but I can't drive and will be spending most of my energy on physical therapy. The bulk of the investigation will rest on Paolo's shoulders, so I'll be helping to ease that load and with handling Apfel."

The front door opened again and Paolo stepped in as if summoned by Jason's use of his name. That was the sort of friend Paolo had become—someone who could comfortably walk into our house without knocking. He said hello to everyone, grabbed a bowl and a beer, and stuffed a slice of sourdough bread in his mouth as he ladled chili into his bowl.

"Is Linc around?" Paolo asked me.

I shook my head. "He's still asleep upstairs. Should I wake him?"

"No, no, not at all. But if he's not awake by the time I leave, can you let him know that I'll bring Jelly by tomorrow? I got a call out to an accident scene while we were working at Sarah's. By the time I got back, they'd finished. One of our techs took Jelly home with her. We'll sort it all out tomorrow, if that works for Linc."

"I'm sure it will."

"I wasn't able to get his clothing, either."

"No problem. I fixed him up with some sweats of Max's. Now, sit. Your chili is getting cold."

Paolo perched on the arm of the couch near Jason's feet. He dunked his bread in his bowl, took an enormous bite, and washed it down with a swallow of beer.

"God, what a day," he said. "Great to see you, Jason. I'm glad you've got my back. I'm fighting Apfel every step of the way. He keeps wanting to stop at some doughnut shop. Drives me nuts—both the stalling and the fact that he's enforcing stereotypes of lazy cops eating doughnuts. He's not doing anyone any good. And his sense of what's important in this case is in direct conflict with what I think."

Jason closed his eyes and sighed. "I hear you, Paolo. But you can deal with it. You know how to handle the interfering public, like the folks around this table, right? That's the most important thing."

Everyone laughed again. We'd become involved in Orchard View's most recent homicide case following the death of a school principal back in September. Luckily, we'd helped more than we'd hindered the investigation.

Jason cleared his throat and the room quieted. "I'll find out which deputy district attorney will be assigned to the case and who will take lead at the crime lab. As soon as I know who the players are I'll have a word with them. If we tell them to contact Paolo or me if they can't get hold of Apfel, that should take care of things. He's not known for returning calls. I'll offer to help Apfel with paperwork he doesn't want to handle. That will keep me in the loop." He frowned and stroked his scruffy chin. He would need to shave soon or commit to growing a beard.

"Paolo," Jason said. "I've heard rumors that Apfel can be more than just an unattractive, lazy nuisance. It's been said he cuts corners, is quick to blame his partner for his own mistakes, and is not above planting evidence. He's fired on suspects at least twice."

"Is that a lot?" I'd grown up in Stockton, a rough-around-the-edges Central Valley city. While my family lived in a quiet neighborhood near a university campus, reports of gunfire were common.

Stephen put his hand on my shoulder and cleared his throat to get everyone's attention. "Most of the Orchard View force retires without ever drawing a gun," he said. "Both times Apfel was investigated after discharging his weapon, his family stepped in and he was cleared of wrongdoing."

Stephen scanned the room. "My take on the situation is that Apfel can be unpredictable and dangerous. Anyone near him should watch their back."

Paolo nodded at Stephen, who turned to me and frowned.

"Maggie, you're already in this up to your ears because you're friends with both Linc and Sarah, and because you found her. But you're going to have to stay far away from Apfel. Neither he nor the new chief will appreciate a civilian tangling with their investigation."

"But Paolo will keep us filled in," Tess said.

"I'll keep you as informed as I'm able," said Paolo. "First, I'm hoping you all can give me some background on Sarah and Linc so I can figure out what's going on here."

We all began talking at once. The noise level amplified as we struggled to be heard. Paolo stuck his fingers in his mouth and whistled, earning a grin of approval from Jason.

"Here's how it's going to work," Paolo said, drawing another laugh. It was one of Jason's favorite phrases. "I'm the cop. You're the civilians." He looked at Tess and me. "And in some cases, the suspects."

I drew in my breath with a hiss. I'd not thought about any of us as suspects. I knew I hadn't done anything wrong and would never hurt Sarah. But Paolo was right. We would become the obvious suspects if we weren't already.

"Let's talk about that," I said. "Who else could have done this? Did anyone have a problem with Sarah? Seriously? They'd have to be nuts—"

"Maggie," said Tess.

"I know, I know. Anyone who thinks killing someone is the simplest solution to a problem is, by definition, nuts. But really, who could have wanted Sarah dead?"

"You're right," Tess said, "but I was going to say that if Paolo is talking about suspects, does that mean Sarah's death is officially a homicide?"

Paolo shook his head. "It's not officially anything until we hear back from the medical examiner, but I don't want to lose any time if we're going to ultimately be investigating a homicide. Right now, the county team is examining the evidence and they'll let us know what it tells them. For the moment, I'm trying to fill in some holes in the picture. Unless anyone thinks she was likely to have committed suicide?"

A murmur rippled through the room. The consensus seemed to be that suicide was very unlikely, if not impossible. Small conversations erupted as they do among gatherings of good friends.

"Detective Apfel is focusing on homicide and looking solely at Linc." Paolo paused and held up the fingers of both hands to make air quotes. "Because it's 'always' the boyfriend."

"What's the story on Boots?" I asked. "I know she runs the community gardens behind the house, but there's something cagey about her. She has easy access to Linc's house."

"Boots is a character, all right," said Elaine Cumberfield, who'd arrived just before Paolo and had been listening carefully, but saying little. "Maybe *institution* is a better word. But I think she's completely honest." Elaine passed around a plate of her famous gingerbread men. Each cookie sported a cast made of icing on its right leg. Each face bore a chagrined expression that Elaine had accomplished with a few swipes of her pastry bag. The woman was an artist with gingerbread cookies and I told her so.

"Consider them an edible get-well card," she told Jason as she settled into a Shaker rocker and smoothed her cloud of white hair. "For the rest of us, they're a warning to look before we leap."

"Ouch," said Jason. "Way to rub it in."

"What you did was stupid, Jason. You're not in middle school any more. You're not invincible and it's time to stop acting as if you are."

We laughed, but Elaine silenced the room with one of her "I'm the principal" looks.

"Here's what I know about Boots," she said. "Her real name is Claire Domingo, but she wears those goofy boots everywhere, so she earned her nickname accordingly. She was a foster mom for many years and she's now helping kids who've aged out of the foster system. So many of them are cut loose as soon as they reach their eighteenth birthday. With no skills and teenaged judgment, they tend to fall through the cracks and Boots is trying to stop that. Many of her unofficial charges work volunteer hours at the garden."

"So, what are you saying?" I asked. "Is she like that guy in *Oliver Twist* who was running a ring of young thieves?"

Elaine smiled. "Nice literary reference, Maggie. But no. She's been known to skate close to the legal edge, but always for a good reason. I can't see her doing something blatantly illegal any more than I can see her wanting to hurt Sarah—or Linc, for that matter. Are we sure Sarah was the target here?"

We all turned to look at Paolo, who leaned back a little under the onslaught of attention. "Like I said," he began. "There's no official manner of death until we hear from the medical examiner."

Elaine frowned and leaned forward. "It's difficult to imagine what could possibly make someone angry enough or desperate enough to resort to murder." She paused and bit her bottom lip. "Although . . . tensions are running high over the need for a new school site. If you combined the gardens with the land from Linc's house you'd have just enough square footage for a public elementary school close to the downtown center."

Uncomfortable laughter filled the room and Stephen said what we were all thinking. "Given the opinions being shared on online forums and letters to the editor, folks around here certainly care enough and are crazy enough to commit murder to find available land."

"I'd say I'd never read such vitriol-filled comments," Elaine said, nodding. "But it's just the angry issue of the moment. The other matter that has folks riled up is the proposed curriculum changes. The back-to-basics crowd, the ones who say we should stick to teaching, readin', writin', and 'rithmetic has been especially vocal this year. I'm sure most of that crowd is peaceful, but when a group of them are at a board meeting, their comments grow particularly strident. It wouldn't be much of a stretch to believe one of them decided the best way to put their ideas into action would be to take out a librarian. Our district is the last one in the county to employ full-time librarians. Their salaries make for a hefty line item the back-to-basics crowd would love to eliminate."

I shivered. "There's a vast difference between crossing out a line item and eliminating a person. Have we all had too much wine? This discussion is getting really creepy. I know that I said we should think about who might have wanted to hurt Sarah, but if we continue speculating like this, none of us are going to sleep tonight. Let's shift gears. We've got Elaine's cookies and I think that Tess stopped at the Japanese bakery. Does anyone want more coffee with their desserts?"

While my guests began clearing our first course off the table, I went into the kitchen to start the coffee. Tess followed me. "Maggie, we've got a problem."

"Bigger than Sarah's death?"

"Of course not, but serious nonetheless. All the pre-publicity for my holiday tea has gone out. My schedule is locked up."

I stole a cookie from the dessert plate Tess was creating. She slapped my hand. I chewed the slightly salty chocolate cookie and thought about what to say next. My business plan depended on the exposure I would get from participating in Tess's holiday tea and upon endorsements from Tess and Linc.

Tess looked up as she peeled the fluted paper off of a cupcake. I raised my eyebrows.

"What?" she said. "It wouldn't fit on the plate."

"You can't be thinking of sticking to the schedule," I said. "Surely that's impossible now. Will anyone want to buy a house where there was recently a fatal accident or a homicide?"

She wiped chocolate frosting from her lips. "We'd disclose it, of course. The law requires it. But it would probably get us a record number of lookie-loos—the gruesome sort who would get a thrill out of Sarah's death."

It made my stomach ache to think of Sarah's memory being defiled by people who were looking to turn Linc's home into some sort of haunted house.

Max came into the kitchen carrying empty chili bowls. "Everything okay in here? Can I help?"

"I'll get these out on the table," Tess said, grabbing her dessert trays and heading back to the dining room. I handed Max another basket of bread. "In case anyone is still eating," I said.

"The boys are," Max said. "But I expect they'll be done as soon as they see Tess's contribution." He picked up the carafe of coffee that had almost stopped brewing. I winced as drops of coffee hit the heating element and hissed, emitting the smell of scorched grounds.

"This won't last long," said Max, lifting the carafe. "Can you start another pot?"

I nodded and he disappeared through the pantry into the dining room. I began loading dishes into the dishwasher. Tears welled up and stung my eyes. I grabbed a paper napkin from the stack on the table and buried my face in it before I had a chance to realize how scratchy and uncomfortable it was.

By the time I'd recovered enough to venture back into the dining room, Elaine had left and Jason was asleep with Munchkin snoring beside him. Belle was curled next to Munchkin, but awake enough to look up and thump her tail when I entered the room.

I gestured to Tess, Paolo, and Stephen to follow me into the kitchen, where we could speak freely without waking Jason. The boys had moved upstairs to finish their homework.

Just as we sat down, we heard Linc and Newton trudging down the stairs. On the last step, Linc yawned and stretched. Newton pushed past him and sniffed at Belle's empty food bowl.

"How long was I asleep?" he asked. "What day is it? Is it always so busy around here?"

I laughed. "It's Monday evening. I probably should have warned you about all our visitors, but you were sound asleep and I didn't want to wake you. Can I get you anything? Leftover chili? A sandwich? Dessert?" I pulled out a chair for him at the table.

"Coffee would be great, Maggie," he said. "Thanks."

I fed Newton some of Belle's food while Max poured coffee into a mug for Linc. He clasped Linc's shoulder in a manly display of sympathy. I put a few cookies on a small plate in front of him, hoping to tempt him into downing some extra calories. I wasn't sure when he'd last eaten.

Everyone chipped in on the cleanup while Linc went through the motions of sipping his coffee and nibbling on a cookie. Paolo filled Linc in about Jelly's location and apologized for the confusion.

We'd all joined Linc at the table when Stephen glanced at the kitchen clock, comparing the time with his watch.

"It's nearly time for Jason's next pain pill," he said. "I hate to wake him, but I need to get him home. Thanks so much for this evening, Maggie, Max."

Stephen, like Max had done, clasped his hand on Linc's shoulder in silent sympathy.

Max helped Stephen get Jason settled in the car. I stood on the bottom step of the porch stairs to wave good-bye.

"Please call, day or night, if you need anything," I told Stephen. "One of us will be here."

Stephen nodded. "Let me know if there is anything I can do for Linc while I'm home with Jason. Make phone calls, maybe?"

"Of course."

He opened the back hatch of his SUV for Munchkin and then settled into the driver's seat. Jason waved from the open window, his teeth clenched. It looked as though it was past time for those pain meds.

Max sighed as they turned at the end of the driveway to make the trip down the hill.

"You can't help everyone, Maggie," Max said, putting his arm around my shoulders. "I'm not sure there are enough hours in the day for you to do all you want to do with your business and help Jason and Linc too."

"I know," I said. "But it's not every day that a dear friend dies, either. I feel like I have to do *something*. April called earlier too. I'm so afraid she's going to ask me to expand my volunteer hours to help keep the library staffed now that Sarah is gone."

"We can talk it over later if you like, and figure it out together," Max said. "For now, let's see to the rest of our guests."

Back inside, Tess and Teddy were getting ready to go and our boys were getting ready for bed. Paolo and Linc were hunched over steaming mugs. Linc looked up as I walked in.

"Maggie, do you still have the electronic calendars you were working on for Sarah and me? They'd help Paolo map out Sarah's daily life and highlight what might have changed over the past few days."

I looked from Linc to Paolo. I knew Paolo was a friend and had Linc's best interests at heart, but he was still a cop and under the disagreeable thumb of Detective Awful, who I was certain would take the laziest and most direct route to nabbing a suspect. I didn't want to do or say anything that would harm Linc. The guidelines of my profession dictated that my loyalties were to the person who hired me. But my clients' confidentiality wasn't protected the way certain conversations with priests and doctors were.

Max shook his head as if he'd been reading my thoughts.

"Linc, I'm not sure it's a good idea to hand all that over to the police without checking with a lawyer first," I said.

Paolo's head whipped around and he glared at Max and me as though we'd betrayed him. I wished I could find a way to help both Paolo and Linc at the same time.

"But Linc's cooperating," Paolo said. "I need him to help me find out what happened to Sarah."

"Maggie's right," Max said. "Linc, let's have you at least talk to a lawyer tomorrow. My college roommate is a criminal attorney in San Francisco. If he isn't the right guy to help out, he'll know who is— more so than any of us, anyway."

Linc closed his eyes, turned away, and said nothing.

I went to him and touched his shoulder. "Linc, no one is suggesting you did this or that you stop helping the police. But Jason said that Detective Apfel can't be relied upon to do the right thing. I think it's a good idea to get advice from someone experienced and objective. If a lawyer tells you it makes sense to talk to Paolo and Jason, and gives you some language you can use to avoid talking to Detective Apfel, fine. But if he or she thinks that's a risky way to proceed, then you'll know. And you'll have someone in your corner in case you have questions later."

"Max, could you call your lawyer friend, please?" Linc said. "Paolo, I'll give you as much help as I can. Maggie has my permission to pass along all the records she has as soon as the lawyer approves it. You could get all that with a warrant, anyway. Talk to her so you know what we can offer. For now, though, I'm going to bed."

He stood, gave Max and me a tiny bow, and climbed the back stairs, followed closely by Newton.

I turned to Paolo, who still looked furious.

"I need to say good night to the boys," I said. "But after that, if you can wait, I'll give you a list of the files I have for Sarah and Linc. I can give you the complete files after Linc talks to the lawyer or after you get a warrant, but for now, you'll at least know what we have."

Paolo nodded, but I could feel him shooting angry looks at me as I followed Linc up the stairs.

Today had started out in the worst possible way. Now, nearly everyone I knew was a little ticked off at me. Paolo thought I was undermining his investigation. Max thought I was spreading myself too thin. April almost certainly wanted more volunteer hours from me than I could spare.

I needed time to figure out what I *wanted* to do, and what I *could* do, as well as what I *should* do. And figuring that out was going to take time. Time I didn't think I had.

Chapter 5

I recommend spending time on Friday afternoons cleaning up your desk, filing stray papers, and organizing
your Monday to-do list. It will help speed your transition
back to the work world after the weekend.

If you've had a hectic day midweek, the same technique
can help you feel more in control of your work environment and is well worth the time spent.

From the Notebook of Maggie McDonald,
Simplicity Itself Organizing Services

Tuesday, November 4, 6:00 a.m.

The next morning, we were all dragging. When we woke at six,
Max texted his friend Forrest Doucett to explain Linc's need for
legal guidance. Forrest phoned back and insisted on talking to Linc
immediately. I took Linc coffee, toast, and the portable phone. I
knew from careful monitoring of the light on the kitchen extension
that they ended up talking for at least an hour.

At 7:30, Max called up the stairs to the boys. "The bus is leaving
in five minutes, guys. Hustle up."

By *bus*, Max meant my car and his. Orchard View had given up
buses in the 1970s.

Max was taking David to school this morning while I'd take
Brian, then stop in to see April. I'd fallen asleep in the midst of going
over my schedule with Max the night before, but the quick gist of our
talk was that he was willing to do more of the kid transport and help
out in other ways if it would give me more time to tackle projects that

were piling up. He still hoped I'd say no to any suggestions April made to increase my library hours, but left the decision to me. We'd agreed to carve out more time to talk this evening and discuss solutions to the fact that physics dictated I couldn't cram more than twenty-four hours' worth of tasks into a twenty-four-hour period.

The kids' footsteps pounded down the back staircase into the kitchen. They were followed by Belle, Newton, and Linc, who was shrugging into his jacket while carrying his backpack and was in serious danger of getting stuck in the stairway. Belle looked back at him and whined. She'd apparently adopted him as part of her pack and thought he was taking too long to rejoin the group. Newton chewed on Belle's ear, then dropped it and barked as if asking for someone to please tell him what was happening next. He tilted his shaggy head and wagged his tail, indicating he was game for anything, so long as he was included. Some days, I wished I were a dog.

"Can you drop me at the house, Maggie?" Linc asked. "I want to pick up my car and stop by my lab before I meet with the lawyer."

I agreed and pulled out my phone as we headed out to the car. I texted April to see if we could move up our meeting, and she responded immediately, telling me to head on over.

I scrolled through the rest of my texts while Brian, Belle, Newton, and Linc got settled in my small SUV.

I was about to put my phone back in my purse when it pinged with a text from Paolo, asking if I could meet him at the school library. He wanted me to look around and see if I could spot any clues to problems in Sarah's life that might have contributed to her death.

"Mom, hurry up," Brian said. "We're gonna be late."

Brian's words knocked me out of the digital world and into the real one. I handed my phone to Linc, started the car, and backed out of the driveway.

"Linc, can you text Paolo and tell him I'm dropping you at your house, but after that I'll come straight back to the library to help him out?" Linc typed at lightning speed. I'd set up his phone earlier with texting, scheduling, calendar, and reminder apps. For clients like Linc who had trouble remembering a schedule and who found phone conversations stressful, the features of a smartphone were a godsend. Linc had taken to texting as if he'd been doing it since birth.

Brian yawned loudly in the backseat and so did Belle, which made us all laugh so hard I had trouble keeping my eyes on the road.

It wasn't eight o'clock yet and we already needed the stress relief of laughing at something that wasn't particularly funny. It didn't bode well for the rest of the day.

"Mom, are you going to work in the library?" Brian asked. "Can you still pick me up after school?"

"Pick you up after school, definitely," I said. "It's the best part of my day." Too soon, he'd be driving himself everywhere and I'd miss these precious minutes in the car. We might speak only a few sentences, none at all, or Brian would chatter nonstop about his day. It didn't matter. I learned more about my kid—and whether he needed help or encouragement or praise or guidance—in those few minutes at the start and end of the school day than I did at any other time in any other setting.

"Is Jason going to find out what happened to Sarah?" Brian asked. "Who is Detective Awful? Is that really his name?"

"Of course Jason will figure things out," I said. "Just because his leg is broken doesn't mean his brain doesn't work. He can analyze the evidence from home as well as he can from the police station." I dodged the question about Detective Awful. The derisive nickname helped me deal with him, but I wasn't proud of using it, especially in front of my youngest son.

I pulled up at the school. Brian grabbed his backpack, lunch, and trumpet case. He kissed Belle on the top of her head, patted Newton, pushed at the top of my head, and jumped out of the car. "Later, Mom. Bye, Professor."

He pulled his backpack higher up on one shoulder, lengthened his stride, and stood up straighter as he joined a group of band kids waiting to stow their instruments in the music room. I pulled away from the curb and tried to be patient as the queue of minivans and SUVs crept toward the parking-lot exit.

"What did the lawyer say this morning?" I asked Linc as we turned left onto the main road.

"Forrest? Linc asked. "He *does* think we need help, or I need help, anyway. He doesn't want us to hand anything over or talk to the police until he has a chance to come down here and find out more about what's going on." Linc looked at his watch. "I'm supposed to meet him around eleven. He has a deposition in Palo Alto and will call me after that. Turn at the next block to avoid the school traffic."

His voice didn't change as he shifted from talking about the attorney to giving directions and I nearly missed the turn before I registered what he'd said.

When I pulled to the curb in front of his house, we stared at it. I couldn't quite believe that it had been only twenty-four hours since we'd found Sarah's body. A piece of police tape attached to the front door had become detached at one end and flapped in the breeze like an advertising banner at a used-car showroom. It was tawdry and grim, and I wanted to run up and rip it off, as if that would bring Sarah back and restore normalcy to our lives.

I frowned. Linc turned toward me with an equally dour face. He shook his head. "I guess there's no way around this except through it," he said, and I nodded. It was one of those statements that made no sense and perfect sense at the same time.

"Thanks, Maggie, for everything." His eyes grew damp and he rubbed them with his hands. "*Thank you* isn't enough. I can't begin—"

"Linc, it's fine. Please don't worry. I understand."

He climbed quickly from the car, waited for Newton to climb out, and shut the door gently, patting his jacket for his keys. I held my breath until he pulled a huge key ring from his pocket. I wondered how he knew which key was which when he couldn't remember where he'd left the key ring.

Linc turned around with a look of desolation on his face. He bent to the passenger window. "Maggie, what have they done with my car? Where is it?"

I gritted my teeth and took a deep breath. I was late to meet Paolo as it was. I didn't have time to deal with the professor's inability to keep track of his belongings nor with the possibility that Detective Awful had seized Linc's car.

Linc stood on the sidewalk in front of his house, staring at his driveway as if it would make his car appear. Newton bounced about, bowing playfully and nipping at Linc's pant leg.

I turned off the engine and got out to help Linc stare at his empty driveway. I felt like I should be looking for tire tracks with a magnifying glass.

"Do you think you should call the police?" I asked him. "To see if they collected it? Or to report it stolen?"

Linc stood with his shoulders hunched, shaking his head and shifting his gaze from his driveway to the street in front of the house. Solving this problem was beyond him this morning.

And then I remembered. I put my hand to my forehead and smiled. I thought I had the solution to both this problem and one of the nagging questions that had bothered me yesterday.

I grasped Linc's arm gently. "Yesterday, you arrived here on your bicycle," I told him. "Do you remember?" He moved his head in what might have been agreement or denial. I couldn't be sure.

"You said you'd gone out in the middle of the night because you had an idea you wanted to test out at the lab. But it was pouring buckets on Sunday night. And the wind was howling. Why did you take your bicycle?"

Linc turned toward me and I was relieved to see a little life returning to his glazed expression. "Because it's not that far, and I can pull up in front." He shook his head. "No, you're right. I looked for my car and didn't see it. So I took the bike. And passed by my car where I'd left it in the parking lot. I was freezing when I got to campus, but there's a shower in the basement and I had a change of clothes."

I didn't know whether to laugh or cry. Linc's explanation was so indicative of the logical workings of his mind: He needed to get to campus. His car wasn't there. His bicycle was. Never mind that it was raining. And, of course he had a change of clothes on campus, because he'd done this sort of thing before. Or because he'd played basketball after work one day and left his work clothes there. It didn't matter. We'd solved the riddle.

Linc looked at me sheepishly and asked, "Would you mind?"

I shook my head. It wouldn't take more than five minutes to drop him at the university.

"Hop in."

Once Linc's immediate problem was solved, I headed back to the middle school and parked in the shade. Normally, Belle hopped into the driver's seat as soon as I left the car, rested her chin on the steering wheel, and snoozed happily until I returned. Today something was bothering her. She grabbed her leash in her mouth and pushed through the door as I was closing it. In a conspicuous show of obedience training, she sat on my left. She hadn't made a sound, but I had the distinct impression she'd clicked her heels like a soldier coming to attention. She looked up and smiled hopefully at me... with a touch of guilt.

I couldn't help but smile. Today, I wanted the comfort of her company and she wanted mine. I hoped that April and Paolo would understand that and allow her to accompany me. If not, I could always give her a short walk and bring her back to the car.

I attached her leash and she trotted beside me in a perfect heel all the way to the library. The door was locked, but I knocked and Paolo opened it.

"Thanks, Maggie," he said quickly at the same time I said, "I'm sorry I'm late."

"I'm sorry about last night," he said at the same time I said, "How can I help?"

We each stopped, took a deep breath, and waited for the other to speak. April bustled over, dressed in deep green this morning, head to toe. A feather dangled from her ponytail in a way that made me think of Peter Pan or Robin Hood. I didn't think the look was accidental. The April I knew thought of herself as Robin Hood: Bending the rules if necessary to help those at risk of falling through the cracks. In that way, she was like Sarah—and I realized, a lot like the way Elaine had described Boots. I tugged my attention away from Sherwood Forest and back to the matter at hand.

"Do you mind if Belle stays?" I asked April. "And would you mind putting off our meeting until after I help Paolo?"

April stooped to pat Belle and Belle responded by licking April's face. "I feel like I should say something clever about how Belle is the Disney character that loves libraries and books," April said. "But I can't quite pull a pithy statement from my brain. Of course she can stay." She turned toward Paolo. "What do you want us to do?"

Paolo looked around the library. "To get a handle on Sarah's death I need to understand her life. You've both spent a lot of time here with Sarah. I want you to look at the room and tell me if anything strikes you as different from the norm or if you see anything that looks out of place or that could be a clue to what happened."

April scanned the room, then stood and walked past the rows of library tables, touching each one. She turned when she reached the opposite end and looked back at us.

"Normally, when I was in here, I'd be observing the kids or getting to know them better, seeing how I could help out," she said. "I left it to Sarah and Maggie to pay attention to the nuts and bolts. With the kids gone, there's not much I can tell you."

She looked pensive and stood resting her hand on Sarah's computer. She patted it. "We can get you access to her records, if that would be useful. Or, we took pictures of the library last year for a fund-raising brochure. Would that help with any anomalies?"

Paolo shrugged. "It's worth a look."

I shook my head. "I wasn't here when the pictures were taken, but I remember Sarah looking around the room one day and snorting with laughter. There were kids sprawled everywhere. Some were asleep on their books and some lounged on the floor working on a project. She said that it wasn't picture-perfect, but that every inch of the library was being used and she liked that. She told me about the photo shoot, and how it was all staged and clean and the kids were all nicely dressed. She guessed that the fund-raising team knew what they were doing, but said she never wanted her library to look that stiff and clean ever again. I don't know if comparing the way it is now to the way it was for the photo shoot would do any good."

Paolo stood and then turned to me. "Okay, then, Maggie. You've seen this room more recently. Take a look and see what it tells you about Sarah."

I walked to Sarah's desk, spun her chair around, sat in it, and surveyed the library.

"It looks . . . like Sarah was behind in her work."

I pointed to the cart of books waiting to be shelved. "There are too many books here. The cart isn't organized. Sarah liked to have the books where students could find them. Shelving books gave her an excuse to move around the room and check on the kids. If she didn't have time to keep up with it, she would have asked a volunteer or a student for help."

I gathered scattered mail and catalogues into a neat pile. "She normally organized her desk before she went home—especially on Friday afternoons. It made her feel ahead of the game when she walked in the door on Monday mornings."

I moved to the front door of the library, trying to remember mornings when I'd arrived earlier than Sarah and watched her walk in.

"If there were any kids here, the first thing she'd do would be to greet them. If there were only one or two, she'd walk right up to them to say *good morning*, touch them on the shoulder, and ask how things were going." I walked to where April was sitting at one of the tables and I acted out part of Sarah's routine. "The regulars were kids who didn't have computers at home and needed to do their homework here before and after school. She always checked to see if they needed help—not just with the computers but general support. Particularly if they needed funding for school projects or trips. She has—I mean, she *had*—a team of people she called if these kids needed anything. Those adult helpers are mostly people who needed extra support when they were in school. They want to give back."

I stopped and rapped on the table with my hand. "The custodian. Valentin Diaz. He was part of that team. He also knows everyone's secrets from emptying out wastebaskets and tidying their rooms. He and Sarah were friends and he often stopped by in the afternoon to talk to her."

Paolo typed the name into his iPad and looked up at April.

"He's helping out at one of the elementary schools this morning, but he'll be back this afternoon," she said. "His kids all graduated from here. He used to run the hardware store downtown, but he turned it over to one of his sons a few years ago. Here, he works shorter hours. It's a pay cut for him, but he's got good benefits and it's his way of giving back to the community that helped him launch his kids. They've all got advanced degrees, I think. When his wife was ill and their kids were young, parents and teachers stepped in and helped out. Ask him about it. It's a great story."

While April was talking, I opened the refrigerator under Sarah's desk. Sarah brought her lunch every day, along with fruit, cheese, and crackers. If kids came in before school or at lunchtime, Sarah would feed them.

I pulled out two paper lunch sacks and held them up. "Linc probably packed these. When Sarah packed her own lunch, it went in her purple Gore-Tex lunch bag. Linc wasn't organized enough for reusable bags, but he was a whiz at packing lunches. He generally packed twice what Sarah needed, but that gave her more to share with the kids."

April looked at her watch and stood. "I need to get back to the front office," she said. "I have a meeting with a parent. Please, let me know if you need anything. I want to help." Paolo thanked her and she went to the door, opened it, and paused. "Maggie, I still need to talk to you about finding a way to keep the library open for the kids."

I grimaced. "I'm sorry, April. I really want to help, but if you're asking me to take over Sarah's hours, or increase my own, I've decided I just can't swing any more volunteer hours or even paid ones that take me away from launching my business. I'd actually talked to Sarah last week about cutting back."

April stared at me, frowning. "I was counting on your help. You're one of the good guys."

"Look, maybe we can get together later in the week and brainstorm ways to get grant money or interns from the library program at Stanford . . ." I stopped talking, because April's face had gone from dour to expressionless. I hadn't known her for long, but I knew she was very angry.

"Do you still want to meet after this?" I asked.

She shook her head. "I don't see much point. Do you?"

She left the library without waiting for an answer and let the door swing shut behind her.

I swallowed hard, feeling guilty. I was sorry to disappoint her and felt that in some way I'd disappointed Sarah too. But Max was right. I couldn't do everything. I focused on how happy he would be to know that I had stood up for my own schedule, instead of turning myself into a pretzel to accommodate someone else's. Maybe that vision of a happy Max would keep me from running after April to tell her I'd changed my mind.

Paolo cleared his throat and I yanked my attention back to the matter at hand. I opened one of Sarah's lunch bags and unpacked it, pulling out a big sandwich on homemade bread with cheese, tahini, and cucumbers: Sarah's favorite. The bag also contained a giant oatmeal cookie, a container of pomegranate seeds with a spoon, and a napkin on which Linc had drawn a heart with a red marker.

"I'm not sure why she wouldn't have eaten this. Or given it to a student." I checked her calendar to see if she'd gone out to lunch or had a meeting, but there were no meetings written in during the previous week—although there was a question mark penciled lightly on Wednesday, and a small circle drawn in Friday's box.

Paolo leaned over the front of the desk and spun the calendar around. He pointed to the marks and turned the pages, looking for similar marks or notes on other pages. "What do you think they mean?"

"I'm not sure. It could be a private code of Sarah's for a calendar that wasn't particularly private."

"Why did she have a calendar, anyway?" Paolo said. "Isn't one of the files you won't give me her iCalendar?"

"Yes, but she was transitioning to it. So was Linc. It's common for someone her age who grew up using a physical calendar to prefer using that—it's the 'If it ain't broke, don't fix it' school of thought. I encourage clients to go as green as possible, but if they've got a system that's working for them, I don't try to change it."

I opened the bottom desk drawer where most workingwomen stash their purses or backpacks. It was empty, as expected. But where *was* her purse? I hadn't seen it at Linc's house. And for that matter, where was her car? How had she arrived at Linc's house? I could see now why Paolo was trying to piece together details of Sarah's life and her movements over the past few days. There was so much we didn't know.

The upper drawer was carefully organized with separate slots for pens, pencils, stapler, rubber bands, tape, small bandages for paper cuts, and other supplies essential for a school librarian. It also held her hairbrush, which was full of hair. I picked it up and stared at it.

"Paolo, this is odd," I said.

"A hairbrush?"

"Not the brush, but all the hair in it. Sarah was one of those people who freaks out over stray hairs—on her clothes, in her face. I often wondered why she wanted a kitten. She always wore her hair in a ponytail at work to keep it out of her eyes. She had a lint roller in her purse and her car. It seems odd that she'd leave her brush full of stray hairs. There's—I don't know—maybe a week's worth of hair here." I put the brush back in the drawer and closed it. "That might be someone else you want to talk to. Her hairdresser. Women tell secrets to their hairdressers."

Paolo typed another note into his iPad and looked up. I gave him the name of the hairdresser Sarah went to in Orchard View. Lily Takahashi cut the hair of most of the women I knew, and Sarah had been after me to make an appointment with her.

I opened the last drawer, the center drawer of the desk, where most people keep odds and ends, and sweep clutter when they don't have time to tidy up properly.

The drawer was empty except for a letter. I picked it up and held it out to Paolo. He nodded. I wasn't sure what that meant. But, since Paolo didn't take the envelope from me, I opened it.

"It's from her gynecologist," I said after scanning it for a moment. "And it's bad."

Chapter 6

When you are worried, stressed, or afraid, talk to someone you trust. Spinning your wheels, hesitating out of fear or making the wrong decisions due to a lack of information, is never efficient. Most of the things we worry about will never happen. Most of the friends we fear are angry, aren't. A good friend, a wise coworker, or a trained professional can help you sort through your roadblocks faster than you may be able to do by yourself.

From the Notebook of Maggie McDonald,
Simplicity Itself Organizing Services

Tuesday, November 4, 9:30 a.m.

I felt my skin flush with embarrassment and quickly handed the letter off to Paolo. "Um, it's private, medical. Maybe I shouldn't have read it." But, as Paolo stared at it, I realized a young man might need more clarification about what the brief note implied. Sarah was gone and her whole life was going to be examined in excruciating detail, including her medical history. Privacy was no longer possible.

"Something's wrong with her mammogram or Pap smear or some other test," I said. "They're asking her to call immediately. They tried to call and couldn't reach her."

Paolo scanned the page and looked up. "The letter doesn't say that at all," he said, reading aloud: "*We'd like to redo your tests. Please call at your earliest convenience.*"

"That's code," I told him. "They don't like to scare people. But if there's anything weird, the office generally calls so they can explain and reassure and schedule immediately. They squeeze you in and find a time that the gynecologist and the oncologist too, if necessary, can see you right away. At least, that's what my doctors have always done."

"I'll call the doctor," Paolo said, blushing. "Maybe it was something less important than that, less urgent, and that's why they sent the letter."

I shook my head. "If it were nothing, Sarah would have tossed the letter. But look at the envelope. It's grubby and creased, like it spent time in her purse."

Paolo frowned. "It's not evidence, but maybe it's a lead. I'll see if we can get a warrant to look at her medical records." He tucked the letter into an evidence bag and put it in his backpack.

"You need to talk to the nurse," I told him. "She's the one who would have had the reassuring conversation with Sarah, encouraging her to come in. She might be willing to tell you how Sarah took the news even if she can't tell you what the news was."

I stopped for a moment. Something was bothering me. A memory that was begging for attention. I took a minute to clear my head.

"Paolo, didn't you ask Linc yesterday whether Sarah was ill? Didn't he say she was fine? But if you put all this together . . ." I waved my hand in the direction of the desk drawers and refrigerator. "Her hair was falling out, she wasn't eating, and she got a strange report from her doctor. Maybe she thought she had cancer? Her mom died from cancer and so did her sister. She had no family that I know of. April's been going through breast-cancer treatment. Sarah might have confided in her if she were worried. What if Sarah so feared cancer treatment that she decided to commit suicide?"

"It's a theory," Paolo said. "I'll look into it."

My brain threw up another memory then, one that made me feel dizzy and cold. I sank into Sarah's chair and leaned my head on my hands.

"Maggie, are you okay?" Paolo asked. "Can I get you anything? What's wrong?"

I shook my head. "I'm just feeling overwhelmed after losing Sarah." I couldn't tell Paolo what I was thinking, not now. According to Linc, the lawyer had suggested we keep everything from the police until he'd had a chance to talk to us. Even the most innocuous detail. And there was nothing innocent about the thought that had erupted in my brain.

*   *   *

After saying a hasty good-bye to Paolo, I dashed to the car with Belle, who pranced alongside me, hoping for a run. She tugged her end of the leash toward the sidewalk, toward Tess's house, a walk we often made after dropping off Brian. Visiting Tess and her dog, Mozart, was a highlight of any day for Belle.

I stopped for a moment and pulled my phone from my back pocket. Belle stared at me, tilting her head and lifting an ear as if to say, "Well, why *wouldn't* we visit Mozart? What could be more important?"

"Don't try that, Belle," I said more sternly than I meant to. "I'm on to your golden retriever mind tricks."

I walked toward the sidewalk and turned right, toward Tess's house, while I punched the number to reach Linc at his lab. But then I turned off my phone and shoved it back in my pocket.

I couldn't discuss what I'd remembered with Linc. It was too explosive. Maybe Linc's lawyer was the person to call. He'd know what I should do. And he needed to know the information I had. I couldn't be sure whether Linc would tell him.

What I'd remembered was earthshaking, or could be, but discussing it with the lawyer would cost money. Linc's money, probably. Was it right for me to use Linc's money to tell his lawyer something that might very well convince him of Linc's culpability? I didn't think so; not yet, anyway.

I phoned Tess, but the call went straight to voice mail. My hands shook as I scrolled through my list of contacts. I checked my watch. It was ten o'clock. I could talk to Jason, but he was a cop, and the lawyer had told Linc not to share anything with the cops. Not yet. But what about Stephen?

I let out a breath I hadn't known I was holding. I knew I could trust Stephen. He was ex–Special Forces, and he'd protected my family and kept me sane back in September.

"Come on, Belle," I said. "Let's go visit Munchkin."

At Jason's, Stephen sat on the front step, looking uncomfortable, twitchy, and unable to settle.

I pulled my car to the curb and opened the door for Belle, who leaped from the car and flew into Stephen's arms. Laughing, he stood and told Belle to sit and stay. She was almost successful. She sat, but certainly didn't sit still. She licked Stephen's hand and nudged it. Belle squirmed forward and head-bumped Stephen's arm, then froze, remembering she was supposed to be sitting. She did it over and over, looking much like a canine version of a bobblehead. I laughed. There is nothing in the world like a dog for helping you to find joy in a rotten day.

Stephen moved off the steps to greet me.

"Jason's therapist rescheduled for this morning, and she's still inside. He's cursing over his physical-therapy routine. His therapist looks about sixteen, but she's tough as nails—stricter than my boot-camp sergeant. I'm not going back in there until she comes out."

"Is Munchkin around?" I asked. "Belle would love to play."

We walked around the side of the house and opened the redwood gate into the backyard. We weren't two steps through the gate before Munchkin plowed through his dog door with a deflated rugby ball in his mouth. He growled, shook the ball, and play-bowed to Belle: front feet forward, head down, rump in the air, and tail waving wildly enough to upend a less sturdy animal. Belle bowed to Munchkin, and they were off, chasing one another around the yard.

"What's up, Maggie?" Stephen asked, inviting me to sit on the cracked concrete back steps. A former owner had enclosed the back porch, and I knew that Stephen and Jason were debating how to create an outdoor living space they could both enjoy. Stephen wanted to re-landscape, creating a stone seating area and fire pit. Jason was pushing for a redwood deck and a pool. Munchkin, as far as I knew, had no opinion on the matter.

I bit my lip and looked up at the hummingbird feeder that hung from an apple-tree branch near my head. A hummer paused and thrummed in the air nearby, apparently gauging whether we posed a threat, and whether he could outpace us if we did.

Stephen put his hand on mine. "You don't have to tell me what's bothering you if you don't want to, but you sure look like you want to."

"It's Linc and Sarah . . ." I began. It was a statement that could go anywhere. I half-hoped that Stephen would think I was talking about the situation in general and pick up the conversation so that I didn't need to go on. He didn't, so I continued. "Stephen, did you know Linc's first wife?"

"Mei? She died about five years ago, didn't she? Of cancer? I moved here shortly after that. Never met her."

"Neither did I, but Sarah told me about her a few months ago. It was just after I found out that April was being treated for breast cancer."

"April's doing well, isn't she?"

"As far as I know. But Sarah was telling me about Mei and Linc. Apparently, Sarah and Linc had been talking about moving in together, but they each had some issues. Sarah's biggest concern was Linc's disorganization and I offered to help them find ways to work with that. But Linc was reluctant to commit because of all he had gone through with his first wife."

I stopped and watched Munchkin and Belle fly around the yard and stop on opposite sides of a redwood trunk that was nearly four feet in diameter. Their tongues lolled from their mouths and they feinted, first one way, then the other. They were about ready for water and a break. But not yet. Munchkin made a move, Belle grabbed the rugby ball, and they were off again.

"Go on, Maggie," Stephen said. "I haven't heard this story."

"I'm not sure I should tell it," I said. "It might make Linc look bad. The lawyer told him this morning not to say anything to Jason or Paolo or any of the other police officers. That applies to me too, I think. The not-talking part, I mean." I sighed, stood, and walked toward the base of the apple tree. Belle walked over, dropping the ball at my feet. I tossed the ball to Munchkin, who caught it but then sprawled on the ground. Belle collapsed, panting heavily.

"You could wait to talk to the lawyer," Stephen said. I nodded and told him my concern about spending Linc's money.

Steven rubbed his hand over his shaved head. "You could talk to Linc."

He whistled to Munchkin and bent to turn on a tap at the side of the steps. He filled a plastic dish tub with water. Munchkin and Belle slurped loudly from the tub, splashing more water on the ground than they got into their mouths.

"Or, you could talk to me," he said, sitting down and patting the step next to him. "We've still got a few minutes before Jason's torture session is finished. I can't promise I won't say anything to him at some point, but I could tell you whether I think it's pertinent to the case and suggest folks you could talk to. I'll keep your secret as long as I can."

"I don't think it's actually a secret," I said. "And Jason may already know. I'm not sure how long he and Linc have been friends. If he knew Mei, he probably knows this story anyway. Sarah didn't have any hesitation telling me and she hardly knew me at the time."

I sighed again and took a deep breath. Not telling Stephen the story was taking a lot out of me.

"Apparently, Mei had ovarian cancer," I said quickly, as if it were all one word.

"Slow down, Maggie."

"It was bad. Stage four before she even knew she had it. There was very little anyone could do. It progressed quickly and spread to her bones. It was incredibly painful and she wanted Linc to help her commit suicide. She'd been involved in some kind of medical research at Stanford and had arranged for Linc to get everything she'd need. I'm not sure exactly how."

"It's not important," Stephen said. "Not now."

"According to Sarah, Linc wanted to help her, but he couldn't do it. Mei was angry. She'd asked Linc to help her because there was no one she trusted more. She saw it as a way of honoring the bond between them and as a last act of complete intimacy. Linc couldn't do it. Mei saw that as a betrayal. But she wasn't the sort of person who could hold onto a grudge. A day or two later, she told him she respected his decision. She was so calm and peaceful he wondered if she'd found someone else to help her. Within a few hours she slipped into a coma and died peacefully the following day."

Stephen didn't say anything. We both looked at the dogs panting and were silent.

Stephen sighed. "That's a lot. Linc's a tough guy. First Mei, now Sarah?"

I whipped my head around. "You knew?"

"Knew what?"

"That Sarah had cancer too?"

"What? No. Really? No, I didn't know. I just meant that he'd lost two people he loved very much."

I pushed my hair back with both hands and looked up at the sky through the bare branches of the apple tree. "I don't know for sure whether Sarah had cancer, but Paolo is checking up on some evidence we found in her desk."

"What then?"

"When Sarah told me the story, she said Linc was reluctant to move forward with their relationship because of what he'd gone through with Mei. Apparently, at least back in September, he still felt guilty about being unable to help Mei with the most important thing she'd ever asked of him. He felt he'd failed her."

My mouth was dry and I wrung my hands together. I looked at Stephen, wishing he would pick up the thread of my fear and run with it, coming to the same dire conclusion that I had.

"So you're terrified that . . ."

"That Sarah had cancer. And Linc knew. And decided to help Sarah end her life before she experienced the same symptoms that made the final stages of Mei's life so difficult that she had to beg her husband to kill her." Again, I blurted it out as if it were all one word. Forcing myself to voice my fears had been more difficult than I'd imagined.

Stephen said nothing. He leaned down to rub Munchkin's belly.

"Okay," he eventually said as he brushed off his hands and slapped them down on his thighs. "A prosecutor could make that look bad. But on the other hand, here's a guy who couldn't help his first wife with an assisted suicide, no matter how much she begged for his help, nor how horrible her symptoms were. Do you really think he'd kill Sarah? Especially before she had obvious symptoms? Linc was meeting with the Nobel committee, right? That's a really big deal. Yet all he talked about in the last month or so was how happy he was about the wedding and how hard he was working on getting his house cleaned out. If he were going to kill Sarah, why work so hard on things that wouldn't matter afterwards?"

Stephen leaned down and tilted his head to stare into my eyes as if he were verifying that my fears were baseless.

"Oh, come on, Maggie. Let's say he actually decided to kill Sarah—he didn't, I'm sure of it, but let's say he did. Electrocution? Seriously? There had to be an easier way for both of them. He'd gone through all the planning with Mei—he'd know what to do to make it easy on Sarah. He might even still have the pills. There's no way he wanted Sarah to go through what she did. No way. You saw her body. Electrocution is horrible. You have to know that."

I thought back and shuddered. "You're right. No one who loved her could ever have set Sarah up to die the way she did. From the outside, her body looked relatively undamaged, but the smell . . ." My stomach lurched with the memory. "It was a vile combination of burned meat and hot metal—a smell that made me want to run away as fast as I could. And Linc's first move was *toward* Sarah. We had to hold him back. If he'd set up the accident, surely he, more than any of the rest of us, would have known how deadly a situation it was. He would have been holding *us* back, not the other way around."

Stephen stood, looking at his watch. "I think it's time to go in," he said. "Feel better?"

I nodded. "Thanks. I'll still suggest Linc tell his lawyer about Mei's death, but it's not eating at me the way it was."

"Thoughts can do that," he said. "Sometimes having an imagination can be a very bad thing."

I felt better after talking to Stephen, but when Belle and I climbed back into my SUV, I started the car, put it in gear, and then stopped. Where would I go from here?

I took a deep breath and let it out slowly, just the way I was told to do in the mindfulness meditation sessions Tess and Elaine dragged me to. The sessions were relaxing, but I was still having trouble remembering to use the techniques in my daily life.

I thought about what I knew so far. Officially, Sarah's death could still possibly be ruled an accident, based on the findings of the medical examiner and Santa Clara County crime lab's expert in electricity and electrocution deaths. According to Paolo, the expert was off hiking the Pacific Coast Trail with no reliable cell access and wouldn't be back in the Bay Area until early the following week. I expected they'd borrow an expert from another jurisdiction. In the meantime, I wondered if we could hire our own expert to look at the scene. After all, if her death could be ruled an accident, Linc would be off the hook, and there would be nothing more for me to do. I made a note to ask Linc's lawyer and Paolo what they thought of the idea. I wondered whether any electrician could look at the scene and render an opinion, or if they needed an official license or certification.

I rummaged in my bag for a pen and a pad of paper to make a list of who had access to Linc's house. I nibbled on the end of the pen. Linc, Sarah, Tess, and I, of course, and apparently Boots. I wrote the names down. Theoretically, anyone could have broken in, but the five of us had easy and explainable access. I knew everyone well except Boots. I circled her name several times.

I needed to look at the garden and rule out, at least in my own mind, the idea that Boots had something to hide. A secret she'd kill to keep hidden. Something Sarah could have seen or overheard, given the proximity between the community garden and Linc's house.

I sighed heavily but stopped myself from wallowing in sadness, which would get no one anywhere. I needed to be doing something. I pushed my hair back from my forehead, and remembered that I needed a haircut.

Sarah had urged me to phone her hairdresser. And as I'd told Paolo, there might not be anyone else in all of Orchard View who would know more about Sarah's life.

I rattled Belle's leash. "Hey, Miss Belle, let's go ask Stephen if you can stay a little longer."

Chapter 7

I try to arrive at appointments at least ten minutes early.
Some people find this practice annoying, but it means
that I don't have to waste time fretting if an accident
slows traffic or I can't find a parking space right away.
But being early might not work for you. All organizational ideas are suggestions. Pick the ones that work
for you.

From the Notebook of Maggie McDonald,
Simplicity Itself Organizing Services

Tuesday, November 4, 12:30 p.m.

I found the garden address on my phone, plugged it into my GPS
system, and drove around in circles for twenty minutes before I
gave up. The garden plots occupied a parcel of land in the center of a
housing development that had been built in the 1920s. Dead ends,
circles, and pedestrian shortcuts made maps of the area difficult to
read and impossible to follow, even with locally grown technological
assistance. I parked in front of Linc's house and approached the garden via his backyard.

I hoped to start my investigation with Boots. I followed a path
through the grass, thinking that we'd need to arrange to have it cut
soon. The house had been the site of a sudden death. We didn't need
to have it looking haunted to add to its stigma.

Overgrown shrubs I should have been able to identify marked the
end of Linc's property. I pushed through a break in the hedge and
frantically wiped a spider's web from my face.

I couldn't see anyone in the garden and took the opportunity to look around. Split-rail fences enclosed the parcel, which I estimated at about four acres—a rare expanse of open land in the overbuilt Bay Area. A small, open patch in the center had park benches laid out in a circle around a recirculating fountain. Nearby plots included bird feeders and what looked like birdhouses.

Most of the hundred-square-foot plots within sight were filled with winter vegetables and well-pruned fruit trees or bushes. A few rangy squash plants held the last of the pumpkins, acorns, and butternuts.

Boots could be using the garden for an illegal activity, but as I wandered the paths that hypothesis seemed unlikely. It was all so peaceful. I passed the trickling fountain and a hummingbird buzzed me—warning me to stay away from his feeder. I looked up to see a woman with a bright pink outfit disappearing into a shed near the official entrance and parking area that I'd earlier failed to locate.

I hurried toward her and nearly tripped on an errant root. Most of the pathways were tidier than a formal French garden and were covered with pea gravel that crunched when I walked. The root seemed to come out of nowhere and I looked around to see if I could figure out which plot it originated in. But then I snorted and shook my head. I had enough to do rooting out clues to Sarah's death without tracking down delinquent vegetation.

"Boots," I called as I approached the shed, not wanting to startle her. I squinted through the door trying to make out shapes within the darkness, which was dramatic given the brightness of the fall day outside.

"Boots isn't here," said a voice. "Can I help? Let me come outside where it's warmer."

A young woman emerged from the dark interior of the shed and held out her hand to shake mine, "I'm Ketifa Hanif," she said. "Boots is working at Legal Aid this morning, but she should be around later this afternoon. Are you looking for a plot to work? There's a four- to five-year waiting list, I'm afraid, but we always need volunteers. And volunteers get first crack at any surplus from the gardens."

I smiled and shook Ketifa's hand.

"Maggie McDonald."

Ketifa looked like a scoop of rainbow sherbet, wearing a long-sleeved pale yellow T-shirt that spread over her obviously pregnant belly. An ankle-length orange skirt and a head scarf in a pattern of shocking pink with flecks of green completed her outfit. Brown eyes looked up at me through long lashes. She shielded her eyes from the sun.

"How can I help, Ms. McDonald?"

It occurred to me that I should have prepared a statement or at least a plan of how to approach someone with my inquiries. There was a reason the police asked amateurs to leave the detecting to them.

"I've been working with Professor Sinclair in his house on the other side of the hedge," I said, pointing toward Linc's property. "I met Claire yesterday, the day we found my friend Sarah Palmer dead in the house. I'm wondering if Claire knew Sarah? Or if she saw anything or anyone that struck her as odd or out of place—if not on that day, the day before, or in recent weeks. Since she's not here, maybe you could help me?"

That was probably too many questions to ask all at once, but I was winging it and hoping I might stumble on information that would help Linc.

"She actually prefers to be called Boots," Ketifa said. "But let me think for a minute. Would you like to walk with me? I need to fill the bird feeders and do some planting."

Ketifa looked very young to be a mother, but she might be older than she appeared. Her age didn't have anything to do with my investigation, though, and was none of my business. I followed her back through the plots.

"I'm very sorry about your friend," she said. "Do they know what happened to her?"

"Thank you. The police are looking into it. I haven't heard anything for sure, yet."

"I'm usually here every day, but something came up on Monday and I didn't make it. We all read about your friend Sarah in the paper." She put down the bucket she was carrying and unhooked a feeder from a hanging bracket. "We like to encourage the birds because they help our organic farming efforts," she said. "Any bugs and insects they eat can't harm the plants. That's what the bat houses are for too."

"Bat houses?" I conjured images of Bat caves and Bat mobiles.

Ketifa pointed back to the garden shed, to what I'd originally thought were birdhouses mounted on the side of the building. "They eat like, a thousand mosquitos an hour. Good guys to have around."

"I hate spiders. Please tell me they eat spiders too."

"Some do. Some don't," said a voice that seemed to come out of nowhere. A second young woman stood up from behind an overgrown rosemary bush. She held a sheaf of weeds in one hand and a trowel in the other.

"New volunteer?" she asked, putting down the trowel and reaching out her hand. "I'm Santana Marimba."

"Pretty name," I said and shook her hand.

"Don't ask her about it," Ketifa said. "She makes up a different story every time and I don't think anyone knows the truth."

Santana smiled and shrugged. "The truth is overrated. Are you going to get those primed spinach seeds in this afternoon, Keef? Do you want me to help? If we wait much longer it will be too cold for them to get established."

"I'm planting twenty every day," Ketifa explained to me. "Taking notes. The climate is changing. If we don't think about adapting our planting schedules, we'll never learn anything. I'm varying the schedules on the kale, spinach, cauliflower, and Brussels sprouts in Boots's plot—all to see if I can figure out an optimum schedule."

"Wow," I said. "That sounds like a university research project. Are you a biologist?"

"An avid amateur," Ketifa said. "But you didn't come here to learn about spinach. Ask Santana your questions."

She turned toward Santana and explained. "Ms. McDonald was hoping to ask Boots about the professor's house. She knew the lady who died and wanted to find out if we'd seen anything out of the ordinary."

"That's right," I said. "Although I'm really more interested in whether you've seen anything unusual over the past few weeks. Anyone strange hanging around?"

"There's been a lot of activity over there this fall," Santana said, pointing toward Linc's house. "Lots of repairs and someone clearing stuff out. Is that the kind of thing you're talking about? Is Professor Sinclair moving?"

"I'm not really sure," I said. "Everything is up in the air since Sarah Palmer died."

Ketifa looked at Santana and frowned. "Didn't you hear Boots talking the other day with the committee members? She told them the property would be changing hands and that the people on the waiting list for plots of their own—folks like you and me—were going to be happy."

Santana looked like a younger, smaller version of Boots, though she wore green overalls and bright yellow rubber boots. Her face, which earlier had seemed open and friendly, now looked secretive. But she volunteered more information without my prompting.

"Boots said she would have killed to get that land," Santana said, "but that now she wouldn't have to. She claimed old Mrs. Sinclair's will stated that Professor Sinclair could live in the house as long as he wanted, but that when he moved out, the land would go to the Master Gardeners, the Orchard View Community Gardens, and the Plotters."

I made a mental note to tell Paolo Bianchi to check Mrs. Sinclair's will.

"Three groups?" I asked. "Would they fight over the land?"

Ketifa shook her head and the wind caught one of the hanging ends of her head scarf, waving it like a flag. "I don't think so. Those groups all kind of overlap. I think they'd contribute money toward improvements that would benefit them all, like putting in more paths and more plots, expanding or rebuilding the garden shed, redoing the irrigation pipes, and installing another toilet."

I considered Ketifa's pregnant profile. "I'd think the toilets would be a high priority, particularly if the membership is going to grow. I guess the professor's bathroom is a lifesaver for those of you who are here all day and work at the other end of the lot."

Santana and Ketifa looked at each other, and I thought I detected a hint of alarm in their expressions. My forehead wrinkled in confusion. I'd obviously stepped into a delicate subject. The girls had been forthcoming about everything else. I lifted my eyebrows in question.

Ketifa responded. "It's nothing, really, but we try to avoid the professor's house. Boots says he doesn't need all of us tromping through his kitchen when he's trying to work or relax."

Ketifa turned and brushed her hands on her skirt. "Santana, what about the Jinn? Tell her about the Jinn."

Santana sniffed and threw up her hands. "Again? Seriously?" She turned to me. "We've had some problems with sketchy electricity, particularly at night. The power goes on and off, and the lights may flicker. Ancient wiring explains it all, in my opinion, but Ketifa says it's ghosts."

"Where are the ghosts?" I asked.

Ketifa shook her head. "Not ghosts, Jinn. I don't think they mean to hurt us. And it's probably just silly superstition on my part. It's just creepy, you know?"

"I imagine it would be scary," I said. "Especially if you were here alone."

Ketifa hugged herself and shivered. I could hear Santana making *tsk-tsk* noises behind me, so I changed the subject.

"But all this talk of renovations would assume a new source of income, right? And would occur after Linc moves and his land passes to the gardening groups?"

Santana nodded, looking at Ketifa for confirmation.

"But I don't think that's actually true," I said as gently as possible, trying not to imply that the girls were misinformed or lying. "The story I heard was that the land belongs to Professor Sinclair, who inherited it from his mother." I made a mental note to tell Tess about the confusion and suggest she verify the land's status before she put the house on the market.

Ketifa gasped and I turned toward her. Her eyes were wide and staring beyond me. I half expected to see a ghost when my gaze shifted back toward Santana.

Boots loomed behind Santana, fuming.

"Enough with the ghost stories, Ketifa," Boots said in a booming voice the whole neighborhood must have been able to hear. "I've told you there is no such thing. And Mrs. McDonald, you are equally mistaken if you think there is any question about the contents of Mrs. Sinclair's will. She showed it to me herself. I've waited years to take over the land. I've got plans drawn up for expanding our organic-gardening education programs and enhancing pest abatement, hybridization, and drought-tolerant plantings. The whole committee is in agreement."

Boots plunged past me into the shed, grabbing my arm along the way and pulling me in to join her. She reached the counter and picked up one of two surge protectors, each of which was filled with electric plugs that made them look like giant mutant insects.

She thrust the surge protector in my face. "Can you see what we're dealing with? This is a fire hazard. The whole place could go up. We've been waiting to go after more grants until we get more land. We need to rebuild, adding toilets, an emergency phone, solar power, a water-reclamation system, and drought-friendly irrigation. The ancient pipes are brittle. Every time we try to fix the old sprinklers, they break somewhere new. We need toilet facilities here and at the other end of the garden. Most of the people who work here are seniors or pregnant or moms with young children. Reliable plumbing is essential."

She reached into a dark corner shelf above the counter and pulled out a binder. Flipping through it, she said, "Look at this. Our waiting list is four or five years long. Moms who want to garden with their kids sign up for a plot, but by the time it's available, they've got teenagers."

She tossed the binder on the counter. "The council has approved all these new apartments without a scrap of green land, and they don't require the builders to add parks. We're raising a generation of kids who may never learn where vegetables come from and may never know what a fresh spring pea tastes like. We need new plots and we need funds to develop a program designed specifically for apartment dwellers. Before anyone ever heard of Silicon Valley, Santa Clara Valley was known as the Valley of Heart's Delight, with orchards as far as anyone could see in every direction. Our residents need to retain at least a tiny piece of their own history."

Boots turned and glared at me, her face as purple as the plums that were once a primary local crop.

"We've requested permits on all of these items and been turned down for one reason or another each time—local residents say more bathrooms will attract the homeless or increase traffic, and more electricity will mean we'll have searchlights on all night destroying the rural atmosphere." Boots lifted her arms and made air quotes with her fingers as she said *rural atmosphere*. I'd learned it was a hot-button issue in Orchard View politics, a term bandied about by those opposed to any and all development, even of parks and recreation facilities.

"But Boots . . ." I began, wanting to suggest they make up smaller plots to take the pressure off the waiting list or work with the planning department to create permit requests that could be rubber-stamped. But Boots's red face and clenched fists made me shift gears.

"Boots," I said, holding up my hands in surrender. "I'm not the enemy. I'm in favor of community gardens and bathrooms and all the things you talked about. I'm just saying that my understanding of the terms of Mrs. Sinclair's will is different from yours."

"I don't care what you understood. I know what I saw."

We were at an impasse. I spoke quickly before Boots could order me to leave.

"Did anyone around here have a grudge against Sarah or Linc? Have the folks from the school-site committee had their eye on the land?"

Boots half-turned away from me, looking like she was ready to sprint to her car to avoid more questions. But instead she scowled and pointed her finger at me.

"Watch what you imply about my volunteers," she growled. "They've all overcome troubled backgrounds and are working very hard to get on stable, adult footing. They don't need you or anyone else stirring up gossip about them. Donations, we'll take, but we've no need of snarky comments."

I opened my mouth to protest her assumption that I was disparaging Santana and Ketifa, but she continued before I could say anything.

"Of course the school-site committee has been drooling over this property. There is no plot of land, public or private, built-up or vacant, that hasn't been scrutinized by them. Our four acres combined with the Sinclair land would make a perfect location for a new elementary school. But they'll have a fight on their hands if they try to take it from us. We've got more than a hundred current gardeners, another hundred on the waiting list, and more who grew up gardening here but no longer hold plots. All of this was once part of the Sinclairs' land and it's time the properties were reunited." She took a breath and smoothed the long sleeves of her T-shirt over her arms. "You need to leave now. You're stirring up trouble. You need to leave or I will call our lawyer immediately." She must have been used to having people obey her every command, because she stomped off to her car and jumped into the driver's seat without waiting to be sure I followed instructions.

From where I stood, I could see her hold up her phone and point to the watch on her wrist. The message was clear: If I didn't take off soon, she would call out the cavalry. I didn't expect the police or her lawyer would be able to keep me from walking in the garden, but I didn't want to antagonize Boots, either.

Santana's mouth dropped open and she stared at me. "I just realized. You're the woman who's been working at the house. What were you trying to find out?" Santana looked hurt and confused.

"I'm sorry," I said. "I wasn't trying to be sneaky."

Santana still looked suspicious. "You fired question after question at us," she said.

"Again, I'm sorry if it seemed like I was interrogating you," I said. "It wasn't my intention at all. I just wondered if any of the garden members had seen anything unusual going on either here or at the professor's house over the past few weeks."

"Of course we haven't seen anything suspicious," Santana said. "We already told you that. Not unless you think my friend Ketifa is suspicious. Some truly ignorant people think she dresses like a terrorist." Santana gave Ketifa's head scarf a gentle tug and went on. "You're as bad as that horrible detective Gordon Apfel. This garden is full of people who do organic gardening, for God's sake, and who are trying to save the bees." She waved at a corner of the garden that held four grayish cubes that I assumed were beehives. "We literally wouldn't kill a fly because flies are also good pollinators. Why on earth would we kill Sarah? We hardly knew her." Santana turned, stomped into the shed, and slammed the door behind her.

"Santana," I said to the closed door. "I'm not accusing anyone of anything."

Ketifa looked at me, shrugged, and concentrated on coiling up a loose hose.

I walked back through the garden and across the professor's yard to my car. I was insulted to the core by Santana's effort to link my behavior with that of Detective Awful, but I also wondered why Santana had referred to Sarah by her first name, yet claimed to have barely known her. This suspect-interviewing process was more complicated than I'd thought.

Ketifa had said that she was an avid amateur gardener and that she volunteered every day. But she also said she hadn't been there on Sunday or Monday. The two statements were mutually exclusive. And why on earth did Boots believe that Linc's property would pass to the gardeners as soon as he vacated the premises? Could that be true? If so, who knew about it? Boots, obviously, and maybe all of the other gardeners and volunteers.

I'd hoped to break the case wide open with my interviews, so Detective Awful would stop pestering Linc and so the rest of us could pick up the pieces of our lives, honor Sarah, and at least *try* to move on.

My efforts at the garden had fallen short of the mark. I hoped my interview with Sarah's hairdresser would go more smoothly.

Chapter 8

The best way I know to quickly find a great hairdresser
in an unfamiliar town is to find someone who has hair
that is similar in texture to your own. If you like their
hairstyle, ask who cuts and styles it. Most people will be
flattered to know you admire their look.

From the Notebook of Maggie McDonald,
Simplicity Itself Organizing Services

Tuesday, November 4, 1:30 p.m.

I leaned against my car and consulted my phone's search engine for
the number of Sarah's hairdresser.

Before it could bring up any information, my phone rang. It was
Elaine, calling from Jason's house. She'd been principal when Jason
was in junior high and when he was a rookie cop working as a
school-liaison officer. Now with her house directly across the street
from the same school, she kept a sharp eye on the property, the students, and visitors to the campus. She and Jason had become great
friends over the years.

"Hey Maggie," she said after I answered. "Jason is fast asleep.
When you come back to the house for Belle, come in the back. The
more he can sleep, the faster he'll heal."

"What are you doing over there?"

"Whatever needs doing. Loading the dishwasher, unloading the
dryer, taking the trash out, answering the phone on the first ring. I
figure the more of those pesky daily details I can take care of, the
easier it will be for both Stephen and Jason."

"It sounds as if your day has been more productive than mine," I said, telling her about my interviews at the garden. Elaine and I had worked together trying to solve the last violent death in Orchard View, and I knew she had an insatiable interest in local intrigue.

"Don't pout, dear," Elaine said. "You may have gleaned more than you know, even if it's only that everyone connected to the garden is innocent."

"I'm not sure about 'innocent,'" I said. "Those girls are hiding something."

"Aren't all young people hiding something?"

I laughed. "Okay, Elaine, you win. You can read a teenager or young adult better than anyone I know. You might want to make a trip over there and see what you think. For now, I'm going to see if I can schedule an appointment with Sarah's hairdresser. Give me a call if Stephen has something else he wants me to do; otherwise, I'll check in later. Do you have any of those broken-leg cookies left? They're delicious. I may need one for a quick sugar fix when I come to pick up Belle."

After we ended the call, I accessed Sarah's calendar on my phone and found the name, address, and phone number of her hairdresser, Lily Takahashi. Luckily, her building was a few blocks from Linc's house. After I dialed I was greeted with:

"Hair Affair, this is Donna. May I schedule a clip, color, perm or facial for you today?"

"Hi Donna, I'm Maggie McDonald. I wondered if Lily has had any cancellations and could fit me in this afternoon?"

"Normally Lily books up two months in advance," Donna said. "But I'd be happy to check her schedule for you. If she's not available today I could give you her first available opening."

"Thanks, Donna." It was a delight to talk to someone who was fully trained in how to make a customer feel special.

"Wow, I'm glad I checked," Donna said. "She had a last-minute cancellation for an appointment in ten minutes. How fast can you get here?"

I looked at my watch. "It will be close, but I think I can do it. See you soon."

I sent a text to Max asking if he could pick up the boys. He responded before I got back to the car. *Leaving now. Will pick them up and bring them back here for dinner. Home 8pm.*

Relieved, I typed back quickly. *Thanks. Love you!!!* I tended to

overuse exclamation points in my texts. Max said I texted like a fif-
teen-year-old girl in love. The boys said I texted like an old lady. I
liked Max's version better.

Influx, like many other Silicon Valley companies, offered dinner
for employees who worked into the evening. Families were welcome.
The boys enjoyed having dinner with their dad and selecting exactly
what they wanted from a wide variety of fresh and locally sourced
food. Google devoted nearly as much square footage to recreational
activities as they did to workspace, and its grounds resembled a resort. Influx was a much smaller company, but they still offered work-
out equipment, exercise classes, a basketball court, and a wide array
of video-gaming platforms. The video games were a draw for our
boys, but I was confident Max would insist they finish their homework before food and games distracted them.

I walked around the back of my car to open the driver's-side door,
but stopped and looked up at the sound of a loudly revving engine. A
swanky black Range Rover stopped at the end of Linc's street. Its
hulking body reminded me of a raging bull from a kid's cartoon—the
kind with red eyes and steam escaping its nostrils, and that pawed the
ground before charging. The vehicle lurched toward me with a
squeal of its tires and I stepped back, molding myself to the side of
my car and wishing I had time to hide behind it. The Rover slowed as
it passed me and I peered through the front window, trying to identify
the driver. I only got a glimpse. All the other windows were darkly
tinted, defying state laws limiting tinting on the front-side windows.
I couldn't identify the driver and the passenger ducked out of view,
but I was almost certain the passenger was Santana.

I stared after the Range Rover as it sped away, then remembered
the phone in my hand. I snapped a picture of the license plate. It was
a little blurry, but I could make out most of the digits. I shivered. The
vehicle and its odd behavior had felt threatening, but grabbing the
image gave me a small sense of control that felt surprisingly good.

Take that, you beast of a car, I thought as I climbed into my SUV,
which in retrospect seemed tiny and not in the slightest bit protective.

Bells above the front door of the Main Street shop rang as I opened
the door to Hair Affair. The woman at the first station raised her eyebrows in greeting. She held a hair clip in her mouth that would have
made it difficult to speak.

"I'm here for an appointment with Lily," I said.

The hairdresser positioned the last clip into a snail curl. "Sorry! Our receptionist stepped out for coffee. She'll be back any moment and will check you in. Please, have a seat. There's bottled water in the back if you're thirsty."

I took one of the three chairs in the waiting area. The salon was small, with only four stations each for cutting, washing, and drying. A spa chair for manicures and pedicures was positioned across from me and I eyed my short and scruffy nails. Maybe it was time for that too, but not today.

Two young women came through the door and the bells announced their arrival. The shorter one took her place behind the counter. I figured she must be Donna. She wore her hair, which was magenta on one side and black on the other, in stiff spikes. She had pixie-like features and the short hair made her look like a space-age elf.

The taller one wore her purple-streaked dark hair in a ponytail. She put down her coffee cup and hung her fuchsia hoodie on a coat tree, exchanging it for a lab coat with her name on the pocket.

"Maggie? I'm Lily. Do you want to change?" She held up a fluorescent green nylon smock. I wondered if there'd been a sale on the cover-ups.

I shook my head and tugged a bit on the hem of my white T-shirt. "Thanks, but I don't think you can do anything to hurt this shirt," I said. "Let's go for it."

She sat me in the chair and finger-combed my hair. "What were you thinking? A shorter style? A trim? Maybe some highlights?"

I looked at my reflection in the mirror and barely recognized myself. The woman staring back at me looked exhausted and washed out. I'd put off some basic self-care. My hair needed serious help.

"I'm open to suggestions, style-wise," I said. "As long as it's easy to care for and will look halfway decent if I need to let it air-dry."

I must have looked a little wary, because Lily laughed and said, "All righty, then. No wild streaks or mohawks for you." She fluffed my hair a little, bit her lower lip, and moved slowly from one side of the chair to the other, glancing between the mirror and my hair.

"Do you still want to be able to put it up in a ponytail?" she asked.

I nodded. "Practical, easy care, and ponytail-able in case it's super-windy or I don't have time to wash it."

"Got it. Let's cut it to here," she said, indicating a point just below my chin. "Nothing too drastic for your first visit. If you don't like it, you can still grow it out, but if you like what I do and want to be more daring, we'll try that next time. Whaddaya think?"

"Sounds great," I said. "You're very reassuring."

"I'd suggest some highlights too, for next time. A bit lighter around your face and enough elsewhere to make it look subtle, natural, and blended. Let's get you washed and we'll get started."

Lily shampooed my hair herself, chatting about how thick and healthy my hair was and how she thought it would be fun to work with and that she hoped I'd come back.

I sank into the cushy chair and put myself in what I hoped were Lily's capable hands. And then I remembered that the haircut was an excuse for my real mission: finding out anything more I could about Sarah. I pondered where to begin. But Lily took care of that for me.

"So, how did you find us?" she asked.

I explained that I was new to town, hadn't had a good cut since July, and that my friend Sarah Palmer had recommended her.

"Oooh," said Lily. "She was one of my favorite clients. I was so sorry to hear about her passing. Do you know if there are funeral plans? How is her fiancé? Do you know him?"

If I wasn't careful, Lily was the one who would get information out of me, instead of the other way 'round.

"It was such a shock," I said. "Last I heard, the police were looking for relatives and investigating her death."

"Investigating? What happened? I'd heard it was an electrical accident in that old house that belongs to her fiancé. For all he's some smarty-pants at Stanford, I guess he must not have been too careful about those old electrics. With all the dryers 'round here, and wet hair and hands, we're hyper-aware of power hazards. I guess it's easy for people to forget electricity kills." She shook her head and her facial muscles drooped, giving her a look of grave sadness.

"Sarah was so excited about her wedding and Linc's move to her cottage," Lily continued. "That's all she talked about for the last few months—the renovations they were making, the dress she'd picked out, who was coming—all the details."

"Did she mention family?"

"Maybe a brother? In Seattle? No, that was someone else. Sarah's sister died pretty young. She had cancer. Her mom did too. They died within a few years of each other, I think. It was really hard on Sarah because they were her only family."

"What about her fiancé? Did she talk about him much?"

Lily laughed. "Linc? I loved hearing those stories about him. She was so madly in love, you know? She was proud of him—all the meetings with the Nobel Prize guys and saving the planet. But then she'd tell me about how he'd put sunscreen on his toothbrush or left the car running in the driveway, because he was preoccupied and all."

"Did that bother her?"

"No, like I said, she was so in love. She thought he was adorable. How did you know her?"

I saw no reason to hide my relationship with Sarah. I explained my volunteer work at the library and that she'd hired me to help consolidate her household with Linc's.

"Oh, my God. Of course. *You're* Maggie. Well, I knew your name was Maggie and all, but I didn't realize you were *Sarah's* Maggie. She was so thrilled to find you. And not just because of all the help you were giving her. She said whenever she and Linc argued about giving something away they'd just say, 'Let's see what Maggie thinks.' And you'd suggest a solution that made 'em both happy."

She stopped cutting and pointed the scissors toward me in the mirror. "Do you have some cards you can give me? I'd be happy to recommend you. Sarah pretty much figured you could walk on water and that's enough of an endorsement for me."

I blushed, thanked her, and dug in my backpack for my cards. I gave her all I had. "I'm glad you said Sarah was happy. She seemed to love her job and when I worked with her at her home or at Linc's, she was almost effervescent. Floating, even. But the police were asking questions like they thought maybe she could have committed suicide. . . ."

"Suicide? Sarah? No way. No frickin' way." Lily stopped the blow-dryer for a moment. "I'm sorry. I shouldn't have said *frickin'*. But you know, Sarah was the most upbeat person I've ever met. Never saw even a hint of depression in her."

"I thought the same," I said. "And I couldn't think of anyone who disliked her."

Lily shook her head again. "Me neither. It had to be an accident, right? Unless there was some family thing she never talked about.

Family she'd run away from, hoping to never see again." Lily's voice took on the tones of an announcer catching up faithful watchers of a daytime drama.

I looked up at her and grinned. "That's a little melodramatic, don't you think?"

"Sorry," she said. "I'm taking some classes up at Foothill—you know, the junior college? Trying to finish my degree. I've got a presentation for Vampire Literature in Diverse Cultures tonight. I'm reading a short story I wrote. I'm wearing a black cape and I want to sound dark and haunting. I guess I've been practicing a little too much. Gives me goose bumps when I think about it. It's one of the last night classes to get out, so I'm afraid to walk alone to my car. The fog settles in up there at night. It's dark and spooky—the perfect setting for a vampire attack."

"Under those circumstances, I think I'd be more worried about an attack from a mountain lion or even a real-live bad guy rather than the undead," I said. "Do you all walk together when you leave?"

She restarted the blow-dryer. "Of course," she said. "One of the girls has some guy she's really afraid of. We all try to park in the same general area and we leave at the same time, chatting all the way to the parking lot. It's a great class. The young guys are really protective of us."

"Did Sarah ever talk about the garden at the back of her house?"

"That community thing?" Lily nodded, sending her purple-streaked ponytail flying. "She had lots to say about that Boots lady. Sarah thought she was abrasive and full of herself. She didn't like the way Linc left the back door unlocked so she could come and go. I guess Boots was a friend of his mother's going way back."

"So Sarah didn't like her?"

Lily stopped the dryer again. "I dunno about that. They weren't buddies or anything, but Sarah admired the work she did with those kids that used to be in the foster system. They were working with similar groups, just at different ages. Sarah was planning on getting together with Boots and coordinating some of their resources. I guess that won't ever happen now, though."

"Was there any truth to the rumor . . ." I hesitated, since the rumor I was talking about was one I'd just made up. I was normally a very truthful person and lying, for however good a reason, made me uncomfortable.

"Go on," Lily said. "We're done with the dryer."

"Was Boots ever accused of doing anything not quite right?"

Lily frowned and stared at me as if I were crazy. "Are you kidding? That would be like dissing . . . I dunno, Glinda the Good Witch. I mean, I don't know her personally, but everyone in town knows *about* her. She may be hard to get along with sometimes, but she gets stuff done. She's always in the paper getting some award for creating yet another program that benefits the community."

"I'm sorry," I said, trying to placate her. "I'm fairly new to town. I just wanted to form a complete picture and make sure that Sarah hadn't seen something at the garden she shouldn't have. I've been trying to come up with reasons someone would have wanted to kill her. It's hard when we're talking about Sarah. Everyone loved her."

"You got that right." Lily gave my hair a final brush. She squinted at my head and trimmed an invisible bit off one side. "If Sarah saw anything illegal going on at that garden, it wasn't something Boots was involved in. I'm sure of it."

She sprayed my hair with a tiny bit of light hairspray and spun me around so I could see the back with the mirror. "What do you think?"

I fiddled around with the mirror until I could see. "I like it." And then I repeated it with more confidence. "I like it. It's very me, but a little . . . different . . . better." I smiled up at her. "It's perfect."

"Highlights next time? Something soft, nothing brassy?"

"Definitely."

We made the appointment and I paid her, leaving a generous tip. I hadn't learned much from Lily that I didn't already know, but she'd confirmed my own impressions of Sarah's life. I'd gotten a great haircut and found that elusive suburban treasure: the hairdresser who would listen to what I wanted and give me a perfect cut. A cut that looked like me, but better.

I sent a little message of thanks up to Sarah and my eyes dampened. I missed her terribly. She would have loved knowing that Lily and I had met.

I glanced at my watch. I had time to check in at Jason's and pick up Belle. After that, I was hoping to spend some quality time with a cold glass of wine and a hot bath.

I climbed the steps leading to Jason and Stephen's front door before I remembered that Elaine had asked me to go around the back. I tiptoed down the steps and around to the side gate. My efforts to be quiet proved wasted. As soon as Belle and Munchkin heard me, they came barreling down the walkway at the side of the house, barking to greet me.

"Sit!" I said, firmly and loudly to make sure they could hear me over the sound of their own voices. To my surprise, both of them slammed their bottoms to the ground. Belle scooted forward a little just to let me know how much she loved me and how hard it was for her to do as I asked.

"Okay, you two," I said, relenting. "Escort me to the back porch."

Belle's leash was coiled up on a redwood picnic table in the back. I was attaching it to her collar when Elaine came out to greet me.

"I'm so sorry," I said. "Did we wake up Jason?"

Elaine shook her head. "He was already awake. Do you have time to come in and say hello? He's going stir-crazy. How those doctors expect us to be able to keep him still for weeks on end is beyond me."

I unhooked Belle's leash, told her I'd be back in a moment, and followed Elaine into Stephen and Jason's front room.

"Maggie," Jason said, pushing himself up to a seated position on the couch. "It's great to see you. I was afraid you might be the physical therapist coming back to torture me some more. We're now working on the exciting skill of getting dressed." He grinned and shook his head. "The bloody tyrant timed me." He tapped his watch. "Sixty-five minutes is the number to beat. Strip, shower, shave, and dress, including socks and one shoe. Socks are the hardest. Think about me next time you put your socks on, Maggie. You don't know how good you've got it."

"I'd punch you for wallowing in self-pity, if you didn't look quite so pathetic." I kissed his head, though I knew the last thing he'd want was to feel that I was mothering him, smothering him, or in any way suggesting he couldn't stand on his own two feet—even though, at the moment, he couldn't.

He grabbed his clipboard from the coffee table and flipped through the pages.

"I know you need to get home," he said. "But do you have time to fill me in on what you've learned? Elaine said you'd been doing some investigating. Did you get lunch? Do you want a sandwich?" He pointed to a plate of sandwiches and cookies someone had made and covered with plastic. "Nice haircut. Looks good."

I grabbed a cookie and chewed while I thought. Jason was obviously revved up at the moment, but I didn't want to overtire him.

"How 'bout just the key points for now?" I said. After I'd filled him in, I asked if he needed anything and promised to phone him tomorrow if I learned anything new.

"Next time you come, be sure to bring Belle. She wore poor Munchkin out today, which means Stephen won't need to walk him. Unless . . ."

Jason was referring to Stephen's practice of taking long walks with Munchkin in the wee hours of the morning, trying to walk off the terrors that had plagued him since he'd returned from Afghanistan several years before. Stephen had told me his symptoms grew worse when he was under pressure, which he certainly was now. Stephen's post-traumatic-stress issues were only one of the reasons I wanted to make sure he had the support he needed while Jason was recovering.

I filled Jason in quickly and headed to my car. I'd just gotten Belle settled in the backseat when Tess called.

"Hey, Tess. What's up?"

"Maggie, I'm so glad I caught you. I wanted to let you know that I'm worried about our schedule. If that Detective Awful creature keeps us out of Linc's house much longer, we won't be able to meet our deadlines for holding the tea there. And everyone knows that I hold my holiday party the weekend following the long Thanksgiving weekend. I can't change the date. I've been looking at other possible locations but haven't found anything yet."

Thoughts raced through my head, including wondering whether Tess would deliver on her plan to promote my organizing business if she held her tea in an alternate location. The whole point of my involvement in the promotion was that my skills had transformed the house and made the event possible. I struggled to find a way to ask her that didn't make me sound like a child left out of a playground game. But it turned out not to matter. Tess kept me from saying anything as she rattled on about her efforts. "I'm not going to panic yet and I don't want you to, either. I just wanted to keep you posted."

"Can you check with the police to find out when we'll be allowed back in? Surely they can't keep us out forever."

"If it were up to Sir Awful the Stupid, they would," Tess said. "I think it hinges on how soon they can get their electrical expert to look at the scene. I called my lawyer this morning and he's looking into it. He thinks we may be able to go around Sir Awful." She paused. "That's probably the attorney now. I've got to take this call, Maggie. Talk to you tomorrow. Don't worry."

If Tess's words were meant to be reassuring, they'd failed miserably. But I started my car and headed home, determined to leave the worries about the tea to Tess. As I drove, I thought about how my own efforts had gone today. My stomach growled and I realized that part of my problem in getting people like Boots to open up to me might be the fact that I hadn't brought cookies. To arrive bearing cookies was an important part of the Orchard View social contract and was a ticket into places where I might not otherwise be welcome.

I'd need a lot of cookies. I'd need to get started baking tonight.

I was nearing my driveway when I saw my neighborhood nemesis, Dennis DeSoto, and his three yippy Pekinese dogs standing by my mailbox. My heart sank. Dennis seemed to put a negative spin on anything happening within my family or on my property. I needed neither his judgment nor his condescension this afternoon. But there was no way to politely avoid him. I stopped in the driveway and walked around the car to check the mail.

"Hi, Dennis," I said in a voice that I hoped seemed cheerful. "I haven't seen you in ages. How are things?"

"Everything *was* fine, but the police are at your house again causing a commotion. I hope you're not bringing *more* trouble to the neighborhood."

I grabbed my mail and looked in the direction of the house, though it was hidden by a dense patch of evergreen trees and shrubs that badly needed thinning.

"I can't imagine what they want with us," I said. "I'd better check it out."

I raced back to the other side of my car, flung the mail onto the passenger seat, waved out the open window, and tried not to squeal my tires as I raced away from Dennis and toward the police, who I very much feared were represented by Detective Awful.

Chapter 9

When you're overwhelmed, step back, get help, and
make a plan.

Repeat as necessary.

*From the Notebook of Maggie McDonald,
Simplicity Itself Organizing Services*

Tuesday, November 4, 4:30 p.m.

Paolo's Subaru was parked in the shade in front of our house. A
marked police SUV with lights flashing blocked access to the
paved area that marked the first stage of our efforts to restore our rut-
ted driveway. One of the vehicle's tires had crushed some of the heir-
loom roses planted by Max's Aunt Kay.

I peered into the shadows on the front porch and spotted the distinctive profile of Detective Awful. I took a deep breath in and out,
and then did it again, bracing myself to approach the abrasive man.
Then I shrugged, engaged my four-wheel drive, and drove around
the SUV into my normal parking spot.

I sighed and briefly wondered how long I could logically remain
in the car, protected from Detective Awful's bombastic personality.
Sometimes it's hard to be a grown-up. Belle growled.

"My sentiments exactly." I got out of the car, opened the back
door, and unhooked her leash. Low to the ground, she raced around
the end of the car, barking and snarling.

By the time I reached the front porch, she was seated by Paolo's
side, held there by his firm grasp of her collar. He showered her with

loving praise. I climbed the steps and tried to ignore the angry words Awful was spewing at my gentle and beloved Belle.

Maybe it wasn't fair of me. Maybe it was. But it didn't matter. If you were mean to my dog—or any dog, for that matter—you made my "bad person" list. Detective Awful was vying for the top spot.

I said a polite hello, anyway.

"You hiding the professor here?" Awful said to my back as I unlocked the door. "Why is no one answering the door?"

Belle stood between the detective and me, growling.

"Untrained beast," Awful said. "Can you put her away or put her down?"

I clenched my teeth and my fists and ignored him as much as I could.

Paolo pushed past the detective before I could invite the men in. I forgave him, because I was sure he was trying to help.

"Hey Maggie," he said quickly, before Apfel could say anything else inflammatory. "What a day. I'm exhausted. Can you offer a poor cop some coffee? And maybe some cookies?"

He made the last statement in a wheedling tone, not unlike my own boys. It made me realize once again that this responsible young man was closer in age to Brian and David than he was to me. I waved my arm in the direction of the kitchen.

"You know where the mugs are," I said. He was already pulling them from the cupboard.

I poured a scoop of kibble in Belle's dish, hoping to distract her from giving Detective Awful her opinion of him. It worked and the room filled with the sound of her crunching. I hoped that with a full belly and all the exercise she had today, she'd be willing to protect me by laying her head on my foot and going to sleep.

I pulled cookie dough from the freezer and plopped frozen blobs on a baking sheet. They would smell great, feed Paolo, and might even begin to thaw the stiff detective.

"Coffee, detective? Cream and sugar?" I waved toward the table. "Please, take a seat."

"Maggie makes the *best* coffee," Paolo said, pulling up a chair. The detective frowned at him, but nodded at me. Licking crumbs of kibble from her nose and snout, Belle curled under the table with her chin on Paolo's shoes. "And the *best* chocolate-chip cookies."

The detective cleared his throat. "This is not a social call," he said, drawing a small notebook from the chest pocket of his jacket. "We're here about the murder."

Paolo and the detective eyed each other. The room crackled with tension and there was a subtext here I didn't understand. I checked on the cookies.

"I've got Jelly, the professor's cat, in her cage out in the car," Paolo said. "And a few things for Linc in a duffel. Shall I bring them in now?"

I nodded. "Linc's at his lab, as far as I know. But sure, bring them in. Leave Jelly in her carrier, though. I'd hate to have her bolt in an unfamiliar place. I'll take her up to Linc's room when we're done here." *And may that be soon*, I thought.

It took Paolo a few minutes to go retrieve Linc's stuff. Detective Awful felt the need to supervise. By the time they finished, the cookies were ready. I pulled the tray from the oven, transferred the cookies to a plate, and placed it on the table next to the sugar.

I sat in my normal spot, took a giant gulp of coffee, and forced myself to wait for the detective to speak. He doctored his coffee with almost all the cream from the little pitcher I'd poured. He added three spoonfuls of sugar and stared at his notebook for so long I was gritting my teeth to keep from talking.

The detective stirred his coffee, placed the spoon on his napkin, and said slowly, staring at me, "We need your help with our inquiries."

The skin on my spine seemed to freeze, contract, and prickle. "Helping with inquiries" in the parlance of the British TV mysteries I watched meant, "We know you're guilty and we're going to do everything in our power, legal or illegal, to bring you to justice." I checked my watch, wondering how much longer I'd have to put up with the detective.

"Are you in a hurry, Mrs. McDonald?" asked Awful. "Or nervous about talking to the police?"

"She's got to pick up her sons from school," Paolo said. "We can talk to Maggie tomorrow. She's not going anywhere."

The detective glared at Paolo. "Neither are we. Not without Lincoln Sinclair."

"He's not here," I said.

The detective's phone rang. He took it and looked at the screen. "This is important. I'll take it in the other room."

As soon as he'd walked into the living room and closed the seldom-used door between the front of the house and the kitchen, I grabbed Paolo's arm.

"What's going on here?" I asked. "Why is he so smug? Who is he talking to? Is it officially a homicide? I thought you were waiting for word from the electrical expert."

Paolo looked behind his back and around the kitchen as if there might be two or three additional Apfels hiding behind him. He leaned in and whispered.

"We found Sarah's car, purse, and cell phone in the long-term lot at San Jose Airport. Her keys were in the ignition and the car was wiped clean and vacuumed. Her death is definitely a homicide and Apfel's got a warrant."

"A warrant? For *my* house?"

"No, for Linc."

"Based on what evidence? What judge would approve that?"

"That's the problem. I tried to slow things down and get him to talk to the district attorney before going to the judge, but Apfel wasn't having it. He and the judge play poker together. Approval for the warrant was a slam dunk. It's a warrant for Linc's arrest."

"But—but—"

Paolo forestalled my sputtering. "Look, Maggie, I don't know how long he'll be on this call. Can you pick up Newton at Stanford? We're headed there next. Apfel wanted to check out your house first, even though I told him Linc spends most of his time in his lab."

I started to ask Paolo again what kind of evidence, if any, Awful had on Linc. But before I could, Awful pushed the door open and let it bang against the wall.

"Let's go, Bianchi," he said. He turned away, then came back to the table. "Mrs. McDonald, I'll tell you this once and only once: Do not phone Professor Sinclair to warn him that we're coming. If you tip him off and we need to chase him all over Orchard View, I'm charging you for the cost of that chase."

I knew that the air-bag detective had no authority to do that, but rather than provoke him further and slow his departure, I laughed.

"In all the time I've worked with Linc, he's never picked up his phone when I've called," I said.

The detective glared at me, gulped his coffee, and grabbed a cookie that he shoved in his pocket. I filled a small, disposable plastic-storage container with the rest of the cookies for Paolo. If the snarly detective hadn't been there, I would have referred to them as a bribe, but Detective Awful had no sense of humor and wouldn't appreciate the joke. I couldn't risk it. He would likely arrest me on the spot. I handed Paolo the cookies without saying anything and he nodded, winking as though he could read my thoughts. I walked them to the door.

"All these comings and goings," Paolo said, shaking his head.

I wrinkled my forehead. Was he telling me something he didn't want the fat detective to overhear? If so, I had no idea what he was trying to say.

The detective sneezed. He wiped his nose on his sleeve. "Damn cat," he said as he left.

I decided I liked Jelly. I headed upstairs with her carrier, litter box, and the food Paolo had brought. "Well, Jelly, welcome to the household," I said to the kitten. "I'm trying to imagine ways in which I could murder Detective Awful and get away with it. Would you like to help?"

Jelly didn't answer, but there is nothing like a kitten for turning a foul mood upside down. I slipped into the bedroom, closed the door, and let Jelly out. She was a cute little black-and-white tuxedo cat, probably just a few months old. Sarah had loved her dearly and talked incessantly about the kitten's antics and her fears that Linc and Newton would be unable to adjust to the little newcomer. I bit my lip. Did she say Linc was allergic? I couldn't remember and decided it didn't matter. Allergic or not, the kitten was the only living reminder Linc had of Sarah. He'd want to keep her close. Jelly dashed under the bed, where I left her to adjust to her new surroundings. I set up her litter box, dry food, and water in the adjoining bathroom, and wished I'd thought to tell Paolo to bring something of Sarah's—an old sweater or sweatshirt to comfort the kitten. Jelly, Linc, and Newton had a long road ahead of them and were going to have to find ways to comfort each other.

"Settle in, Jelly," I said. "Linc will be home soon." When I heard my words aloud I realized I had no idea when Linc would be home. Apfel, I was sure, would keep him locked up as long as possible.

I trudged back down the stairs and looked at my watch. All I wanted was to snuggle into the cushions of the sofa with a cold glass of wine in my hand and Belle at my feet.

But I couldn't. I had to pick up Newton.

* * *

Despite using the GPS app on my phone, it took me ages to locate parking at Stanford. The university seemed to constantly be building new parking garages that were invariably several steps behind the capacity required. I plunked all the change I had into the meter and hoped twenty minutes would be enough time to find Newton and get him back to the car.

As Belle and I walked the three blocks to the building housing Linc's lab, I became aware of heavy footsteps following mine. The man the footsteps belonged to stopped beside me as we both waited to cross Campus Drive. I took the opportunity to latch onto a possible tour guide. Belle leaned toward him. I knew she was hoping to snuffle his hand and get a pat on the head.

"Hi. Am I heading in the right direction for the Environment and Energy Building? I'm afraid I got turned around in the parking garage."

The man smiled and held out his hand while taking a half-step back to avoid Belle.

"Walt Quintana. That's where I'm headed. Shall we walk together?"

I shook his hand. "Maggie McDonald."

"What brings you to us? Are you interviewing? Visiting?"

We crossed the street and I forced myself to pay attention to stepping up on the curb safely. Stanford's campus boasted hundreds of fragrant eucalyptus trees, which dropped acorn-like buds that could make walking treacherous. Because of Walt's obvious discomfort with dogs, I moved to put him on my right while Belle heeled on my left.

"I'm picking up Linc Sinclair's dog," I said, hoping Walt hadn't heard of Linc's arrest.

"I'll take you straight to his lab. We work on the same team, Linc and I."

"Team?" I didn't know there was a team. Sarah had told me it was Linc's research that caught the attention of the Nobel committee.

Walt apparently didn't feel the need to answer my question. I nodded my thanks as he held open the door to Linc's building. I waited as another professorial type came toward the door in a rush just behind us, screeching to a halt to admire and pat Belle. We chatted briefly about how golden retrievers are the best dogs. Belle thumped her tail in agreement and nudged the professor's hand with her nose.

He laughed, wiped his hands on his jeans, and strode down the hall.

"Harrumph," said Walt, his face contorted as though he'd been sucking on a lemon. "He's an upstart. A junior professor. Thinks his research is more important than anyone else's. He's dying to nudge us—Linc and me—out of the way and dazzle the Nobel committee with his whiz-bang formula to—" Walt waved his hands in front of his face as if brushing off a cloud of pesky mosquitoes. "Never mind what he does. It's not important. Not compared to our climate-change solution." He paused at a door marked *Global Climate and Energy.*

"Here we are." He opened the door to Linc's lab and office. "Linc? You in here, buddy? You've got a visitor."

Walt's words indicated he'd expected to find Linc in his lab. That meant he hadn't heard about Linc's arrest. I knew better than to assume that Apfel and Paolo hadn't picked the professor up, but I was glad to know that at least so far, Linc had escaped becoming the subject of widespread campus gossip. I hoped to keep it that way.

A student working at a lab bench was the only one inside. He turned and held up one finger, indicating that we should wait. After a few deft movements with a soldering iron, he set aside his instruments, and walked toward us.

"What can I do for you?" he asked. "Linc's not here right now."

"Slacking again?" Walt laughed. But I had the sense it wasn't a joke. The student winced almost imperceptibly and turned to me, tilting his head and raising his eyebrows.

"Sorry," I said, reaching to shake his hand. "I'm Maggie McDonald. My husband and I are friends of Linc's. I'm here to pick up Newton. He's staying with us while . . ." I couldn't make myself finish the sentence.

"I'm Allen Zander, Linc's lab tech and one of his grad students."

Before I could reply, the jovial professor we'd run into earlier emerged from the back of the lab carrying a steaming mug and what looked like a sack lunch.

"So glad to see you again," he said. He put the mug and bag down on a lab bench and held out his hand. "Keenan Barnaby."

"Maggie."

"And this lovely girl?" he asked, kneeling in front of Belle.

Belle thumped her tail and licked his face. Keenan seemed honored by her attention.

Walt, however, looked disgusted. "What are you doing over here, Keenan? You'll never be promoted from assistant professor if you don't spend more time in your own lab."

Keenan turned to Walt as though he'd just noticed the older man was in the room. "Oh, hey, Walt. You forget that we all can't fit in the cushy digs in this building. I'm over in the shared annex, remember? We can't all be on the fast track like you. Congratulations on your promotion to associate, by the way. At this rate, you'll make full professor by the time you hit seventy."

Walt puffed up when Keenan mentioned his promotion, but immediately deflated at Keenan's well-aimed barb.

Walt stepped back. "Well, I'll leave you in Allen's excellent hands, Mrs. McDonald. It was delightful to meet you." Had he been wearing a hat, I was sure he would have doffed it. While his accent held a hint of Texas, his manners had an Old World formality.

"Bastard," Allen said under his breath as the lab's hallway door swung closed behind Walt. "Who is Quintana to accuse Linc of slacking?"

"Never mind, Allen. He does that to everyone," Keenan said, opening his lunch bag or, considering the hour, I guessed it was more likely his dinner. He pulled out an enormous sourdough roll stuffed with meat I couldn't identify.

Allen looked at me and blushed. "I'm sorry you had to hear that. I'm tired of Walt—his snide remarks and his determination to convince the university and the Nobel committee that he should be recognized for work that Linc did on his own."

"Can he get away with that?" I asked. "What does Linc say?" Allen hadn't mentioned that Linc had been picked up by the police and I wasn't about to mention it. Besides my desire not to fuel gossip, I wasn't sure I could talk about it reasonably. The mere thought of the professor's arrest made me as steamed about Detective Awful as Allen was about Walt Quintana.

Allen looked at me and pushed up the sleeves on his lab coat. "Mrs. McDonald, would you like some tea? Keenan and I were about to take a break."

"I can split my sandwich with you," Keenan said. "Do you like pastrami? You aren't vegan, are you?"

"Does Newton need a walk first?" I looked around the lab but didn't see the enormous wolfhound.

"No. I just took him. He was upset when . . ." Allen looked around the room and his face flushed.

"It's okay, Allen. I know already. That's why I'm here."

"And I'm up to speed too," Keenan added. "I saw Linc when he was leaving with the police. He asked me to put away some of the papers he'd been working on."

Allen's shoulders lost their tension and he let out a long sigh. "Word will get out soon enough, but I don't want to add any fuel to the fire."

"I feel the same way." I shook my head as Keenen offered me half of his sandwich.

"Newt's such an old softy, but I was afraid he was going to take a chunk from the rump of one of the detectives who came to get Linc," Allen said, rubbing Belle's ears.

I could picture the dog's reaction easily. "Good for Newton."

"I put him back in Linc's office," said Allen, rising from his lab stool. "Newt has a bed there and feels more secure. I think he's asleep."

Allen grabbed a wheeled office chair from a desk-level counter that was home to an electron microscope and other lab equipment I didn't recognize. "Have a seat, Mrs. McDonald. If Linc trusts you enough to leave Newton with you, I know I can trust you implicitly. What kind of tea do you like?"

"Something caffeinated, please."

Allen walked across the lab to a small counter and washed his hands as if he were going to perform surgery. He plugged in an electric kettle, selected two mugs from a rack above the sink, and turned toward me. Keenan chewed his sandwich, closed his eyes, and didn't comment, but I didn't think he was missing a word of what Allen and I were saying.

"Thanks for coming. I live in an apartment and didn't know what to do with Newton. I love that guy almost as much as Linc does. I would have crashed here with him if I'd had to, but Officer"—Allen reached into his pocket, pulled out a business card, squinted, and read—"Paolo Bianchi. He said that you'd take Newton."

"I'm happy to do it. Newton and Belle are old friends." At the sound of her name, Belle thumped her tail.

"Thanks for not mentioning Linc's arrest to Walt," I said to Allen. He nodded and blew on his tea.

"How is Linc?" I asked. "You were here?"

"That jerk told me not to say anything," Allen said.

"I know who you mean. Gordon Apfel. I call him Detective Awful."

Allen snorted, in danger of spraying tea across the room. "He was also here yesterday looking for evidence and asking lots of questions about security. I assume they've looked at key-card records and security cameras."

I remembered Paolo's cryptic words as he was leaving my house. Something about comings and goings. Maybe he'd been hinting that I should be looking at security in Linc's lab.

Allen sipped his tea and stretched his arm toward the bottom drawer of the desk next to us. He pulled out a sleeve of chocolate-covered British biscuits and offered me one.

"So, the police?" I asked.

Allen thought for a moment. "They spoke to all of us." He looked at Keenan, who nodded agreement. His mouth was full of a large chunk of Delicious apple.

Allen went on. "Their questions were all over the map. Who was where and when? Who could account for the whereabouts of anyone else? What kind of security systems do we have? Who hated Linc? Was Linc happy with Sarah? Did they have problems? It was what you'd expect from watching a TV show."

I chewed my cookie and swallowed. "Do you have any ideas about what happened?"

Allen didn't answer, but lifted the tea bag from his tea and dropped it in a nearby trash can.

"Surely you've thought about it," I prompted.

"Of course," Allen said. "I've worked for Linc for two years and we're here at all hours checking on our tests and data." He blushed. "It's natural to consider, just for a moment, whether you've been working with a murderer, right?"

I nodded.

"I also thought about whether, with Linc arrested, I'll be able to continue my research. I've wondered who I'd work with, where I'd find funding, and what would happen to Linc's funding. We're supposedly using scientific principles to solve the problems of the world. But you'd be surprised how much time we waste chasing after grants and worrying about where our research money will come from. I'm convinced that's why we're not flying around in solar-powered cars, really, because of the paperwork and time required to lock in funding." Allen shrugged and smiled.

I nodded. "I sometimes think I'd make a deal with the devil if only my paperwork would vanish. Of course, helping people manage their paperwork is my job, so I shouldn't complain."

Keenan, who had finished his apple but seemed hesitant to join the conversation, slid from the counter. To Belle's delight, he sat on the floor beside her and began stroking her ears.

"I'd love to have a dog like you," Keenan said to Belle. "But I'm afraid you wouldn't have much fun in my tiny apartment. Belle is such a good name. Much better than Newton."

I thought the Newton comment was an odd non sequitur, but Allen laughed.

"I asked Linc about that. He said he named his dog Newton because the wolfhound looked like a canine reincarnation of Sir Isaac. They shared the same long snout and sixteenth-century wavy, unkempt hairdo. Linc had no worries about the scientists who put forth the notion that Sir Isaac was a self-centered jerk. His dog, the professor said, had a strong sense of his own identity."

Keenan chuckled. Allen smiled and continued recounting the story. "He said if I felt uncomfortable with the name, I could pretend the dog was named after the cookie."

Belle's ears perked up at the word *cookie*, and Keenan pulled a dog biscuit from his pocket. "Do you mind if I give her one?" he asked.

Belle scooted forward, thumping her tail. "Thanks," I said. "You know the way to a golden retriever's heart."

We watched Belle destroy the cookie and fall more deeply in love with Keenan.

Then Allen leaned forward. "Linc said he was talking to someone named Maggie about coming in here and streamlining the paper flow. Was that you?"

"Yes," I said as I rummaged in my purse for my business cards. I handed one to him and another to Keenan.

I sipped my tea while they examined my cards. Normally, at that point in a conversation, I'd launch into a short pitch for my business. But I wanted to get back to discussing Sarah's death.

"Can either of you think of any reason that someone would have wanted to kill Sarah? Or implicate Linc?"

Allen shook his head. "I don't think anyone around here knew Sarah very well. Aside from a few awkward department holiday parties, we don't get together much outside of work."

He turned to Keenan. "You've got a family, right? I've never met them."

Keenan rubbed his chin in a gesture I'd often seen in men with beards. I wondered if he'd ever had one. "Allen's right, come to think of it. We aren't a very social group."

"What about Linc? Could anyone have wanted to kill him but killed Sarah by mistake? Maybe that Walt Quintana? You said he was nipping at Linc's heels, begging to get in on the Nobel work?"

Keenan nodded. "I wouldn't put it past him. That guy is no good. All caught up in his own career path and how he can sabotage everyone else."

Allen shook his head and looked at the ceiling. "Linc told me that Walt's research was really promising, maybe ten years ago, but he spent all his time going to conferences, presenting papers, and promoting the work he'd already done. He didn't spend enough time in the lab or snagging grants so he could take his work to the next level. Now, instead of going back to his original research, he bounces between our lab and another one. He figures one or both teams will be nominated for one of the other big prizes. He wants a piece of that."

"But isn't science collaborative?"

"Of course," Allen said. "In fact, the first part of any project is researching what others have already accomplished. But there's a protocol to research and papers and snagging lab space. It's cutthroat, but seldom dishonest. Walt's actions lean toward what could be called . . . maybe not dishonest or unethical, but not squeaky-clean, either."

"Do you think he'd stoop to murder?" I asked.

"Hmm. Probably not. But even if he did, why would he kill Linc's fiancée? And why do it at Linc's house? Walt has access to the labs here. Linc spends all his time here. It would have been easier to fiddle with this equipment." Allen pointed to safety signs posted around the lab. "There are very strict rules about lab safety here. We don't let in the undergraduates. They have their own labs and are always supervised. Graduate students have to take a weeklong class before they start work and if they're caught making any mistakes or cutting corners, they're out."

"Is it really that dangerous?"

"Not if you follow the rules, but how easy would it have been to stage an accident and cover it up by saying that Linc had been working long hours and was distracted because of his upcoming wedding?"

Pretty easy, I figured, so I tried another tack. "So what's the story with the key cards? Linc said he was here almost all night on Sunday. Or rather Sunday night going into Monday morning. Surely there are cameras or key-card records that could verify that."

Keenan laughed. "It was pouring rain that night. Everyone entering the building would have looked the same." He demonstrated: "All hunched over with their hoodie pulled up."

I looked from Allen to Keenan. He had a point. Both young men were dressed in jeans, running shoes, gray T-shirts, and dark hoodies.

"Were either of you here that night?"

"Part of the night," Allen said. "But as your Detective Awful pointed out, time of death isn't an exact science. Sarah could have died before or after the time that I can vouch for Linc."

"And the key cards?"

"The detective got excited about that but—"

Keenan shook his head and interrupted Allen. "Key cards are useless as evidence. We're nerds here. The absentminded professor is a stereotype, but every stereotype has a basis in fact. My lab annex is in a building about a half-mile from here. If I forgot to bring my card with me, it would be ridiculous to waste time going back to get it when I could just have someone let me in. If Linc forgot his, but needed to run out to his car to get something, he'd grab my card. We're always swiping someone else in or propping the door open. It's a major breach of campus security rules, but we're engineers and we're stereotypically pragmatic. Security hates us."

He took a sip from his mug and added, "For that matter, key cards aren't that hard to clone. Almost anyone in this building could turn a plastic hotel key into a key card. I'm not saying this to implicate any-one, but I don't think the key-card data is as strong a clue as that de-tective thinks it is."

"Linc's lawyer ought to make short work of that evidence," I said.

"I tried to tell the detective that," Allen said, looking miserable. "But he didn't listen."

"He never does," I said.

Belle decided she'd been patient enough with this tea business. She sat up, sniffed the air, and barked. Newton let out an answering *woof.* Belle strained at the leash, pulling my wheeled chair a few feet away from the counter. Newton stood on his back legs and planted his front paws on the wired-glass windows of Linc's office.

"I think that's my cue to go," I said.

"Do you need any of his stuff? Food? Bed? I can help you carry it to your car."

"Newton's spent some time at our house. He's not too picky, so I think we're good. Do you know where his leash is?"

"It's in the office. Let me get him. I don't want him to run out and bounce around in here. He's usually pretty good, but with Belle here and Linc missing, I'm not sure how reliable his safety protocol will be."

Allen got Newton ready. He was a little squirrely, so I took Allen up on his offer to walk with me to the car.

"Nice to meet you, Keenan," I said.

"Same here. Nice to meet you too, Belle."

Belle wagged her tail and we followed Newton and Allen out the door.

As we left the building, I noticed that the door was propped open with an old tennis shoe.

"Is that the sort of security breach Keenan was talking about?" I asked, pointing toward the shoe. "Is it really that common? I would have thought that with the dangers you mentioned in the lab, you'd all want to be a little more safety conscious and restrict access."

Allen shrugged. "Keenan probably overstated the situation. Linc's absentminded about some things, but never about safety. And allowing unlimited access to this building isn't safe." Allen looked over his shoulder, back at the door to the lab, and shook his head. "For that matter, I'm not sure that I believe Linc asked Keenan to look after his papers. Linc took the time to lock up everything securely in his office before he left with the police."

I frowned. "Does he usually eat with you and Linc, or was he making excuses to be here right now and pump you for information about why the police were here?" I shuddered. "I hate the feeling that Linc and Sarah's life has turned into some sort of tabloid drama, being exploited for other people's entertainment." I stopped and rummaged in my pocket for a Kleenex. Belle turned, whined, and snuffled my hand, and I knelt to bury my face in her fur.

Allen sniffed next to me, and Newton whined, leaning firmly against my back. *Pull it together, Maggie,* I told myself. *Either that or upset the dogs and this nice young man.*

I stood and held out my hand for Newt's leash. "Thanks so much, Allen. I can find my way from here."

"You'll let me know if there's anything I can do? Tell the professor I know he didn't do this?"

I nodded and turned before Allen could see another few tears spill from my eyes. "I'm sure he'll be happy to hear that," I said as I strode briskly toward my car.

Chapter 10

I allow time each day to check my schedule and plans to
make sure they'll still work. If not, I adjust accordingly,
delegating, dropping, or delaying goals that can no
longer fit in the available time.

From the Notebook of Maggie McDonald,
Simplicity Itself Organizing Services

Tuesday, November 4, 7:00 p.m.

By the time I got home, I was ready to be done for the day. I took
a shower, poured myself a glass of wine, and sat at the kitchen
table surrounded by yellow legal pads, trying to pin down everything
I needed to accomplish over the next few days.

On one pad, I made a list of what I needed from the grocery store.
Another was for all the ways I could juggle my schedule to make
time to thwart Detective Awful and get Linc out of jail.

But I quickly got distracted, replaying my discussion with Allen
and Keenan. For now, I discarded their theory that anyone who was
trying to sabotage Linc's career could hurt him at the lab more easily
than at his home. Maybe the murderer deliberately set a deadly trap
at Linc's house to shift attention away from any of his Stanford colleagues.

I pulled my computer from its bag and fired it up. I knew that
there were all sorts of expensive online services that could reveal details about people's lives that at one time were considered private.
But I also knew that with my library research skills and a few targeted search criteria, I could discover nearly as much as was available through those fancy programs. Enough to get started, anyway.

I began with the names of the three men I'd met at Stanford: Keenan, Allen, and Walt. After only a few minutes, I learned that they all lived nearby and had all published articles in various academic journals. Allen, still a graduate student, had published the least and was almost always a secondary author. Keenan and Walt both had long lists of author credits in academic journals and popular science magazines. They'd been on panels at conferences and interviewed on network news programs and by national and local newspapers.

Digging deeper, I learned that Keenan was one of the youngest assistant professors in Stanford history and had published more than I would have suspected for someone his age. Yet, he'd referred to Walt as being on the "fast track." I wondered if Keenan had meant that remark to be sarcastic. I replayed the conversation in my mind, but couldn't come to a conclusion one way or another.

I looked more closely at the publication dates. *Interesting*. After years of regularly churning out articles and papers, Keenan Barnaby had published nothing in the last year.

My fingers flew across the keys. Looking at his Facebook page, I discovered he was married with an adorable young son he obviously doted on. I smiled as I clicked through the pictures, remembering Max's joy in playing with David and Brian when they were small.

Keenan had mentioned that he lived in a "tiny apartment" with no room for a dog. A man with a family to support who was living in a compact apartment with a rambunctious toddler might be desperate to boost his career and focus on gaining a secure position and a larger paycheck. But desperate enough to commit murder? I didn't think so. Lots of people might, on occasion, consider that their life might be simpler if they could eliminate one of the worst people in their lives. After all, I'd thought more than once about bumping off Detective Awful. But fantasy is a long way from reality. And thinking is a far cry from doing. I wanted to believe that Stanford professors would be smart enough to come up with alternative solutions to the problems they faced.

Belle liked Keenan. For now, I'd trust her judgment.

I turned my attention to Walt Quintana. He'd published widely, but was often not the first name on the paper. I wondered whether that was an indication that, as Allen had suggested, he had a tendency to ride on the coattails of others, neglecting his own once-promising research.

Or, could it just mean that he was generous in helping graduate students hungry for publishing credits?

I shifted to Stanford's list of recent press releases. One release distributed in March said Quintana had been named to a research group that was "working in parallel with" the group Linc headed.

Was "working in parallel" academic code for "in cutthroat competition?" I wasn't sure. My parents had both been professors at the university in Stockton, as had Max. Every university was basically a gossip factory—even lofty academic minds were subject to human frailties. But I'd never heard of professors having the level of competitive zeal that might lead to murder. I made a note to ask Max about it when we both got home.

Next, I checked into Allen. I found his address and the fact that he'd gone to University of California at Berkeley for his undergraduate work. I wondered which team he'd pick to win when archrivals Stanford and Cal faced each other in football.

Other than four years spent at Cal and a reasonably sized list of publications for a graduate student, I couldn't uncover many details about his life. I found a number of photographs of him with Linc in the lab and one of them playing in a fund-raising golf tournament. There was also a picture of the two of them laughing and wearing seventeenth-century wigs and knee-length pants that I couldn't begin to figure out.

I leaned back from the table and thought about Allen and what clues to his personality he might have dropped during my visit. He'd tried to shoot down my hypothesis that someone within the department had wanted to derail Linc's research by murdering the love of his life and framing him for the crime. Had Allen been trying to deflect attention? Could he be the guilty party? Could there be other lab assistants who might be suspects, but who weren't listed on Stanford's online list of department members? I couldn't think of any way to find out.

Belle stirred under the table at my feet, stretched, and walked to the back door. Newton scrambled to join her. Seconds later, I heard the car. Max was home with the boys.

Confusion reigned while the boys greeted the dogs and filled me in on their day. Quickly, though, they clamored up the stairs to practice their instruments and still have time for a rematch in the great video-game battle they'd begun at Influx. Belle and Newton followed.

Max hung his jacket on a hook by the back door and put his computer bag on a shelf next to the stairs, ready to be picked up the next time he went out. He kissed me and pulled a bit of cupcake frosting from my hair.

"I found a few leftovers from last night," I said.

"More wine?" he asked.

I nodded and Max pulled a wineglass from the cupboard. He poured himself a glass, refilled mine, and sat down at the table.

"What are you working on?" Max pulled one of my yellow pads closer to him.

I filled him in on Linc's arrest, Detective Awful's dreadful behavior, and my visit to the lab to pick up Newton. After telling him about the strange dynamic at the lab, I asked him about university-level competition.

"I have no idea how it works at Stanford," Max said. "But there's competition everywhere. You don't get to be a university professor unless you're passionate about your subject. Research grant money has been getting tighter and tighter, and has increased the pressure even more."

He took a sip of wine and stroked his chin where he'd once grown an admirable, but itchy, professorial beard. "One of the reasons I stayed in Stockton was that it's a smaller institution. Grants were smaller but the professors had collegial relationships." He paused and winked. "Most of the time, anyway. In general, we avoided the glaring spotlight of the large research universities and focused on teaching."

Max twirled the wine in his glass. "Are you thinking competition might have played a role in Sarah's death?"

I nodded and pushed the computer away so I wouldn't be tempted to continue typing while Max and I were talking.

"I was only in the lab for a few minutes when I went to pick up Newton," I told him. "But there was definitely an undercurrent of tension. And the kind of conversation that could be laughed off as friendly banter, but seemed more like targeted barbs meant to inflict real pain."

"That's the kind of fighting that academics normally do," Max said. "Clever insults. But in my personal experience, there just wasn't enough time in the day to accomplish everything I wanted to do. As soon as I got back to my lab or my office, I was very quickly enmeshed in research puzzles or my students' problems or trying to meet a deadline. Those skirmishes between colleagues didn't occupy much of my time. I certainly didn't have the leisure hours required to plan a murder."

I laughed at the idea of the optimistic Max considering a situation so dire that the only solution would be to kill a colleague.

Max put his palms on two of the yellow pads. "Mind if I take a look?"

"Not at all. Feel free to add to either one." Sometimes, my work with my clients was confidential, but these lists concerned him as much as they did me. "And thanks for getting the boys."

"No problem. We had fun."

He wrote *chocolate ice cream, chocolate chips, pecans* on the grocery list. The man was addicted to chocolate ice cream and chocolate-chip cookies with pecans. He pulled the second list toward him.

"Better put eggs, butter, and sugar on the list if you're thinking of cookies," I told him.

He made the additions to the first list and picked up the second. "*Get Linc out of jail*" he read out loud, then looked at me with one eyebrow raised. "Are you planning a jailbreak? What's this list going to be when it grows up?"

I laughed and took a sip of my wine, giving myself time to figure out a way to respond. It was a simple question that required a complex and multilayered answer. *When in doubt, lead with the truth.*

I sighed. "I don't know, Max. It's meant to be a list of all the things I need to do this week, but I'm getting nowhere with it."

"Want to dictate while I play scribe? We'll figure this out together." It was my turn to give Max a quizzical look. His ideas would be great, but his handwriting would make it nearly impossible for me to decipher his notes later on.

"I'll print carefully," he said. I shrugged my shoulders and stood to grab an emergency package of Oreos from the freezer. They were my go-to antianxiety medication. I offered the package to Max. He took two and I popped one and put three more next to my wineglass. The cookies would make the wine taste weird, but I didn't much care.

"Have you talked to Forrest?" I asked. "I'm so glad you got those two together when you did. At least we know that Linc had someone to consult with."

"Forrest is a brilliant attorney. Linc is in good hands. And helping him is Forrest's job. There's nothing we can do to make Linc's situation better tonight. So let's see what we can do for you."

"Tomorrow, I want to head over to Linc's house and make some progress on the last of his clutter. There's only one room left. I can move the entire contents to Sarah's cottage. I'm hoping that will make it easier for Tess and Linc to set their plans in motion as soon as the police cut him loose. They can't really keep him in jail long, can they?"

Max sighed. "I don't know, Mags. I'm not a lawyer or a cop or a district attorney. The evidence seems thin to me, if that helps." He sipped his wine. "But isn't the house locked up? Because it's a crime scene, I mean. Can you get in with your old key?"

I considered Max's words. I'd forgotten that the house had been locked up pending the arrival of the county's electrical expert—or a hastily drafted substitute.

"I'll text Paolo to ask, but even if I can't get into the main building, there are bags and boxes in the old carriage house there that are marked for donation, consignment, and trash. I'll get those cleared out tomorrow." I yawned and propped my head up with my hand.

Max stood, took my glass and his, and put them in the sink. He came back to the table and held out his hand. "But now, I think the best thing you can do for all of us, including Linc and yourself, is to get some sleep."

He pulled me gently up from the chair and hugged me. "Let's go shut down the boys' marathon gaming session. We could all use an early night."

The next morning on my way to Linc's I stopped at the Starbucks off Foothill Expressway. The café was Orchard View's unofficial conference room and mobile office. I ordered coffee and a hot croissant, then headed to Linc's.

I parked in front of the house and looked over the yard. The house looked empty and sad. The crime-scene tape was gone, but a lockbox like the ones Realtors use was suspended from the front doorknob. I didn't know whether my key would still work, or whether the lockbox just enabled various members of law enforcement to access the scene.

I texted Paolo to ask for permission to enter the house. While I waited for a reply, I ate my breakfast and checked email on my phone. By the time I'd finished both tasks and was brushing crumbs from my lap, I still hadn't heard from him.

I didn't want to do anything that might disrupt the official investigation or cause any delay in uncovering clues that would help nab Sarah's murderer. Especially if those clues pointed to someone other than Linc. But I needed to make progress on my own work for Linc.

Instead of entering the house, I unlocked the garage, which Linc called the carriage house. I'm not sure it had ever actually held a carriage, but it might have. The house dated back to horse-and-buggy days. Three pairs of wide doors opened into three broad bays. On the right end of the building, closest to the house, an open wooden staircase led to a three-room loft apartment that might have once housed a chauffeur.

It had taken us weeks to clear out the loft area, which was full of dusty, moth-eaten pieces of used furniture that weren't worth the extensive repairs that would have been required to renovate them. We'd hired an antiques expert to tell us which furniture in the house was valuable, what should be donated, and what could be safely recycled or discarded.

I tugged on the heavy door furthest to the right. It creaked open despite the fact that I'd oiled all the doors when we'd started working in the building. Stacks of boxes, bags, and other items filled half of the floor space. My heart sank. I'd remembered this pile of discards as much smaller and more manageable.

I grabbed a handcart and started moving the boxes, three at a time, to the curb. A local charity I'd called the night before had promised to pick up everything we had for them at about ten o'clock. When they'd come and gone, I'd take the discards and recyclable items out to the curb to be picked up by the local garbage company. After that, if there was anything left, I hoped it would be easy for me to figure out where it belonged.

I'd taken two trips to the curb with the handcart and was heading back for a third when I heard a car revving its motor somewhere down the street. I wrinkled my brow and looked up. I'd taken a few steps hesitantly toward the curb when I stopped and dropped the handcart. The black Range Rover, or at least one that looked just like it, was back. It slowed in front of Linc's house. The driver pulled to the wrong side of the street, and gunned the engine.

I reached for my cell phone in my pocket, hoping to get a better picture of the license plate, but the angle was wrong. I looked around to see if there were any neighbors who could call for help if the Range Rover driver took exception to having his picture taken. I didn't see anyone. I straightened my back and took a deep breath, grabbed the handcart as if it could offer me both protection and camouflage, and walked deliberately toward the curb, hoping to get a better angle on the SUV and its license.

I pulled my phone out again, searched for the camera app, and was all ready to take the picture when the Range Rover sped away, leaving me with a second blurry picture of what I was fairly sure was not a California plate. But it was difficult to be certain. California had so many specialized plates: whale tails, Lake Tahoe, Yosemite.

Before I had time to scowl at the picture, the now-distressingly familiar vehicle of Detective Awful pulled to the curb in the Range Rover's place. I turned with my handtruck and headed back to the carriage house for another load. If the detective had business inside Linc's house, he didn't need my help. And I certainly didn't need any of his assistance with my own efforts.

"Mrs. McDougal!" he called with his chainsaw-rough voice. "Stop right there. Right now."

I turned and then promptly wished I hadn't. The detective lumbered up the drive, rolling from side to side as if he were the captain of a ship on stormy seas or, more likely, was in need of a hip replacement. He adjusted his pants, brushed crumbs from his jacket, and tugged at his stained tie as he approached.

"Good morn–" I began.

"Mrs. McDougal, you know better. You're disturbing a crime scene. I ought to have you arrested. I told you to stay away from here."

"I—"

"No excuses. I don't want to hear them. You need to stop what you're doing, get into your car, and drive away. With your pal Linc in custody, you couldn't resist trying to muck up the evidence, could you?"

"What evidence?" I broke in when Awful stopped to take a breath.

"The garage is not a crime scene. I'm just finishing up the job Linc hired me to do. He labeled all this for disposal weeks ago."

"Weeks ago, eh? If you're such an efficient organizer, why's it still here? Huh?"

I ignored his question. "There is still a bit of work to be done in the house, Detective. Do you know when your people will be finished with it?"

"When we're finished."

I shook my head. There was really no point in going toe to toe with this man. He was a hopeless mess of a human being and I stood zero chance of changing him for the better. In fact, if both Paolo and Linc's futures weren't so closely intertwined with his, his constant obstruction and childish vying for supremacy would have been laughable.

"Detective," I began in what I hoped was my most patient, compliant, and polite tone. "I've arranged for a charity service to pick up those boxes and a few more of the ones in the garage at ten this morning. Did you want your men to look them over before the charity truck arrives? Or do you want to call the charity and tell them not to come? I'm happy to help find Sarah's killer in whatever way I can."

"I told you to stay out of it," he said.

"Would you like to take all this down to the station? Or to the county crime lab?"

Logging in every item in every bag and box in the garage and dealing with the paperwork required for evidence in a felony trial was, I expected, more than the detective wanted to get into. It would be a big job with a big price tag.

Paolo had told me that the detective had boasted that he could solve any crime faster and with less expense than any of Orchard View's current detectives and their fancy modern methods. All it took, Gordon Apfel had said, was good, old-fashioned police work— something I suspected he knew little about.

I pointed at the garbage bags stacked in a lopsided pyramid next to the remaining boxes. "Those are all discards for recycling," I said. "I want to get them out to the curb as soon as the charity picks up the boxes." I checked my watch. "Orchard View Refuse usually hits this neighborhood at about noon with its trucks."

Detective Awful stared from me, to the boxes at the curb, and then to the remaining stacks of discards in the carriage house. He wiped sweat from his forehead with a large bandanna.

"You need to stay out of the house," he said, shaking his finger at me. "And clear out as soon as your little housekeeping chores here are done."

"Absolutely." I was going to add *sir* to appease the detective, but couldn't bring myself to do it.

"Mrs. McDougal—"

"It's McDonald, actually. Maggie McDonald. But thank you so much for letting me finish up here. Please let me know if there is anything I can do to help you out."

"Just—stay—out—of—my—investigation."

I nodded, gritting my teeth to keep from saying anything that he could take the wrong way.

The detective's phone rang. He turned his back on me and walked toward the street while he took the call.

I'd started loading up the handcart with the last of the boxes when I heard the Range Rover's engine again. As before, the driver revved the motor at the end of the street and drove slowly past Linc's house. Perhaps because of the police vehicle parked at the curb, this time the Range Rover didn't stop.

I pulled my phone from my pocket and ran toward the detective.

"Did you see that? That black Range Rover? That's the third time I've seen it around here, doing the same thing—gunning its engine and driving slowly past the house, like it's stalking Linc. Do you know if someone is threatening him? Maybe someone who doesn't know you have him in custody? I have a picture of the license plate right here. It's a little blurry, though." I punched rapidly at the screen with my forefinger to bring up my stored photos.

"Mrs. McDougal—"

"McDonald. Mrs. McDonald. Maggie."

"Right. What did I tell you?"

"Stay out of it?"

"Exactly." Detective Awful turned abruptly and stomped to his car. Before I could think of anything else to add, he was gone. I wondered why he'd come to the house in the first place this morning. Had one of the neighbors seen me and dialed 911, thinking I was robbing Linc's house? If that were the case, surely dispatch would have sent a uniformed detective, rather than the head of a murder investigation? There was no way I could find out. Not while Awful was telling me to stay away.

The best thing for me to do, I decided, was to focus on the job at hand and get Linc's discards stacked at the curb.

The charity truck's driver was writing me a receipt when Paolo pulled his Subaru to the curb.

"Hey Maggie," Paolo said after the truck pulled away. "I got your message about the house. If you need to get inside, I can let you in or . . ." He looked up and down the street as if he was expecting spies to jump out from behind the nearest shrub. "The locks haven't been changed," he said in a whisper. "The old keys will still work."

I shook my head. "I don't need to get in today and I did tell Sir Awful I'd stay away . . . for now." I thought for a moment and started tapping on my phone. "There is something you can do for me, though. I keep seeing this black Range Rover. I saw it at the garden yesterday and here at the house twice today. It might be someone from the neighborhood, but it's coming and going at odd times and is making me nervous. I suppose whoever is driving could be a teenaged boy, high on testosterone, doing some drive-by stalking of a girl he has a crush on. But a shiny new Range Rover? For a teenager? It doesn't add up. And the driver seems . . . aggressive. There's lots of tire squealing, engine revving, rapid stops and starts. That kind of thing."

There were a few kids at the high school who drove showy new cars or their parents' pricey castoffs and drove with that "notice me" kind of behavior. For the most part, though, the parking lots were full of Toyotas, Hondas, and other vehicles almost as old as the teens who drove them. Cars that wouldn't be ruined by a few more dings, but that could safely transport kids in a town without school buses. And most, though inexperienced, were conscientious adherents to the vehicle code.

Paolo nodded and peered at my blurry photos. "I don't know if there's anything we can do with these pictures, but from your description of the driver's behavior, it sounds like he's up to no good. We'll keep an eye out and I'll check to see if there are other complaints. Can you send me the photos?"

I tapped the screen on my phone to send the images to him. "If he keeps coming around, I'll try to get a clearer picture of that tag," I said.

"Don't, Maggie. I'm worried that the driver may realize you're taking his picture and try to stop you. Don't engage him." Paolo looked me in the eye, which I knew was difficult for him. He excelled at the analytical aspects of police work but—though he was working on it—interpersonal interactions still didn't come naturally to him. "Please? Promise?"

I did.

Paolo helped me carry the last bags out for pickup by the garbage and recycling truck, then went back to work.

I returned the handcart to the garage in case we needed it for hauling out the equipment in Linc's workroom. Then I swept the floor clean and locked the garage door.

Brushing my dusty hands on my jeans, I looked toward the back of the house. Yesterday, when I saw the Range Rover, I thought I'd seen Santana in the passenger seat. If she was volunteering this afternoon, she might be able to identify the driver for me. Unless the driver seemed as aggressive and threatening to her as he seemed to me. I'd ask her. If she was willing to provide the name of the guy behind the Range Rover's wheel, it would allow me to solve that mystery without breaking my promise to Paolo.

I set off across the grass and ducked through the hedge.

Chapter 11

GPS Systems, online calendars, contact lists, and other digital organizational tools can be wonderful things–but only when three conditions are met:

1. You learn their features.
2. You use them.
3. They work.

Use the strategies, technologies, and applications that work for you, not those that work for your next-door neighbor's tech whiz kid, nor those that work for your best friend.

From the Notebook of Maggie McDonald,
Simplicity Itself Organizing Services

Wednesday, November 5, 10:45 a.m.

Once through the hedge, I stood still, examining the garden as a whole. Instead of turning left, toward the shed, I turned right. I surprised a small cottontail rabbit, which froze and then bounded into the shrubbery. Rustling vegetation told me the rabbit was putting lots of distance between us, probably along a familiar escape route.

My own path wound between the plots, which were heavily planted with winter vegetables or strewn with compost, ready to be turned over to restore the soil. I walked the path until it meandered back to the parking lot on the residential street in front of the garden shed. I heard water running into a metal container and saw Santana bending over the spigot.

I watched her as I approached, aware that she probably wouldn't be able to hear my footsteps on the gravel over the sound of the water sloshing against the metal sides of her watering can. Like most teens and young adults, Santana was better looking than she probably thought she was–strong, fit, and slim, and with long, straight blond hair escaping her ponytail.

I cleared my throat and she nearly dropped the watering can. She stepped back, startled.

"Good morning, Mrs. McDonald. You scared me!"

"I'm sorry, Santana. I wanted to come back and have another look around. I came the long way past the gardens at the back."

"Did you see Mr. Haskell's herb garden? It's my favorite. He's asked me to water it while he's on vacation. I love the smell of the herbs—like a perfume or something."

"I must have missed it. Are you going back there now? Maybe you could show me?"

Santana nodded and waved politely for me to precede her on the path. It made for an awkward walk, since I had to keep looking back to verify I was headed in the right direction.

I didn't take me long to realize that Santana was also checking the path behind her, as if she was afraid someone was following her. She caught me noticing and startled, much like the rabbit had earlier.

"Go on, Mrs. McDonald, Maggie," she said. "We'll turn left just before we get to the end."

Mr. Haskell's garden was as fragrant as Santana had described. Each well-pruned stand of perennial herb was marked with its own stake: rosemary, lavender, lemon thyme, verbena, and chives.

Santana watered the plants, closed her eyes, and breathed in deeply. Her shoulders relaxed and she smiled. "You're a skeptic and you think I'm nuts, I'll bet, but do it. It's so relaxing. It makes me believe all that aromatherapy stuff."

I did as she asked: Closed my eyes and took a deep, slow breath layered with the scent of the herbs and rich, warmed soil. I took a second breath and opened my eyes to see Santana staring expectedly with an amused look on her face.

"Told you so," she said.

"You did. And you were right." I broke off a bit of lavender and rubbed it between my fingers. "I can see . . . er, *smell*, why this is your favorite."

Santana knelt to pinch off a few branches and clean up dead leaves, which she put in the now-empty watering can.

I pulled out my phone, selected my photo app, and scrolled to the picture of the Range Rover. Santana spent a lot of time here in the garden. If the Range Rover belonged to a neighbor, she would almost certainly have heard and seen it.

"Would you mind looking at a picture I took?" I said, holding out the phone. "It's a little blurry, but I think you might be able to identify it."

Santana brushed her hands on her overalls and took the phone from me. She enlarged the picture, then shaded her eyes to peer at it.

"It's a black Range Rover and relatively new," I said. "I've been seeing it around Linc's house, and the other day it was in the parking lot here. Do you know the driver? Is he local?"

Santana gasped, turned pale, and shook her head. She handed the phone back to me, still shaking her head.

"What is it? Do you know him?" I asked as I took the phone and looked at the picture to see if it had changed into something more alarming than a big, black SUV.

Santana backed away and walked quickly toward the shed, mumbling something about finishing her chores.

The gravel behind me crunched and I turned to see a silver-haired man in his late seventies, doffing a crumpled felt hat that was a good match for Indiana Jones's Stetson fedora.

"Morning, ma'am," he said. "I thought I heard voices here. Were you talking to yourself?"

I smiled. "No, Santana was here. She just left. Do you know her?"

"Of course. She's always a big help. My big bag of mulch was getting a little too awkward for me to lift from the car to the wheelbarrow and she took care of it for me. Chatting all the while like a little sparrow. Made me forget I'm an old man."

I started to respond, but he went on talking. "Seeing you're here, can you use any of these vegetables? I overplant and get way more than I can eat by myself."

He thrust forward a flat basket artfully arranged with carrots, turnips, shiny green kale, and bright rainbow chard.

I looked to see if he really meant for me to take it. He nodded and I selected a carrot and a bunch of chard.

"No, no. Take it all. I picked some just yesterday that will last me the week. Where's your car? I'll walk you to it."

"I—well, I—" I stammered. "I've been working over at the Sinclairs', cleaning out the garage for the professor. I'm parked in front of his house. You don't want to go all the way over there."

"No," he agreed. "I'm about done for the day. Take the basket and bring it back to the shed next time you come." He held the basket out and raised his eyebrows when I didn't take it from him right away. "Go on, now. Take it. I can't hold it here all day. I trust you. What would you want with a dirty, empty basket? Bring it back and I'll fill it again. If I'm not here, just leave it at the shed. No one will take it."

I smiled at the old-fashioned system of trust and gentility. "I'd be delighted," I said and nearly curtsied.

His face lit up. "I'm grateful to be able to share. It's my pleasure. My pleasure, indeed." He lifted his hat, brushed his hands on his worn trousers, and headed down the path toward the shed and the parking lot beyond.

Too late, I realized I should have shown him the picture on my phone. I followed after him, hoping to see Santana again before I left.

When I got to the shed, the older man had left and Santana was locking up. She carried a forest-green backpack heavily loaded with what looked like textbooks.

"Santana, are you on your way to a class? Can I give you a lift?"

The girl visibly relaxed and let out a breath. Hoisting the strap of her backpack up on her shoulder, she took a step toward me.

"Would you mind? I'm headed up to Foothill College. I was going to catch the bus, but I'm running a little late."

"Of course I don't mind. My car's over in front of Professor Sinclair's house. I'll have you there in ten minutes."

"Thanks," she said. "Wednesdays are slow around here. Other days I can get a ride from one of the other volunteers, but Wednesdays I count on catching the bus."

I switched the vegetable basket to my other hand, and we walked side by side on the path that led back to the opening in the hedge. Once we'd settled in the car and were on the road, I looked over at Santana, sitting comfortably, but with her hand still tightly wrapped around the strap of her backpack the way she might protect her belongings among strangers on public transportation.

"What classes are you taking?" I asked, expecting her to mention the general-education classes most kids took to figure out what they were interested in and to prepare for transferring to one of the four-year state schools.

"Calculus three and physics," she said. "The professor is so cool. He works at Stanford part of the week and teaches a class or two at the junior college. He says he'll write me a recommendation for Stanford. I want to do engineering. Maybe aero-astro or biomedical."

"Wow," I said, making the turn onto Foothill Expressway and dodging a car that changed lanes without looking. "I was expecting general-education courses like English or history or something."

"I'm taking a vampire-lit course at night, but it's super-easy—and fun too. The other students are really nice."

"I think I know someone else taking that class—Lily Takahashi. Do you know her?"

"Yeah. Lily, anyway. I don't know her last name."

I remembered that Lily had said there was a girl in the class who was afraid of some guy and that was why they all walked in a group to the parking lot. I wondered if I should mention that to Santana. I didn't know her very well and asking about an abusive partner was personal. On the other hand, if Santana was trying to get out of an abusive relationship, she might well need some help. She was a young girl with few resources other than the fiercely protective Boots. I forged ahead.

"Lily said there was someone in the class who was afraid of a stalker or someone like that," I said, hesitating and waiting for a response.

Santana stared out the side window, tightened the grip on her backpack, and chewed on a hangnail.

"Was that you? Is someone bothering you? Is he the one who drives the Range Rover?"

She turned to me, her eyes damp with tears. Her chin jutted out and she crossed her arms in front of her. "I told him it was over. I told him I was done and to leave me alone."

"But he drives through the neighborhood all the time and revs the motor so you'll know he's here."

Santana nodded.

I kept my eyes on the road. We weren't far from the junior college, and I was afraid that if we arrived before the conversation was finished, Santana would leave the car and I'd miss my opportunity to learn about her stalker or help her in any way.

"That's stalking, Santana, and it's illegal. Is he dangerous? You can report him. The police need to know."

"Uh-uh. No way. You can't tell."

"I could phone the police for you, if you're afraid to, or if you've promised you won't."

Santana squirmed in her seat. "You can't tell. Promise me you won't. Promise. It will only make things worse."

She was crying in earnest now, so I assured her I wouldn't report her situation to the police. "I've already told them about the car, though. I thought it could be a clue to Sarah's murder."

Once we were on the campus, Santana directed me through a maze of alleyways to the student union near the center of campus. She looked behind my car before she opened the door.

"I checked, Santana. No one has followed us."

She looked at me skeptically as she moved to open her door. "Um. Thanks for the ride."

I leaned over the passenger seat. "Santana, wait." She paused, looking again like a terrified, cornered animal.

I handed her one of my cards. "Call me if you need a ride anywhere. I want you to be safe. If you need help, call me or call the police."

Santana took the card. "I think you've done enough already." She swung her backpack onto her shoulder, slammed the door behind her, ducked behind a dumpster, and was gone.

I'd started to back up when a campus police car pulled up next to my bumper, preventing me from backing or making any kind of a turn.

A security officer in a green uniform stepped from the car and rapped on my window.

"Ma'am, you can't park your car here. The alley is restricted to special permits for delivery vehicles." He pointed to a sign saying the same thing in big red letters.

"I'm sorry, sir," I said. "I was giving a neighbor a lift. She's having trouble, uh . . ."

"Walking? We can get you a temporary disability permit if you need one, and there's a drop-off spot you can use to get her closer to the building."

"Thanks, I'm sure her regular driver has all that. I'm just filling in and didn't know I needed any paperwork. I'm really sorry."

"No problem, ma'am, but I won't see you here again now that you know, right?"

I nodded. "That's right, thank you." He patted the roof of the car and started to walk away. "Officer?" I called after him. "Can you show me how to get out of here and back onto the main campus road? My neighbor gave me directions on the way in."

He laughed. "I'll back up my car and let you get turned around, and then you can follow me out. It is a bit of maze. I think it's deliberate."

I thanked him, followed him out, and then headed back home, thinking about Santana's predicament. Dealing with young adults was tough. I wanted to respect Santana's request and allow her to make her own adult decisions, but I was sure she was wrong not to involve the police. Stalkers often escalate into violent behavior with no warning. If Santana was working in the garden, it was likely that she was one of Boots's projects—a former foster kid with no family support system. I should not have promised to keep her secret.

As I pulled into our driveway, though, I realized I'd promised Santana I wouldn't say anything about her situation. Technically, that promise wouldn't stop me from telling Paolo the little I now knew about the Range Rover's driver. Knowing that he was in some way connected to Santana might help the police track him down. I dialed Paolo's number, but before I could say anything about the Range Rover, Paolo started speaking quickly and with great enthusiasm.

"Maggie, I'm glad you called. I've got *great* news!"

Chapter 12

The best-laid plans go out the window in any
emergency. Having an emergency plan sketched out and
shared with every family member can help diminish the
impact of any disaster and speed the return to normal.
Some professional organizers specialize in creating tai-
lored emergency plans to streamline and individualize
that process.

From the Notebook of Maggie McDonald,
Simplicity Itself Organizing Services

Wednesday, November 5, 1:00 p.m.

"Linc's been released and all the charges have been dropped,"
Paolo said. "One of our patrol cars is taking him back to your
house as we speak."

"Thank heavens. But how on earth did that happen?"

Paolo laughed in a way that was almost a snicker . . . or even a
giggle. "Don't repeat any of this, but one of the assistant district at-
torneys was looking at the case, preparing for the arraignment, I
guess, and had a question. She went to the district attorney, who blew
a gasket because it was the first she'd heard about a high-profile
murder case that she should have been pulled in on from the begin-
ning. She found out that Apfel went to the judge for an arrest warrant
behind her back. She was livid. Especially since there is really no evidence against Linc. I mean, there is a witness statement about con-
flicts between Linc and Sarah, but it's weak at best. And we couldn't
find anyone else to corroborate the story. The DA tore 'em—er, blis-

tered the ears of everyone from the chief and the mayor to Apfel himself."

"Is Apfel gone?"

"If only. He's furious. To hear him tell it, the DA is an upstart kid who gave him a slap on the wrist to flex her power. He says she let the murderer loose, and if Linc runs, it will be the DA's fault."

"But Linc isn't going to run—he's got all his research at Stanford."

"I know. But Apfel's trying to sell himself as the poor cop, working his fingers to the bone, only to have his hands tied by the prosecutor's office. I overheard him laughing with some of the older guys on the force who were teasing him about being schooled by a woman."

"She's the district attorney. How far is he going to go before his old-school politics catch up with him?"

"Exactly. Cops have to work with the prosecutors. We don't always get along, but everything goes more smoothly when we at least respect each other and the procedures. The way Apfel is throwing his weight around will make it more difficult to work with anyone in the prosecutor's office in the future. They've got long memories too. It will take eons to repair the damage."

"So what happens now?"

"Same as before. Apfel keeps harassing Linc, trying to stir up some new evidence, and I keep working the case to find Sarah's real killer."

"What about media coverage?" I asked. "Are the news crews going to be harassing Linc too? Has he made any statements? Has Apfel?" I heard crunching from the other end of the phone.

"Sorry, Maggie. I don't mean to chew in your ear, but I've got an energy bar. I can't remember when I last ate. I just needed to call you right away."

"That's okay, Paolo, I understand. You need to eat. So, about the media. Should I expect to have news trucks blocking my road? That will make my neighbor Dennis very unhappy."

"I doubt it," Paolo said. "That's why one of our patrol officers is driving Linc to your house—there was a big media presence here when they released him, but if there is any more coverage, I think they'll focus on Stanford or Linc's home address. They don't have a way to connect you and Linc. You should be fine."

I hoped so, but knowing how easy it was for me to find information about the three men I'd met in the lab, I doubted that resourceful news crews would be kept away for long.

"Thanks for calling," I said. "I hope you find the real killer soon, so Apfel and the news crews will leave Linc alone. He's grieving. He doesn't need to be harassed."

"I'm on it," Paolo said and ended the call.

Immediately afterwards, I realized I hadn't had a chance to tell Paolo about the driver of the Range Rover. I phoned him back, but before I could leave a voice mail, send a text, or write an email, the dogs started barking and Newton pawed at the door. He dashed from one window seat to another, scratching on the glass as if he meant to go through it.

All the barks were happy ones, though. Linc was home.

It was a tumultuous homecoming. Even moving around the house was difficult, because Newton glued himself to Linc's trouser leg and went wherever Linc did. Some of our doorways and hallways weren't quite wide enough to accommodate a large man and his enormous and exuberant dog.

Thursday morning we repeated our routine from Tuesday, with Max taking David to the high school and me dropping off first Brian and then Linc and Newton. Linc was anxious to get back in the lab and asked me to drive him there.

We saw one news truck interviewing Walt Quintana in front of Linc's lab, so I went to the loading dock on the opposite side of the building. I waited while Linc swiped his card and opened the door. Linc hadn't had a chance to talk to any of his departmental or university administrators about his arrest or Sarah's murder. Neither one of us was sure whether his card would still work.

Later, after I'd been to the grocery store, put away the groceries, made fresh coffee, and was thinking about hiking one of the trails behind the house with Belle, my cell phone rang. It was Linc.

"Hi, Linc," I said. "Are you settling in at the lab? Dodging reporters?"

He didn't answer immediately and I grew alarmed. "What's wrong? Are you there?" As I said the words, I felt sheepish. I'd overreacted. It was probably just a bad connection with a long delay.

"I'm fine, Maggie. I've had a little trouble with my bicycle, I'm afraid. I took a tumble and Newton's hurt. I'm reluctant to ask for another favor, but would you be willing to pick us up at the house and take us back to campus? My vet isn't far from here, but I don't think Newton will be comfortable walking."

"I'll be right there," I said, knowing from experience with the kids that it was more important for me to arrive quickly in a crisis than it was to have answers to all my immediate questions.

"Don't hang up, Maggie. Are you still there?"

"Still here," I said as I scrambled for my keys and my backpack.

"Do you have an old sheet or a beach towel we can put on the seat for Newt? I don't want him to stain your car."

"I'll find something." I hung up the phone and tore down the basement steps to the laundry room. I'd cleared out our oldest and most worn sheets before we'd moved, not thinking that moving often requires painting, and painting requires tarps and cleaning rags. But the kids had changed their beds over the weekend, and I'd thrown the clean ones in the dryer this morning. I reached in and grabbed an armful of red and blue plaid cotton and raced back up the stairs. I wasn't too worried about my car's upholstery—I knew a million ways to remove bloodstains.

Fresh, clean sheets would be better than old rags or towels at sopping up blood without introducing foreign material into Newton's wounds. I tried not to worry as I drove as carefully as I could, repeating a police driving-course mantra that Jason Mueller had once told my boys: "Slow is smooth. Smooth is fast." The phrase had originated in the armed services, he'd told them, and referred to aiming and shooting a firearm. But it applied equally well to driving.

What he didn't say was that slow is also really difficult. I cursed under my breath at every red light and slow driver and tried not to think about Newton bleeding out. I pulled in front of Linc's house on the wrong side of the street, just as the black Range Rover had done.

I saw Linc and Newton on the front lawn. Newton whimpered and tried to lick his flank where he'd lost both fur and skin across an area nearly as large as a dinner plate. While most of the wound had the meat-like appearance of bad road rash and would be painful but not serious, several lacerations were deeper and oozing blood. Linc was using his sweatshirt to apply pressure. His bicycle lay abandoned on the grass with its front wheel bent like a taco. One of the pedals was missing.

I opened the back hatch of the SUV and pulled out the sheets, dropping a pair of my underwear on the pavement in the process. I had no time for shyness. I picked up the pink microfiber blob and stuffed it in my pocket.

"Let's wrap him up and move him into the back, Linc. You can sit in there with him to keep him quiet. Do you know if anything's broken?"

"His leg, maybe. He cried when I touched it. But it could just be that abrasion. It's bad."

Newton thumped his tail and licked my hand as I worked to tuck the sheet under him. I knew that even the most loving dog could bite when in pain, but Linc was here and I hoped that would calm the wolfhound.

"Linc, can you move up by his head? I trust Newton, but if we hurt him when we move him, he's less likely to bite you than he is me."

Linc looked shocked and moved slowly.

"What about you? Do *you* have anything broken?"

Linc looked gray and sweaty and didn't answer. *Uh-oh.* I needed to get both of these patients medical care as quickly as possible. I didn't think I needed to call 911, but I didn't like the look of Linc's ashen skin and his swollen left wrist and thumb.

When we picked up Newton, using one of the sheets as a stretcher, I was glad I'd brought the newer sheets. Discarded linen could have easily ripped and dropped poor Newton in the street. As it was, we moved the now-shivering dog gently into the back of my SUV as if we'd been canine EMTs all our lives. Linc jumped in after Newton, and I flipped the levers on the backseats to make more room for both of them before I got behind the wheel. *Slow is smooth. Smooth is fast.*

I didn't want to inflict more pain or injury on either one of my passengers as I sped to the vet's office on El Camino. "Linc, call ahead and let them know we're coming. Describe Newt's injuries as best you can."

I knew the vet was theoretically open twenty-four hours, but I was certain Newton was going to need anesthesia before anyone could get the deeply imbedded road debris out of his road rash or stitch him up safely. I wanted to be sure that every doctor and technician Newt needed would be there to take care of him when we arrived. Linc would want to stay with his dog—his only remaining family member besides Sarah's cat—but I was going to ask the vet techs to help me determine whether he needed trauma care of his own.

Chapter 13

When you're in the care of emergency professionals,
take note of the way their pockets and equipment storage
are organized and labeled. Relax, you're in good hands.

*From the Notebook of Maggie McDonald,
Simplicity Itself Organizing Services*

Thursday, November 6, 10:00 a.m.

The veterinary team whisked Newton away for X-rays, stitches, and whatever else he needed. Linc had completed the required paperwork and had his own wounds assessed by a vet tech who said he'd seen worse wounds on those who'd tried to give a de-skunking bath to a feral cat. I still didn't like the look of his left hand, but no amount of urging on my part made him agree to let me have a "people doctor" take a look.

I'd encouraged him to leave his cell number with the front desk and take a break to grab some fresh clothes that weren't covered with Newton's blood. When he insisted on staying, the staff found him a set of scrubs to change into so that he wouldn't scare the other patrons. And we waited, while I tried to distract Linc from his worries.

He didn't take his eyes from the swinging doors through which Newton had disappeared.

"Why don't they tell us anything?" he asked. I had no answer to give him. Instead, I tried to distract him with questions of my own.

"Do you want to tell me what really happened here?" I asked. "I'm no physicist, but it seems to me that Newton's injuries tell a story that involves way more force than a simple fall or skid on a bicycle. Did someone hit you?"

Linc adjusted his glasses and looked around the room before meeting my gaze. He pushed back his hair and flushed. "I'm sorry, Maggie. I should have told you."

"You *were* hit." I frowned and pulled my cell phone from my pocket to show him my pictures of the Range Rover.

"Is this the car?" I asked. "A black Range Rover? Did it hit you? Have you seen it before?"

Linc peered at the screen. "I don't think so. The car that hit us was a pickup truck. Silver, I think. Not one of those little imported ones and not one of the giant ones with huge tires. Just a standard big truck. Probably American. Like a cowboy would drive. I think it was reasonably clean."

Reasonably clean was a pretty precise descriptor. In the middle of the drought, most people were foregoing washing their cars until they had to worry about soiling their clothes if they brushed against the side panels. Clean cars were few and far between.

I typed his thorough description into the notes app on my phone.

"Would you recognize it if you saw it again? Have you seen it anywhere before?" I asked.

Linc put his hands on his thighs in an unsuccessful effort to stop his knees from jiggling. "I'd recognize it again. But I don't think I've seen it before. Or, if I have, there was no reason for it to stand out. Show me the picture again. Why did you think that was the guy that hit us?"

"I've seen him near your house," I said, deciding to hold off on telling him about the connection to Santana until I had to. "I was cleaning out the garage yesterday and he drove by twice." I leaned back in the turquoise plastic chair and let out a frustrated sigh. "He's super obnoxious. If he'd sped by when you were home, you would have noticed. He revs the engine to get attention, squeals the tires, and drives down the street at about twenty miles an hour over the speed limit. Then he parks on the wrong side of the street in front of your house."

Linc laughed. "So he's not exactly sneaking around. I'd say it was a hormone-addled teenager trying to get some girl's attention, but the only young ladies on our street are preschool age, and I don't think there are too many teens who could afford a Range Rover."

"Exactly what I thought," I told him. "But I asked Paolo to keep an eye out for it, just in case." I chewed my lip and thought for a moment. I'd had about enough of people in trouble keeping secrets from one another. Especially when they were secrets that, once shared, might keep everyone a little safer. "He's been harassing one of the girls from the garden. According to her, he can be dangerous. It sounds like whoever hit you is no choirboy either. The pickup that hit you didn't stop. You were injured and so was Newton. That's a hit-and-run. He had to have been lying in wait, watching for a chance to hit you. That's illegal too. This guy could face a number of serious charges, including vehicular assault and reckless endangerment."

Linc looked at me as though he didn't understand what I'd said. "I figured it was just someone who was texting and didn't realize he'd hit us. Why would you assume it was deliberate?"

"He'd have to have been pretty darned distracted not to see Newton. And with the damage done to the two of you, he must have hit you pretty hard. That's something any driver *had* to have heard and felt. Yet he drove off."

I plowed on. "If someone is trying to hurt you, I think it plays into Sarah's death. What if whoever murdered Sarah was trying to kill you and hasn't given up? You need to tell the police about the silver truck. We can call the department or contact Paolo directly. What do you think?" I picked up my phone and held it out to him.

Linc shook his head. "Why would someone want to hurt me?" he said. "All I do is go to work and come home. Eat, sleep, work."

"Jealousy? Money?"

Linc stood and walked over to a cage filled with five young kittens awaiting adoption. They were splashing water from their bowl and had drenched themselves, their food, and their kitty litter.

Linc sneezed, then walked back and sat down next to me. "It makes no sense, but then, nothing has made much sense lately."

"I know. It's terrible. But look at it this way: Detective Awful hasn't given up on wanting to arrest you. If anything, he's more determined now than ever before. Telling him that someone ran you off the road surely makes it more likely there's a murderer out there and less likely that *you* are that murderer. Have there been any other similar incidents that you can think of? Ones that might have looked like nothing at the time, but in retrospect may have been an attempt on your life or Sarah's?"

"But why?"

"Could someone want to prevent you from meeting with the Nobel committee? Someone who thinks another team deserves the prize? From Stanford or somewhere else?"

"That's ridiculous. I mean, I guess there are always crazy people whose thinking defies logic, and we can't ever completely rule them out, but every year there are people who believe that they or their colleagues are more deserving of a Nobel than whoever actually wins the prize. There will always be people like that, but as far as I know no one has ever been killed." He stared at the doors again, then stood and walked closer to peer through the portholes before returning to his seat. "No one's dog has ever been attacked over the Nobel Prize."

Neither of us said anything for a moment.

Then Linc turned toward me. "Will you call Paolo for me?"

"Of course. Do you mind if I call him right away? He may want to ask you some questions, since I didn't see the incident."

"That's fine. I don't suppose the police are going to jump all over this anyway. Honestly, Maggie, academia is not known as a hotbed of homicidal mania."

I left the waiting room and went outside to make the call. The sky had grown dark and the wind had come up. I wondered if we were going to get some overdue rain. Paolo didn't answer, but I left a detailed message about the accident and the injuries Linc and Newton had sustained. I had finished the call and had my hand on the waiting-room door when I had another dreadful thought: If someone was trying to kill Linc and learned he'd been staying at our house, were we going to be safe if he remained with us? I considered phoning Paolo back, but instead I called Max and told him everything that was happening, including that fact that I'd called the police.

"I'm glad you're able to be there for Linc," he told me. "Sounds like he's in no condition to drive. Will you be able to bring him home?"

"Yes. He seems remarkably calm, scary calm, but I'm afraid he may crumble at any moment."

"And how are you? You also seem remarkably, scary calm."

"I'm fine, I guess. Newton's injuries looked dreadful and they've been working on him for a long time. But . . . Max?"

"Spill it, Maggie. What's worrying you?"

"What if someone really is trying to kill Linc? Will we be in danger too? Will the boys? Did I do the right thing when I invited him to stay with us?"

Max was quiet for a moment. I was just about to ask if he was still on the line when he spoke. "Good question. But I don't think we're the best ones to judge. After everything that happened in September, we're both a little prone to panic. That rainstorm last Sunday had me pacing the living room holding a golf club. Every time a branch fell I jumped."

"You didn't tell me that. I like the idea of you defending us from bad guys in your T-shirt and boxers with a golf club."

"The cats didn't like it, either," Max said. "They kept watch on the window seats with their tails twitching."

I laughed, but I was still nervous and so, I guessed, was Max.

"I'm going to phone Stephen," he said. "He'll have a better sense of whether we should worry and whether we should get one of his veteran friends out here to stand guard with another golf club, or if Linc needs more protection than we can provide."

I let out a breath and muscles I didn't know I'd tensed relaxed from my neck and shoulders to my toes.

"That's a great idea. Be sure to ask Stephen how Jason's doing and whether they need any help."

Max agreed. I felt better and ready to return to support Linc.

When I went back inside, a technician was speaking to another customer about his elderly cat, whose name was apparently Fred. Fred, it seemed, was going to be just fine following a course of antibiotics.

Another tech came through the doors with a clipboard, consulted it, and stepped toward Linc. "Dr. Sinclair?" he asked.

Linc stood, but the tech motioned for him to sit down. He knelt in front of us with his clipboard.

"Dr. Davidson is finishing up with Newton now. It looks like he has a cracked rib, but no internal bleeding or organ damage. The doctor thoroughly cleaned all the wounds and is stitching them where he can. Once he's done with all that, he wants to take another set of X-rays to make sure nothing's changed. On the first set, there was some question whether Newton may have a hairline fracture in his right ulna that would require a cast."

Linc nodded and grabbed his own right forearm in sympathy. He winced. I didn't want to interrupt, but I was determined to find a way to convince him to get his left hand examined.

"He's a lucky boy, Dr. Sinclair. Dr. Davidson would like to keep him here overnight and most of tomorrow to keep an eye on him. If all goes well, we can bandage him up and send him home with you tomorrow afternoon. You'll need to restrict his activities and keep that abraded area clean. Keep watch on it too. Let us know if it shows any sign of infection."

"Can we see him?" I asked. The technician shook his head. "Dr. Davidson isn't finished with him yet, and he'll be under the anesthesia for a while. After that, we'll keep him sedated to prevent him from ripping out the stitches or hurting himself further." The technician went over medication schedules with Linc and my attention wandered. I yanked it back when I heard the tech say "police."

"This was no accident," the tech said. "And even if it was, the driver left the scene when there were injuries. Dr. Davidson urges you to phone the police. He'd be happy to provide an assessment of Newton's injuries if it will help."

I assured him I'd just called.

"Great," he said. "The doctor will be glad to hear it. Please tell the police to call us if they have any questions. Now, I'm supposed to tell you to go home and tend to your own injuries so you're ready to look after Newton when he's ready to leave." He consulted his clipboard. "Is this the right number to phone you tonight and tomorrow morning with an update?" he asked, showing the paperwork to Linc.

When Linc agreed, the tech assured him he'd receive a call if anything changed between tonight and the following morning, and that Newton could not be in better hands.

I stood and Linc followed. On the way home, my message signal pinged. I asked Linc to read it to me.

"It's from Max," he said. "*SL says OVPD will patrol. SL will send someone. Name is Rocket. We won't see him, but he'll be there.*"

I glanced at Linc, who was staring at me and the phone. "Care to explain?" he asked.

"Sorry, that's pretty cryptic. Max and I were talking, wondering how safe it was for you to be staying with us when there had been several attempts on your life."

"Do you want me to move to a motel?"

"Of course not," I said, though the thought had crossed my mind. If Stephen or Max had thought that the boys were at risk, I would have driven Linc to a motel myself. A nice one. That allowed pets.

"Well, then. Who is SL and who or what is Rocket?"

"SL is Stephen Laird. After we talked, Max called Stephen to consult with him about the level of risk and how we could reduce the danger to all of us. He has friends from the Marine Corps. Retired Special Forces guys like him. Rocket's one of them, I'm guessing."

"We won't see him, but he'll be there? What is he, a ninja?"

I laughed. "If Stephen says this guy is good, he's good. But not all of his friends like to be social. Some of them have considerable scars, both internal and external."

Linc nodded and sighed. "I wish we could treat the mind as well as we can the body. Someday, maybe." He stared out the window for a moment. "Okay, then. Rocket it is. If Stephen vouches for him, that's good enough for me."

"The police will be patrolling too," I reminded him.

"Great. But I'm not going to live in fear. Do you mind being a nursing home for a wolfhound for a while? Or, with all those stairs, maybe it would be easier for Newt to be at Sarah's."

He slapped his right hand on the dashboard and I jumped at the sound. "Arghhh! This is so frustrating. That lawyer, Forrest Doucett, was going to check to see when I can get into Sarah's house or my own. It's ridiculous that we've been kept out of my home for so long."

He rummaged in his pocket for his phone, pulled it out, and stared at the screen. "No messages."

"There's time enough to worry about that after Dr. Davidson updates you on Newt's condition tomorrow."

I decided to shift the subject. "Linc, who has access to your house? I know that Tess and I have keys. Sarah did, and so does Boots. But is there a neighbor or anyone else who could get in without breaking down a door or a window? Do you keep a spare key anywhere?"

"Hmm. If there are any other keys out there, I'm not aware of them. But I haven't changed the locks. They've been the same for the last sixty years. Maybe I should rethink that. Oh, wait. As far as access goes . . ." Linc chuckled for a moment. "There's a kid over at the garden. I don't know what her background is, but she's real sharp and motivated. At Boots's request, I've been tutoring her in chemistry and physics. I get the sense that whatever schooling she's had in the past was hit-and-miss. Either she moved a lot—most of the foster kids do—or she was homeschooled by someone who didn't have much of a math and science background. She's quick, though, and fun to teach."

"And she has a key?"

"Santana? No. Actually, she climbs up that huge live oak on the side of the house. The one with the limb that extends over the porch roof. From there, she drops down to the roof and opens the window to my office. She comes and goes like the character in a kid's book. I'm glad I'm not her foster parent. You'd never be able to keep her out if she wanted in, or in if she wanted out."

"I've met Santana. She's a character. How much have you taught her? Could she have been doing an experiment that backfired and caused Sarah's death?" Once again, I cursed the fact that we didn't have access to the forensic report on the house's electrical system.

"I don't think so. She's careless sometimes, but she's never done anything deadly."

I was thinking that if Santana could get in, anyone could get in, but I didn't say anything to Linc.

We were stopped at the light just before I needed to turn off Foothill Expressway when Linc asked if we could visit an ATM. He also wanted to get some kitten food for Jelly. I took the next left, parked in the Rancho Shopping Plaza, and we agreed to meet at the car in twenty minutes. I picked up more milk and orange juice along with a rotisserie chicken, premade salad, and precut fresh vegetables to stir-fry for dinner. It wasn't the best meal we'd ever eat, but it would be quick.

Back in the car, I was wary of seeming like I was interrogating Linc, but the questions I'd asked were distracting him from his worry about Newton, so I pressed on.

"You've told me a little about Santana," I said. "But what about the other kids at the gardens. Do you know them? Are they all volunteers?"

"The older kids are all volunteers, and I think they come to the gardens on Boots's recommendation. There are some younger kids around, but they're mostly preschoolers who come to dig in the dirt with their mothers." He laughed. "I think the gardens could do with a shower for them. They are delightfully grubby when they go home."

"Grubby is good for kids."

Linc nodded. "I don't know all the volunteers, just the ones who've stopped by to bring vegetables and flowers. But they seem like nice kids. Sarah was fascinated by what Boots was doing over there. Sarah thought it mirrored what she was doing at the middle school—trying to create a safe place and a safety net to keep kids from falling through the cracks. There could always be some bad apples, I guess—that's what you're after, isn't it?"

I tilted my head from side to side to ease the tense muscles in my neck. "I'm not sure. I was at first. I thought maybe Sarah had seen something illegal happening in the garden from the upstairs windows of your house. I thought someone might have killed her to keep her from saying anything."

"But now?"

"Everyone I've talked to has only good things to say about Boots. The kids I've met seem polite enough. I haven't completely given up my suspicions, but I'm leaning toward being more like Sarah—just plain interested in all the things Boots is trying to accomplish."

I pulled in front of the house. Linc and I got out with our groceries. He carried his with his right hand, protecting the injured left, but I knew better than to suggest the medical attention he'd rejected earlier. It wasn't until after dinner that I had a chance to think about the rest of my unanswered questions and how to address them.

I phoned Stephen to find out what, if anything, Jason knew about updates in the case. It turned out Stephen was more interested in updates from me.

"Max called me earlier about Linc, so I'm up to date on that," he said. "But what else have you learned?"

"Actually, that's something you can help me with. I did some computer snooping on some of the people I've talked to so far, but I don't know anything about their legal history. I'd ask Paolo, but I think he's getting nervous about his job security and his workload."

"He's got his hands full with your Detective Awful."

"How hard would it be for you or Jason, if that's better, to run the names through the police department's databases and see if any of them have an arrest history?"

"Super-easy," he said. "I can do that for you myself. The armed services have access to law enforcement and FBI records to weed out bad recruits. I can't tell you who has a record, or what those records might entail, but I can tell you who is squeaky-clean, if that would help."

"And could you pass along the names of anyone with a record to Paolo?"

"Absolutely."

Later, after saying good-bye to Stephen and in between hearing about what the kids had been up to and warming up our premade dinner, I was able to compile a list of potential suspects and send it off to Stephen. As the rest of our hectic weekday evening schedule unfolded, I had a blissful few hours of laughter and normal family life before I thought again about the threats to Linc's life.

Chapter 14

Many of my clients, particularly teens, have trouble remembering to charge their phones. I recommend investing the time and the money in finding a solution that works so that phones are reliably charged.

Multiple chargers in bedrooms, homework stations, and cars may help. Some families establish a policy that dictates stashing all phones in a charging device right inside the front door so that family time isn't spent staring at phones.

It's worth experimenting. Your teen is working on establishing lifelong organizational systems.

From the Notebook of Maggie McDonald,
Simplicity Itself Organizing Services

Friday, November 7, 1:00 a.m.

I'd been restless for a long time before falling asleep and when Belle's barking woke me, I sprang immediately into alarm mode. Max and I collided at the doorway to our bedroom, shrugging into sweatshirts and dashing across the hall to make sure our boys were safe. Linc met us at the base of the attic stairs, holding his phone.

"I'm afraid my phone woke Belle up. I'm sorry to have disturbed the whole household. It was security. Stanford." He took a deep breath, squared his shoulders, and started again. "The Stanford Department of Public Security. There's been a small explosion in my lab and they want my help to secure the site. I'm the emergency contact for our building."

"Was anyone hurt?" Max asked.

"Not as far as I know. I've got to get dressed and drive over there."

"Is there anything we can do?" I asked.

Linc blinked and looked at the ceiling as though he'd find the answer there. I suspected he was not as awake as he'd first appeared.

"Do you want a lift over there? Your car is still at Stanford, isn't it?"

"No, no, I've asked too much of you already. I'll ride my b—oh, right. It's banged up and still at the house."

Max reached around the edge of our bedroom doorframe, grabbed his keys from the dresser, and tossed them to Linc. "Take mine," he said.

"Go on up and get dressed," I told Linc. "I'll make you a sandwich and coffee to take with you. Who knows when you'll get another chance to eat?"

I dashed down the stairs before Linc could protest. Max came with me and brewed the coffee while I threw a sandwich together.

"That was nice of you to lend Linc your car," I told him.

"It wasn't nice. Not at all. I didn't want you to drive him at this hour, and I didn't want to go out, either. If he's not back by the time I need to go to work, I'll work from home."

"I'm not sure whether you're clever or lazy, but it was still a nice gesture."

Max dodged the compliment. "That looks great," he said, nodding to the sandwich I'd finished and was cutting into two halves. "Would you make me one? Please?"

I chuckled. "Look and see if there are any cookies left too."

I decided I might as well make sandwiches for the kids' lunches too, since morning was going to come way too quickly following this impromptu midnight snack.

Linc flew down the stairs. I gave him his sandwich and a travel mug. Max handed him a flashlight from the lineup on the counter at the back door. Flashlights were Max's thing. He made sure we had fully charged and fully operational flashlights at the ready for any disaster. He referred to his obsession as "earthquake preparedness," but the kids and I suspected he just liked flashlights.

We'd only just gone back to sleep when our house phone rang.

Bleary-eyed, I patted the side table until I connected with the phone and located the *on* button in the dark. "Hello?"

"Maggie McDonald?"

"Who is this?"

"Stanford security. Do you know Professor Sinclair?"

I sat up straighter in bed and turned to drape my feet over the side and shove them into the worn shearling boots I used as slippers.

"Yes, of course. He's at his lab. Didn't you call him an hour ago?" I squinted at the clock to check the time. It was after two a.m. "Surely he's there with you?"

"He never arrived."

"I'm sorry, did you say he's not there? How long has it been? Did you try phoning him?"

"He's not here yet. We've tried calling his cell phone, but there's no answer. We hoped maybe he'd just gone back to sleep."

I shook my head, trying to force myself to be a little more awake. Max shrugged into his sweatshirt for the second time and mimed that he'd go downstairs and heat up the coffee.

"I saw him leave," I explained. I thought for a moment, searching for a logical and benign explanation for Linc's absence. It wasn't as though he'd have any trouble finding his own lab or that there would be any traffic at this time of night.

"Maybe the car ran out of gas." I tried to make myself believe the words as I spoke them. "I'll hop in the car and drive over there. I'm sure I'll run into him on the way."

I was about to hang up the phone when I had another thought. One I wished I hadn't. "Are you still there? Did you call the Orchard View police?" It seemed unlikely that Linc might have crossed paths with the silver truck that had run him off the road, but I would feel better if I knew the police were looking for him. I could give him a lift in my car if his had broken down, but if he'd tangled with the silver truck, chances were we'd need the police.

"We have, ma'am. They're also on the lookout for him. If you're coming this way, would you mind phoning me or checking in with me once you get here?"

He texted me his name and contact information. I dressed quickly and pulled my rumpled hair into a ponytail.

"Maggie, let me go," Max said. "I don't like the idea of you driving all over Orchard View alone in the middle of the night."

"But I already know where Linc's building is. You know what a labyrinth the campus is. It's so easy to get lost, especially in the dark. It will be faster if I go. Can you stay here and hold down the fort?"

Max peered into the dark outside our bedroom window. "If I can't, Rocket is out there."

"I forgot about him. Should we take him some coffee or something?"

"I'll call out into the darkness after you leave and see if he wants anything. I'll feel ridiculous, but I'll do it."

Like Linc, I dashed to the car, barely giving Max time to blow me a kiss and urge me to be safe. He followed me to the car and handed me a sandwich and travel mug.

I cursed the time it took for the windshield to clear and tried to remember "slow is smooth and smooth is fast." It's more difficult than it sounds.

I pulled the car out of the driveway and headed down the hill toward Foothill Expressway, peering through the bottom of the windshield where the defroster and the windshield wipers had cleared the condensation.

Halfway to Stanford, I saw flashing lights, flares, and heard sirens. I slowed for the cop who was directing what little traffic there was in the middle of the night. He waved for me to drive on, but I stopped and rolled down the window.

"Please keep driving, ma'am. We want to keep the lane clear for a tow truck."

"I'm sorry, Officer," I said, forcing myself to speak slowly and more calmly than I felt. "But Stanford security asked me to try to locate Professor Linc Sinclair. He's driving my husband's Prius. Can you tell me whether he's been involved in this accident? Is he hurt?"

The officer looked nervously over his shoulder, which scared me more than the news that a tow truck had been called.

"Can I park over there, off the road, and check with your supervisor?" I asked, pointing to the right-hand shoulder beyond the cluster of emergency vehicles. When you're new on the job, I knew, it's difficult to answer questions that weren't included in your training. And this officer looked brand-new.

He agreed and waved me on.

I found Linc seated on the back deck of an ambulance, where a paramedic was patching him up with Steri-Strips and gauze bandages.

The parts of his body that weren't banged up from his previous crash sported fresh wounds. I stood to the side to let the paramedic complete his work.

"You're pretty battered and bruised here already, sir," said the paramedic, palpating some of the worst of Linc's injuries. "And I really don't like the look of that hand. It needs an X-ray and a splint, maybe a cast. Have you had a doctor look at it?"

Linc nodded, although I knew that the closest he'd come to a doctor were the veterinary technicians he'd seen while Newton was receiving treatment.

"Are you safe at home, sir? Is someone hurting you?" The paramedic knelt down and looked Linc in the eye while he waited for an answer.

"What? Safe?" Linc asked, but then his brain must have kicked in. "Oh, thanks. No. I'm safe at home and at work. No one is abusing me, if that's what you mean."

I stepped forward and put my hand on Linc's shoulder. "He's been staying with me for the past few days," I said. "Is he good to go? Do you need to take him in?"

"I'm recommending we transport him to Stanford Hospital for X-rays and observation," the paramedic said. "He hit that fence hard and his Prius is totaled."

"No, no," said Linc, putting his hand on my shoulder and standing up. He winced as he stepped forward. "I borrowed that car. Oh, Maggie. I'm so sorry. Max will kill me."

"Max will be glad you walked away from the crash," I told Linc. "Don't worry about the car."

"Sit back down, sir. I'd feel more comfortable if you went to the hospital, but if you refuse medical attention, I'll need you to sign a form. And I strongly recommend you see your own doctor tomorrow. If you'd sit right here, I'll get that paperwork for you."

"Ma'am?" The paramedic gestured to me to join him a few steps away from where Linc sat.

"He was getting agitated in the patient compartment when we were working on him, and asked to stay outside where he could see what was going on with his car. Does he have mental health issues we should know about?"

I explained Linc's recent history and told him that Stanford security was waiting for us. When a patrol sergeant introduced himself, I gave both of the emergency responders the name of my Stanford security contact and asked them to call him and let him know where we both were.

After a quick consultation over an interagency communications system that reduced all conversations to a series of squawks and coded terms I couldn't understand, both the sergeant and paramedic said that we could go after Linc took a Breathalyzer test and had signed a ream of forms that he flipped through without reading.

In between forms, the patrol sergeant asked about the accident. Linc told him about the silver pickup that had pushed him off the road. At first I thought he was talking about the previous accident. But then I looked at the side of Max's car and saw the long streaks where it had collided with the silver pickup.

But Linc had been driving Max's car. The only way the driver of the truck could have known Linc was in the car was if he'd been spying on us, waiting for Linc to leave. I shivered and felt violated, knowing that someone had been watching the house and my family.

"Sergeant, that silver pickup has been stalking this man," I said. "That's where his other injuries came from. Paolo Bianchi at Orchard View PD knows all about it. Do you know him? He's got the background on the truck."

The patrol sergeant nodded gravely with a look on his face that gave nothing away. I wondered if he'd practiced the expression in the mirror, or if they gave lessons at the police academy.

"Sergeant, the silver truck," I said, tamping down the hint of hysteria I heard in my voice. "Are you aware that you're supposed to be on the lookout for it? Should you call in to indicate it's been in what could have been a very serious accident? Please tell me you're taking this seriously."

"Of course, ma'am," the sergeant said. "We take all the cases we investigate seriously. We've already called it in." He gave Linc his card and said someone from the department would call in the morning to talk about the accident, give him the papers he'd need for the insurance, and address any follow-up issues.

"The car actually belongs to my husband," I said. "Max McDonald."

The sergeant turned to me with an indulgent smile and I suddenly felt very sheepish. "Of course," I said. "I'm sorry, Sergeant. You already know that from the registration, don't you?"

"Mrs. McDonald. It's late and we're all tired. That's the thing about accidents. They shake people up and they never happen at the right time. Please, don't worry about it. And here, give my card to your husband too."

I pocketed the man's card and noted how refreshing his manners and attitude were compared to Detective Apfel's.

"And get those injuries looked at," the sergeant told Linc. "You may find them a good deal more painful after the adrenaline wears off."

Linc traded the blanket the emergency crew had given him for a warm jacket Max had stashed in the back of his car. I found gloves and a warm cap in the pockets of my jacket, which I didn't recognize in the dark. Max must have handed me the first available jacket hanging on the pegs by the door.

I turned my car's heater on full blast as Linc gave me directions to his lab.

"Linc, I'm going to hang around and give you a ride home. Your car has been sitting in the lot for ages. Anyone could have gotten to it. You shouldn't drive it or even start it until the police have had a chance to look it over."

"Maggie, I think you watch too much television," he said.

I turned to look at him with the "do as I say I'm your mom" look I used on Brian and David. It must have been scarier than I thought.

"Okay, okay. You can drive me home," Linc said. "Turn right up here at the stop sign."

Stanford liked to encourage walking and discourage driving. It would have been impossible for me to find a direct route to the building, especially in the dark, but Linc knew a few shortcuts of dubious legality. We stopped at a blinking barricade in the road. Linc flashed his badge and the security guard waved us through as he clicked his shoulder mic and let his supervisor know we were on the way.

As we drew closer to the building, another officer wearing a reflective safety vest and super-cool glow-in-the-dark gloves directed us to park in the back of a building next to the one where I'd picked up Newton.

A smoky smell permeated the air. In the beams of the bright generator-powered emergency lights, I could see that the same air was filled with particulates. I covered my mouth with a gloved hand and looked around to see if the security team was wearing masks.

And that's when I spotted Detective Awful. I ducked into the shadow behind one of the generators and felt ridiculous. It was too late to hide. He'd seen me and my effort to avoid him.

But, before he could approach us, a young woman with a remarkable resemblance to Kate Middleton introduced herself as the university's chief of police and showed us her identification.

"Professor Sinclair?" she asked.

"Linc, please."

"Are you all right, sir? You look pretty banged up. Do you need to sit down?"

"No, no, I'm fine. But someone called me—hours ago by now—about securing the lab? Was anyone hurt? My graduate students work late. Was anyone injured? The night cleaning staff?"

The chief took Linc by the elbow and moved him away from the crowd. I trotted after them, wondering what my role was here, but determined to learn as much as I could. Tonight's attack on Linc's car was, I thought, the third attempt on his life, and I wanted to be sure the chief would give it the attention it deserved. The explosion at the lab couldn't be a coincidence, either.

I sidled up next to Linc just as the chief explained that the Santa Clara County Arson Squad had arrived on the scene an hour earlier. "They've found no sign that anyone was inside the building when it exploded. My own campus investigators are making sure everyone with access cards has been accounted for."

"They told me on the phone it was a small explosion," Linc said. "It doesn't look too bad from here . . ." Linc's voice broke, and I grabbed hold of his hand to lend him what strength I could.

The chief looked at me as if seeing me for the first time. "And you are?"

Linc blinked and stepped forward. "May I introduce Maggie Mc-Donald? She's a friend. I've been staying with her family for a few days. Maggie, this is Chief Katherine Trent."

I reached out to shake hands, but the chief ignored my gesture and turned to Linc.

"As far as the building goes, don't let it fool you," Katherine said. "The inside is a mess. We'll start escorting researchers in one by one tomorrow to retrieve their belongings, but no one will be working here for a good, long time."

Then the chief turned toward me and held out her hand. I shook it.

She'd ignored me before, but she was balancing a number of priorities and I could easily forgive a minor lapse in social protocol.

"Mrs. McDonald, it's very nice to meet you. I am, however, going to have to ask you to step behind the yellow tape. Our crowd of onlookers is growing, and I need to keep this area clear for law enforcement."

"Linc?" I wanted to respect the chief's wishes, but he was still emotionally fragile and after several attempts on his life, physically fragile as well. If he needed me to be here with him, I was going nowhere, chief or no chief.

Linc patted the air, as if he were trying to keep me from getting riled up. "I'll be fine."

"Professor Sinclair," the chief said. "I'd like to ask you some more questions. Alone."

Linc looked at me and I looked back. We both shrugged. "I'll be right here when you're finished," I said. "I'll take you home when you're ready."

Chief Trent escorted Linc across the rubble, guiding him with her hand on his elbow. I turned back and ducked under the crime-scene tape. I'd spotted a concrete bench where I could wait for Linc and observe the movements of the emergency professionals and the crowd.

I texted Paolo to let him know about Linc's accident, my suspicions about the silver pickup, and the explosion in the lab. I knew that Stanford, Orchard View, and Santa Clara County law enforcement shared information, but things were happening so fast, I wasn't counting on anyone's ability to keep up. Besides, texting Paolo gave me something to do while I was waiting.

While I texted, a shadow loomed over me. I looked up. It was Detective Awful. I looked down again. "Just a moment, please, Detective," I said.

He growled under his breath, and for the first time I wondered if he'd ever thought about what he sounded like to others. Did he intend to be as obnoxious as he seemed? I finished my text to Paolo and then sent a quick message to Max to assure him I was okay.

"Where's your professor?" Awful asked. "What are you doing here? Returning to the scene of the crime?"

The crowd around us gasped and Awful appeared to notice them for the first time. What was he thinking, blurting out information like that on a university campus? Before he could adjust his pants again, the news would have raced around the dorms twice.

"Get up and come with me, Mrs. McDougal."

I sat, waiting for some semblance of manners from Awful and wondering if I'd wait all night. I was so tired of his constantly combative nature. And his inability to remember my name. I deserved respect from him. Everyone did. But this time I was going to insist upon it.

"Are you deaf? Come with me. Now," he commanded.

"Please?"

"Aw, for crissake—*puh-leese*, Mrs. McDougal. Won't you *puh-leese* join me beyond the crime-scene tape. Don't trip now, ma'am. Watch your step." He took my arm but I shrugged it off. I tried another strategy.

"I'm glad you found me, Detective. Did Paolo pass along my messages? Linc's life is in danger. Someone's been targeting him and tried to run him off the road."

"Mrs. McDougal. The police are not in the habit of seeing threats when an uncoordinated fool falls off his bicycle, or fails to maintain his automobile."

"But you'll look into it? Now that someone tried to blow up his lab? A lab he habitually worked in past midnight?"

The detective sneered and started to respond, but I suddenly had the sense that I was being watched. I looked over my shoulder at the crowd, which had doubled in size in the last few minutes. Of course I felt like I was being examined under a microscope. Hordes of students were monitoring me and everyone else working beyond the barriers and tape. Half of them were taking video or snapshots with their cameras. The other half were texting.

"Why are you here, Mrs. McDougal? If it's to tell me how to run my investigation, I'm quite sure that I've told you to stay. *Out. Of. It.*"

"It's Mrs. Mc*Donald*," I reminded him. "And is this, in fact, your investigation, Detective? I was certain that Chief Trent told me she was coordinating her investigation with the Santa Clara County Arson Squad. Is Orchard View here in a support role? To help with crowd control?"

Detective Awful reached for his handcuffs and I stepped back, fearing I'd pushed him too far. Lucky for me, his radio squawked and he stepped away to answer it. While his back was turned, I ducked under the crime-scene tape and sat on the bench in the shadows, pulling up the hood on my coat. I'd be able to spot Linc when he came back out of the building, but I hoped it would be difficult for Detective Awful to find me.

I looked at the clock on my phone. Where had the time gone? It was nearly four in the morning. I yawned, shivered, and tugged my coat more tightly around me.

"Evening, Maggie," a voice said from just over my shoulder.

I turned and saw one of the scientists I'd met when I picked up Linc's dog. I searched my memory for his name.

"Keenan Barnaby," he said. "You're here tonight without the beautiful Belle?"

"This isn't really her kind of adventure," I said, wrinkling my nose at the smoke, lights, and crowd. "No one has a ball to throw." I stood to shake hands, then looked at the ground and rocked from my heels to my toes, trying to keep warm. "I'm sorry," I said, shrugging. "My conversational skills are at low ebb at this hour."

"No worries. I spotted you in the crowd and figured I'd say hello."

"This is pretty incredible. A bomb? I didn't know people actually planted bombs in academic buildings. When I was in school people would call in bomb threats to disrupt the campus, but no one was stupid enough to actually plant one."

"It's the first time I've been happy to have my lab in the annex," Keenan said. "But this will be a major disruption for the whole department." He lifted his chin toward the building. "The dean is over there and I want to see if there's anything I can do to help, if you'll excuse me?"

I nodded and he left. "Good luck," I called after him as he pushed through the crowd. I glanced around me to see if there was anywhere I could get warm. My hands and feet were freezing, although the temperature was a reasonable 45 degrees and the wind was low. I searched my sluggish brain for something to distract me, and remembered that Stephen was often up late at night and early in the morning. Sleep sometimes eluded him completely. It was a problem for him, but tonight it might work in my favor. I phoned him and left a message when he didn't pick up.

"I hope I'm not waking you. I'm at Stanford. There's been an . . . incident at Linc's lab. When you get a chance can you let me know if you got that list of suspects? Oh, and do you have a number for the Santa Clara County District Attorney's Office? I've completely lost my patience with Gordon Apfel. He's getting increasingly obnoxious, which I might be able to tolerate if he were any closer to finding Sarah's killer. This case goes beyond Orchard View. Apfel is over here at Stanford mucking up an investigation that involves Stanford and Santa Clara County. He's neither use nor ornament and someone has to do something about it." I took a breath and realized I'd been ranting. "Good morning—and—I hope Jason is doing better. I spent just a few minutes with that awful man and my manners have become almost as dreadful as his. Sorry. Call me."

I ended the call and looked up to take in my immediate surroundings. I still had that itchy feeling between my shoulder blades that made me feel I was being watched. I moved through the crowd to be nearer the back entrance through which Chief Trent and Linc had disappeared.

Chapter 15

You can't break the laws of physics. Entropy dictates
that any system, unattended, will move in the direction
of increased disorder.

For proof, look no further than your sock drawer.

*From the Notebook of Maggie McDonald,
Simplicity Itself Organizing Services*

Friday, November 7, 4:00 a.m.

By the time Linc was finished, we were both ready to drop.
"Keep me awake on the way home," I told Linc as I backed the
car out of the loading area and we found our way to Campus Drive,
approaching Foothill Expressway one stop sign at a time. "Do you
know what happened?"

"It was a bomb. In my office. Under my desk. If we'd been there,
Newton and I would have been injured very badly, or . . ."

Linc coughed to try and conceal a sob. He covered his face and
his head dropped.

"What is it? What's wrong? Do I need to stop?"

Linc shook his head, unrolled the window, and leaned his head
against the seat back.

"Maggie, it's my fault. Sarah's death too. Someone wants me out
of their way and they don't care who gets hurt in the process. Who's
next? You? Your family? One of my grad students or colleagues?
It's not even safe for you to drive me. Stop here and let me off."

Linc reached for the door handle and I feared he'd jump out while the car was moving. I flicked the lever to activate the child locks on his door and kept driving.

"It's not your fault, Linc. You didn't kill Sarah and you didn't detonate the bomb. Whoever murdered her and caused the explosion is at fault. Not you."

He looked unconvinced.

"If anyone else is blame-worthy here, it's Gordon Apfel. He short-circuited the investigation into Sarah's death and refused to look at any suspects other than you. She died in your house, Linc." Linc made a cry of pain and I quickly backpedaled. "No, Linc. I didn't mean that. Just because it was your house doesn't mean it was your fault. But wouldn't it be reasonable to think that whoever set a trap in your home had been hoping to murder you? Sarah typically spent Sunday nights at her own house. If she was the target, wouldn't they have gone to her house?"

"That's logical thinking, Maggie. But who's to say that a murderer would be rational?"

"You've got me there, but we have to start somewhere."

My phone interrupted as it rang and vibrated on the console between us.

"Can you get that? I think it's Stephen. Put him on speaker."

"Hi Stephen, I've got you on speaker in the car with Linc," I said once Linc had answered the phone.

"I got your message and left a message for the district attorney on your behalf. I know that she's been following Apfel carefully, particularly after he did that end-run around her to get the warrant for Linc's arrest. I expect she'll be on the phone to the Orchard View chief first thing in the morning."

"That's great news, Stephen. Thanks."

"My pleasure. I'm not sure how soon you'll see action on this. There's always a bit of friction between the DA's office and the police."

"And how's Jason?"

"His fever was up a bit. I'm taking him to the doctor in the morning."

"I'm sorry to hear that. I thought he was doing so well."

"I'm sure he'll be fine. He's tough. But enough about us. I haven't had a chance to run those suspects' names for you. I can't do it remotely, but I'll head over to the VA in the morning."

"I'll call you then. Right now Linc and I are fighting to keep our eyes open. We've been up since the wee hours with—well, it's a long story. Can I bring you some food this afternoon? I can explain then."

"No more food. Our fridge is overflowing. If you want to visit, that would be great. Or if you want to come and get some food to take home, we'll welcome you. But no more food."

"Give your guy a hug for us."

We ended the call and I turned to Linc while we waited at a red light. "Sounds like the DA is on your side."

"Maybe. But Maggie, do you want to turn left up ahead and take me to Sarah's? I'll crash there and grab her car in the morning—if you don't mind taking care of Jelly."

I signaled for a lane change, checked my mirrors and blind spot, and frowned. A silver pickup truck with darkly tinted windows followed us as closely as if someone had tied it to my bumper.

"Check your mirror. Could that be the truck that ran you and Newt off the road?"

Linc looked in the passenger-side mirror, then turned and squinted into the high beams of the truck.

I sped up to catch the end of the left-turn light at El Monte Road. My tires squealed as I went through the intersection on the yellow light. My phone, my notepad, and the assorted detritus of a busy "mom car" flew off the console and into the darkness of the backseat and beyond.

"He's still on our tail," Linc said, peering into the right-side mirror.

There was no traffic as far ahead as I could see, so I sped up, trying to lose him. I considered turning left or right into the residential neighborhoods but rejected that idea. Too many Orchard View pet owners walked their dogs early before leaving for work. With few streetlights, and at the speed I was going, my chances of seeing them before I ran them over were nil.

"If you can get to El Camino, you can head to the police station in Sunnyvale," Linc said. "If you drive this fast, you may even snag the attention of a patrol car. They've been cracking down on speeders."

"Good idea. In the plus column, I'm not sleepy anymore."

I took another squealing turn right onto El Camino and my SUV rocked from side to side before it settled enough for me to push the accelerator to the floor. My suburban kid-transport vehicle wasn't designed for a high-speed chase.

"Keep an eye out for cross-traffic," I told Linc. "I going to run the red lights unless you see someone I can't avoid."

"You're doing great."

The car swerved for no reason and I feared I'd blown a tire. But the car quickly stabilized, and I figured I'd hit a defect in the road surface. Even if I'd seen a pothole, I wouldn't have had time to avoid it.

"Watch out. He's right on your bumper."

The truck rammed us and I struggled to maintain my grip on the steering wheel. "Where are all those people who call about loud parties? Can't they hear my tires squealing? They should call the police."

Linc patted his pockets. "I'll call. If I can figure out where I put my phone."

"Don't. Don't take your eyes off the road and don't light us up with your phone screen."

Before we were even halfway to Sunnyvale, before we heard a single siren, the pickup backed off, and I thought we were safe. I started to let out a breath, but froze again as the pickup's lights blinked on and off and its engine revved.

I felt the truck ram us before I heard it. He hit the left rear corner of the car and the taillight broke with a pop. I fought to keep the car from heading into a spin, but the wheels bounced up over the curb and into a large parking lot. It was empty of cars, but full of parking berms. I struggled to avoid them, but was afraid to hit the brakes. If I slowed, the truck would catch us. I half-remembered instructions from my driver's-education classes about not braking during a skid. I wasn't sure if those rules applied during a car chase.

My attention faltered and I bounced off a parking berm and scraped the front driver's-side tire on another one. A bang I felt as well as heard, along with a shudder from the wheel, told me I'd blown a tire. Unless that sound was a gunshot?

"Tire," said Linc as if he'd heard me. "Not gun."

I spotted an alley between two of the buildings and turned down it, nearly clipping the front of the car as the tires squealed, desperately trying to hug the road as they made the turn. Trying to regain control, watch the truck, and the alley ahead of me all at the same time was too much. I bounced from one wall of the alleyway to the other, knocking off first one mirror, then the other.

By the time I got the car back under control, I was sweating and breathing hard.

"I think he's gone," Linc said, trying to peer between the seats while keeping his head down.

I let the car wobble to a stop. When some part of the engine let off a hiss that sounded like a human sigh of relief, Linc and I both laughed until tears flowed down our cheeks and our sides ached.

My giggles slowed and I shivered as the adrenaline wore off. I had absolutely no idea what to do next. Nor how long we'd be safe here. Would the truck come back? Would my car restart? Was it drivable with the blown tire? Was it legal to drive a car with no mirrors?

"I'm calling Paolo," Linc said, grabbing my phone from the floor of the backseat and dialing.

"Paolo, it's Linc on Maggie's phone. We're in trouble." Linc put the phone on speaker and said in a low voice to me, "He wants to know if we're okay."

"Hey Paolo," I said, barely recognizing my hoarse voice. "We're shaken, but unhurt. I think my car is totaled."

"What? You're not kidding, are you? Where are you? Are you safe?"

"That big shopping center at El Camino and . . . and . . ." I looked to Linc for help.

"El Camino and Grant, center of the lot, on the back side of the buildings."

"I'm sending a patrol car and a tow truck, and I'll get there as soon as I can. Call dispatch immediately if either one of you feel any pain after the adrenaline wears off. You're right near El Camino Hospital and we can get you there in a flash."

"Thanks, Paolo," I said, but he'd already ended the call.

"There are the sirens," Linc said, and a second later I heard them myself.

Paolo arrived minutes after the tow truck and patrol cars. I was dimly aware that officers were measuring skid marks with retractable tape measures and laser devices. Others took carefully-lit photos. I tried to get out of the car at some point, but the world outside, now lightening up as dawn approached, didn't seem safe to me. I climbed back into the car, pulled my coat around me, turned the heat on high, and tried to keep my teeth from chattering.

Paolo knocked on the window. "Maggie?"

I unlocked the doors and pointed to the backseat. Paolo opened the passenger door and climbed in, scooting to the center of the bench seat. He put one hand on my shoulder and his other hand on Linc's.

"How are you two? That must have been some driving, Maggie. Linc, are you all right?"

I tried to answer and in my mind I replied, "We're fine. We had a bit of an adventure, like a theme-park ride, but we're fine." But saying the words out loud seemed too difficult. I closed my eyes, leaned back against the seat, and listened to the sound of my own breathing.

Linc answered Paolo's questions in a low voice. "I think she's just exhausted. We've been up most of the night."

Paolo rummaged around on the floor of the car, then held up my travel mug and shook it. "There's a swallow or two here that hasn't spilled. Think you can drink some?"

He held the cup out to me, but I shook my head again. "I just want to go home and sleep," I said.

"Hang on here. Let me see what I can get you." Paolo patted my shoulder and got out of the car, walking toward one of the patrol vehicles. I put my hands up to my face and leaned forward. My chest was sore and I wondered briefly if it was from slamming repeatedly against the shoulder belt, or if it was from holding my breath.

"Do I look that bad off?" I asked Linc.

"I don't think you're ready for the prom."

I laughed and was relieved to find that I was able to stop and no longer felt hysterical.

"You're no prize yourself." Linc's face was streaked with dust and tears and he smelled of fear. I sniffed my own clothes and made a face.

Paolo was back and knocked on the driver's-side door. This time, I opened the door for him. "I've got a cola here for each of you. The caffeine and the sugar will help. Can you pass this over to Linc?"

I followed instructions and Paolo opened another can and handed it to me. I took a tentative sip, and then two large ones. I hadn't realized how thirsty I was, and the sugary drink hit my bloodstream like rocket fuel. "Wow, Paolo," I said, looking at the label, surprised to discover that it was a well-known brand rather than some ultrasecret EMT formula. "That's like magic."

"After the EMTs check you out, let's get you in my car and I'll take you home. You first, Maggie." He took my hands and helped me stand up. "Steady. We're going to take this slowly. Linc, stay there. I'll come spot you after I get Maggie settled."

I looked over my shoulder at Linc. He opened the car door, stepped out, and stood, leaning against the side of the vehicle. "Yikes, Maggie, I don't think there's much paint left on this side. When they find the truck, it will have your paint all over it. Lots of evidence."

The EMTs looked us both over. While they recommended transporting us to the emergency room and insisted that Linc consult a doctor about his hand in the morning, they let us go. Paolo got us both settled in his Subaru, the floor of which was covered with the remains of fast-food meals. "Sorry," he said. "I've been catching meals wherever I could while this investigation is going on. Just shove all that stuff to the side."

He pulled out a tape recorder, turned it on, and placed it in a cup holder. "The official procedure here would be for me to take you in and question you each individually about what happened," he said. "But if you don't mind, I'll tape our conversation and talk to you again when you're good and rested. Seems to me that as tired as you two are, sleep is now a medical necessity." He rattled off a description of the time and location, had us each identify ourselves, and say that we knew we were being recorded and had given our permission.

As we described what had happened, I realized that the explosion at Stanford was news to Paolo. "I've been closed up in the conference room, trying to make sense of Apfel's paperwork, and didn't get called to the scene. If he was there, though, I should have been too. We're supposed to be a team, unless maybe he shouldn't have been there, either."

He pounded the flat of his hand against the steering wheel. "I've had it with that guy. He's by the book when he wants to be and throws the rules out when it suits him, but nothing he does has much to do with the people we're supposed to be serving. Jason has spent months teaching me that taking care of people comes first. That's the kind of cop I need to be. If the department doesn't like it, screw it. I'll find some other way to serve."

I wondered who would transcribe the recording, whether Paolo's words would be included, and what that would mean for his career.

But before I could think too hard about it, he jumped back in with more questions.

By the time we reached the house, he'd done a thorough job of debriefing us and eased us into remembering more details about the silver pickup than either one of us thought we'd noticed.

He'd called for patrols to swing by the house periodically and asked an off-duty friend to stake out the house in case the silver pickup driver returned. He helped us into the house and said he'd stay until his friend showed up.

Max was sound asleep when I went upstairs. I kissed him and told him we were home and that everyone was fine. There would be time enough in the morning to tell him about the danger we'd been in, and that his Prius was no more.

When I woke up hours later, Max was no longer in bed. A quick peek out the window told me Paolo's Subaru was still parked in front of the house. It was time to pick up the pieces and try to figure out who wanted Linc dead. But there was so much to explain. I scrubbed my face with my hands and realized I was almost afraid to go downstairs.

Chapter 16

Paper and pencil are not dead. No matter how many tricks your phone can do, it's dangerous and often illegal to use it while you're driving. I keep a notepad on the driver's console to jot notes down when I'm at a red light or waiting to pick up the kids.

From the Notebook of Maggie McDonald,
Simplicity Itself Organizing Services

Friday, November 7, 9:30 a.m.

Downstairs in the kitchen, I looked for Max or a note he'd written to tell me where he was. I found neither and part of me was relieved. I brushed back my hair with my hands and rubbed my eyes. I needed coffee and wanted to savor at least one cup by myself, without anyone asking questions or demanding explanations. But poor Paolo had been up as late as Linc and I had, and had been run ragged the past few days. He needed coffee too. I set up the pot, inhaled the scent impatiently as it brewed, and poured two cups.

Once I was outside, I walked around the car to the driver's side and peered in. Paolo was asleep with his head on the steering wheel. I hated to wake him, but as I moved closer, he must have sensed my presence. He lifted his head, blinked, and went through the same face- and hair-scrubbing motions I'd gone through to try to force myself to wake up.

"Morning, Paolo," I said in a whisper. "When you're ready, come on in and get some breakfast and we can figure out what happens next."

He nodded and took the coffee mug. Leaving him to finish waking up on his own, I went to the kitchen, where both Max and Linc had apparently appeared out of nowhere while I was talking to Paolo.

"Where did you come from?" I asked.

"Good morning to you too," Max answered while whisking a bowl of eggs. "I am your darling husband who is making you a spectacular breakfast."

"Sorry," I said, stopping to kiss him on my way to the coffeepot. "I checked in here just a moment ago and didn't see you."

"I must have just missed you. I was getting the bread from the freezer in the basement," he said, still whisking. He'd already cut thick slices of the cinnamon bread we bought from a local bakery and froze to have on hand for French toast.

Linc sat staring at a pitcher of orange juice and three glasses as if he could pour our drinks with telekinesis. He looked up at me.

"Morning, Maggie. Max took the day off and had our breakfast planned, prepped, and ready to go."

"He's the best," I said, taking a seat at the table. I poured the glasses of orange juice, since whatever psychic abilities Linc had seemed to have failed him.

"Paolo will be in shortly," I said. "He must have fallen asleep waiting for his friend to show up. Poor guy. We could have offered him a much more comfortable bed." I looked at the clock but couldn't make sense of it. "What time is it, Max? Where are the boys?"

Max glanced at the clock. "At school. Tess picked them up. You slept through the whole morning ritual and chaos. Linc, your phone rang and I took the liberty of answering it when I saw it was the vet. Newt is healing well and ready to come home, though you'll need to try to keep him quiet for a few more days. They've immobilized his leg. They chose a regal purple cast for him."

"Thanks. That's a relief. Would one of you mind driving me to Sarah's? I'll need to drive her car for a while."

"What happened to your car?" Max asked. "And for that matter, what happened to mine? I didn't see it in the driveway this morning. Actually, I didn't see any of our cars. What happened last night? How did you get home?"

Before either Linc or I could answer, we heard a loud yawn from the doorway and turned as Paolo walked in. "It smells wonderful in here," he said. "I'd be happy to drive you to Sarah's. Max, Maggie— do you need a lift anywhere?"

I looked at Max, who was in the process of flipping slices of French toast onto each of our plates. "I don't know if I need a lift," he said. "I'm still trying to find out what happened to my car."

When no one jumped in to explain, Max continued talking as he cooked. "I'm working from home today, Maggie. Tess is picking up both boys after school and feeding them dinner at her house. Paolo, if you want to shower here, or even get some more sleep, you're welcome to do that."

"Thanks, but as soon as Linc's ready, I think I'll take off. I need a change of clothes before I go into work." He sniffed at his shirt and scowled.

Linc took that as his cue to get ready. He winced as he stood from the table.

"Okay, that's enough," I said in my sternest mom voice. "Linc, sit down. Roll up your left sleeve and show Paolo your hand and your thumb. Unless it looks a lot better today than it did yesterday, one of us is taking you to see a doctor. A people doctor. You get to choose who takes you."

"Maggie, Linc's a grown man—" Max stopped scolding and gasped when he saw Linc's hand and wrist, now swollen to nearly twice its original size with purple, blue, and yellow bruising.

Linc shook his head. "I'm just stiff," he said. "I want to get Newt from the vet and see how he's doing."

"You can do that, Linc," Paolo said. "But first we need to get you taken care of."

"Maybe you can get a cast that matches Newton's," said Max.

Linc looked at his left hand, compared it to his right, and tried to flex both hands. He winced, cupped the left hand in the right, and blinked rapidly.

"You win, Maggie. It hurts a lot more today than it did yesterday. I'll go. But first, can we talk about Newt? I'm supposed to keep him quiet. I'm not sure how to do that with Belle around. Fewer steps would be good too. Would you mind if I took him back to Sarah's and stayed there? I'll get Jelly later."

I told Linc that whatever he needed was fine with us, and he limped upstairs to shower and change.

I stared into my coffee mug. I wanted to tell Max about what had happened the night before, but I didn't know where to begin. I also wanted to question Paolo before he left. The details of the car chase seemed unreal to me when faced in the daylight. I wanted to ask how he thought all the wild events of the last few days were related. Sarah's death, Linc's "accidents," and the lab explosion. Were they all connected? In a town known as a place where nothing ever happened, was there even a tiny possibility they weren't linked?

I held off, though. Both Paolo and I deserved to finish our breakfast and pour a second cup of coffee before we tried to do any serious analytical thinking. And I hoped Paolo or Linc or both of them would help me tell my poor husband how much danger I'd been in. I tucked into my French toast.

I'd finished the last swallow of my juice when my phone rang from the depths of my backpack. Max answered it, asked the caller to hold, and handed the phone to me.

"This is Maggie . . . Hello . . . I'm sorry, can you repeat that? The connection is bad and you're cutting out . . . Stephen? . . . Now?"

I shook my head and ended the call.

"It was Stephen, I think," I told Paolo and Max. "The connection was dreadful. I'd asked him for background information about some of the Stanford scientists, the garden volunteers, and the plot holders at the community garden. He's got the information, I guess—I couldn't really tell what he was saying. I'm going to call him back." I hit the speed-dial number for Stephen, but it went to voice mail.

"Why don't you head over there, Mags," said Max, as he cleared our plates from the table. "Tess is picking up the boys from school this afternoon so you won't be tight on time. I'll make some bread and soup for dinner. It looks like we're going to get some rain and it will be a good night for soup."

I turned to Paolo. "How long will the lab need my car?"

"Wait—what?" Max said. "What happened to your car?"

Paolo held up a finger to ask Max to wait, then looked at me and shrugged. "It's hard to say. I'll call them for you. Talk to your insurance. They may give you a loaner. Your car was pretty bad off, though. Totaled, probably. Driving over parking berms with a flat tire when someone is chasing you is not generally recommended."

The color left Max's face and he sank into a chair at the table and grabbed my hands. "*Chasing* you? Your car was totaled? *Totaled?* And you all sat here and let me cook you breakfast without telling me?"

I looked at Paolo and then back to Max. "I wasn't trying to hide it.

Truly, I wasn't. I was just searching for the right break in the conversation."

"Are you sure you're not hurt? How did Linc break his wrist? It's broken, isn't it?"

Max looked at Paolo, who nodded. "I think so."

"Which one of you is going to start?" Max asked, glaring at each of us in turn.

Paolo answered before I could. "Maggie is, because the first part of the story is the part I don't know."

Max and Paolo both stared me down. I sighed, took a big sip of coffee, and placed my hands flat on the table.

"The first part is really Linc's story. But I know enough to give you the highlights. He took off from here after he got a call from Stanford saying that there'd been a small explosion in his lab. Security must have been downplaying it to keep from alarming him, because the explosion was big enough to make the building uninhabitable."

I took another sip of coffee and Max poured me more. "Before Linc could get to Stanford, though, the silver pickup truck ran him off the road."

Paolo hissed. "The same one that ran him off the road yesterday?"

I nodded. "We think so. I'm sorry we didn't tell you this last night. You too, Max. We were just so exhausted. And there was so much to tell. It's all mixed up in my head too. Maybe I should let Linc tell it."

"Not a chance, Maggie. Keep going," Max said, scooting his chair near mine and holding my hand.

"The Prius is totaled," I told Max. "When Linc went off the road he crashed into a chain-link fence. The whole front of your car was smashed."

"I'm glad no one was hurt. That's a pretty fine endorsement of the Prius, don't you think? We should get another one just like it," Max said.

I was used to Max's relentlessly positive approach to life, but Paolo seemed shocked. "You might need to hold off on that," he said. "We towed it to the lab in Santa Clara, and they'll need to take a look before you talk to the insurance company."

"I'll see if I can get a loaner, then," Max said. "But go on with the story."

156 • *Mary Feliz*

"I tried to get Linc to go to the ER," I said, "but he wanted to get to the lab."

"Linc was going to drive home in his car, but I didn't think that was a good idea. It's been parked at Stanford in an unsecured lot. Anyone could have tampered with it. So, I drove him back. I was about to drop him at Sarah's house when the silver pickup showed up again."

I shook my head. "I can't make any sense of what came after that. Really, I can't."

Paolo took over. "That's natural, Maggie. It's your brain protecting you from the trauma. Your memory will come back when you've had time to process what happened."

Linc entered the kitchen from the back staircase, rubbing his wet hair with a towel. Paolo turned toward him. "Maggie was right when she warned you not to drive your car. Don't touch it until we have our experts look it over. I'll call Stanford security and warn them."

Linc nodded and Paolo shifted his attention to Max. "I wasn't there, but from what I learned from Maggie and Linc last night, it sounds like the driver of the truck was waiting for them to leave and followed them, probably from Stanford. A major vehicular chase ensued."

I involuntarily smirked at Paolo's use of technical cop jargon. Paolo ignored me and continued the story. "Maggie evaded the truck with driving worthy of a Hollywood stunt expert."

Max grew paler and tightened his grip on my hands.

"But I'm fine," I said as gently as possible. I took my hands from Max's and patted his shoulder.

"We're getting two new cars just like the old ones," Max said. He stood and cleared more dishes. Ordinarily I would have helped, but I knew it was his way of dealing with his fear as he absorbed the news that I'd been in grave danger.

"I'm not going to let this bad guy keep me locked up in my own home, shivering in fear," I said. "I doubt very much he'll attack again in daylight—especially since his car must be almost as badly scraped up as mine and will be very easy to identify. Paolo, if you can drop me at Jason's, I'll pick up that printout Stephen ran for me, assuming that's who just called me. Elaine is there and should be able to give me a ride home or take me over to Tess's so she can bring me home after she picks up the boys from school."

I started to go upstairs, knowing that it would be awhile before

Max would be ready to talk to me about what had happened. I figured I might as well get dressed. But then I turned back. "Max, how much do the boys know about what happened last night? What did you tell them?"

"I didn't tell them about it because I didn't know anything. I said that Paolo had brought you and Linc home from Stanford because there'd been a problem with the car. A problem with the car, Maggie. That's all you told me last night."

I sighed. "We can tell them more tonight."

"I would have told them more if I'd known," he said.

"I know, hon. I know."

Max had more questions before he was ready to let us leave. He was going to make some calls and find out how quickly we could replace our cars and whether we'd need a rental or two in the meantime.

As Paolo drove Linc to Sarah's and then took me on to Jason's, none of us spoke. There was really nothing more to say about the car chase, but neither could any of us think about anything else. I found myself self-consciously scanning my mirrors and the other cars more than usual. I looked for damaged silver pickup trucks and black Range Rover SUVs. It turns out a very large number of people drive silver pickup trucks, but none of them had the telltale side scrapes and bashed-in front ends that I was watching for, and I was relieved. That was one part of this investigation I was happy to leave to the police. I hoped never to see the truck in my rearview mirror again.

Paolo pulled to the curb in front of Jason and Stephen's house. I thanked him for the ride and for his help the night before. I turned toward the house, squared my shoulders, and walked to the door. Elaine's car was in the driveway behind Jason's, but Stephen's car was gone and I assumed he was running errands or volunteering at the Veterans Hospital. I climbed the steps to the front porch and tried the knob. Elaine had been leaving it unlocked so friends could visit without disturbing Jason.

But Jason wasn't in his usual spot on the sofa in the front room. Munchkin raced to greet me, tail wagging. I knelt down to give him a thorough hug and massage his ears.

"Where are your people, Munch? They didn't leave you alone, did they?"

Elaine walked into the room from the kitchen, drying a tumbler with a white kitchen towel.

"Good morning, Maggie. I hear you had a rough night. Do you have time for coffee?"

"I'd love to sit and chat, but Stephen called me a little while ago about picking up the reports he ran for me on our likely suspects. Is he around?"

"Come on back to the kitchen," Elaine said. "I've been baking and I'll pack up some of the cookies for the boys."

She turned and I followed her. "Have a seat," she said, pulling out mugs and plates even though I hadn't said I was interested in coffee.

"What's going on, Elaine? Has something happened I should know about?"

Elaine sighed. "I don't know who called you, but it wasn't Stephen."

I waited for her to say more. She looked out the kitchen window, then back at me.

"Did you hear that Jason's back in the hospital?" she asked.

"What happened? He's going to be okay, right?"

"He spiked a fever late yesterday. Stephen made him an appointment with the doctor, but when his fever hit a hundred and four early in the morning, Stephen drove him to emergency."

"I must have talked to him just before that. Have you heard anything since then? Can we help?"

"Pray if you've a mind to," Elaine said. "And if you don't, think good thoughts, wish them luck, cast a spell, do nice things for other people—whatever works for you. I'm praying my heart out and scrubbing their grout."

"That ought to keep you out of trouble. Do you have any updates on his condition?"

"It's not good. Stephen's been texting me and he's worried. Jason's leg was swollen and they're not sure whether it's a reaction to the materials in the rods they put in, a local infection of the surgical wound, or a systemic infection called osteo—osteo something."

"Osteomyelitis? That's serious."

"That's it. They're pumping him full of antibiotics. His stomach is upset and he's hallucinating from the fever, so they've got him on antiemetics and tranquilizers to keep him from thrashing about."

"Oh . . . wow," I said, kicking myself for having no words that were more appropriate to the situation.

"I know. Stephen says our patient is off in la-la-land. I asked if he wanted us there, but he said there's nothing we can do. He called the orthopedic surgeon from the Veterans Hospital, who apparently plays golf with the trauma surgeon who initially treated Jason at Valley Medical."

"Is that where his is?" I asked. "Valley Medical?"

"No, Stephen drove him to Stanford. They've got an infectious-disease doctor looking in on him, on top of all the surgeons."

"I can understand why Stephen doesn't want anyone else there. Will you let me know if he needs anything? Anything at all?"

"Absolutely." Elaine poured the coffee I hadn't wanted and I held the warm mug, soaking up the warmth and comfort. Today's cookies were molasses with white frosting hearts on them.

"Good choice," I said, saluting her with one of the cookies.

"Yet another way of praying, in my opinion." Elaine's voice broke and she stared into her coffee mug, not meeting my gaze.

I gave her a moment. I needed one too. I thought about how terri-fied Stephen must be. I pondered my next step and wondered who had tried to contact me. I tried to remember what the caller had said, but the words had been so garbled. I pulled my phone from my pocket and looked at the call log. I found the one call I'd received earlier. It listed the caller as *UNKNOWN*.

I showed it to Elaine. "It definitely wasn't Stephen, or even Stephen's phone. Since he's in my contact list, his calls always dis-play his name. I wonder why I didn't notice that before?"

Elaine patted my hand. "With all the things you have going on, I'm surprised you remember how to use a cell phone. But who would have called with a message that made you assume it was Stephen? And why?"

I told Elaine about the explosion at Stanford, the wild car chase, and Linc's accidents. Her eyes widened and her hand went to her throat.

"I'm amazed you're both unhurt."

"I was expecting Stephen or Jason to phone this morning. Stephen said he would when I talked to him last night. It was a bad connection, but I could tell it was a man calling and I just assumed it was one of them. Max, Linc, and Paolo were at the house with me."

"Could it have been that detective?"

I snorted. "He's had nothing to say to me other than 'stay out of my investigation.' And the voice sounded upbeat, just as if it were someone whose call I'd been expecting."

"Why did you come here? Did he give you an address?"

I took another sip of the coffee. "I can't believe I thought I didn't want this. It's wonderful. Just what I needed." I took another cookie from the plate. "If he'd given an address, I'd have been suspicious." I dug around in my memory, but couldn't be sure what the caller's exact words had been. "He must have said something like 'Come by the house,' and I assumed he meant to come here. But why?" I put down the uneaten portion of my cookie and brushed the inevitable crumbs into my hand and transferred them back to the plate. "Maybe it was someone calling on Jason or Stephen's behalf? Should I text and ask? Or should I not disturb them?"

Elaine shrugged. "If they're in the midst of something, they won't return your text. But if Stephen's sitting around worrying while the doctors work with Jason, he might appreciate the distraction. Go ahead."

I typed on my phone with my right index finger. I'd yet to manage the double-thumb technique my sons used. *Did you phone me with database results earlier? Do you have them? No rush. Got a weird msg from unknown phone. Were you calling from hospital?*

A distinctive *bloop* told me the message was sent. With nothing to do but wait for an answer, I looked at the plate of cookies. "If I sit here all day, I'll eat cookies all day. Do you have more grout for me to scrub?"

Elaine laughed. "I'm nearly finished and I'm not sharing. Do you really think it was a call from the hospital? Wouldn't Stephen have used his phone or Jason's if he were going to call from there?"

I smiled. "Rats. You're right. I was thinking way back to the *olden* days, when we had pay phones. You know, those things you put dimes into? Or quarters, I guess."

"It changes almost too fast to keep up. But I keep trying."

"If this were happening on television, it would turn out that someone had fiddled with the cell phones. What do they call that? Cloning? I should ask Paolo or David about cloned phones. Do you think someone's been listening in on my calls and knew I was waiting to hear from Stephen and Jason?"

"Slow down, Maggie. Take a breath. I think you're making this way too complicated. Where were you when you called Stephen? Did you mention his name? Could someone have overheard you?"

"You're right. I was outside Linc's lab after the explosion. I was in a huge crowd of students who wanted to see what the fuss was about. Any of them could have overheard me. I was probably talking too loudly anyway. What is it about cell phones that make people do that?"

Elaine shook her head.

"Wait a minute," I said. "I had that creepy feeling of being watched when I was in the crowd. I moved across the parking lot closer to the lab building and looked back to see if anyone was staring at me. But, of course, they were all staring in my direction. The building and the parking lot were where all the action was."

"Well, there you have it. You know how, but not who, or why. The person must have known you well enough to know your name and find your phone number. Or do any of your suspects already have your number?"

I thought for a moment.

"Think out loud, Maggie," Elaine said. "I want to follow along."

"Linc's lab assistant has my card."

"You're making enemies all over town. Who else?"

"Boots has my name, it would be easy to look up my number. I guess the same would be true for Linc's colleagues at Stanford. I introduced myself when I picked up Newton. And the kids at the garden, they could probably find any phone number on the Internet."

"Too many suspects and not enough answers."

"Elaine?"

"What is it, dear?"

"Would you be interested in doing some snooping at the community gardens with me? If you're not too busy?"

"I'd be delighted to, but how would that help? Are you just missing Tess? She's been running around like a madwoman trying to find an alternative to using Linc's house for her event."

"No, no. I really need *your* expertise," I said. "Well, your expertise and your car. Something is going on there that I can't put my finger on. I was hoping you might spot something I'd missed. You might know some of the older people who work the plots. They may well have been parents of students from your time at the middle school. The volunteers aren't that much older than your former students. If you give them your principal look, it might make them come clean with what's bothering them. I riled Boots when I was asking questions, and I thought with you there she might not be as dismissive. I'm hoping she has a copy of Linc's mom's will that we can look at."

"The will?"

"Boot believes Linc's mother's will left him the house only as long as he wanted to live in it. Upon his death or if he were to move, she says the house would go to the community gardens—or maybe the three garden groups that run the land."

"Boots has leadership positions on all three groups, so essentially, the land would go to her and her pet projects," Elaine said. "Are you thinking that would make her a suspect? I've always thought of her as beyond reproach."

"I know, but we don't even know if she's right about the will. If we knew for sure, it would help tailor the investigation."

"And you don't trust the police to do this, because?"

"You heard us talking about Detective Awful. He's the one who arrested Linc. And now that the DA has released Linc, Awful is more determined than ever to put him behind bars. He's every bit as dreadful as we described, maybe worse, and Paolo has neither the clout nor the job security to overrule him." I took a sip of my coffee, sighed, and combed my hair with my fingers. "Jason says Apfel has ties to political movers and shakers all over the county. It's only a matter of time before he finds some other way to go over the head of the district attorney."

"Okay, but what else?"

"Huh?"

"There must be some other reason you want me to go over there with you. What else are you looking for?"

I couldn't answer right away. I hadn't slowed down enough in the last few days to think my reasoning through. Elaine waited.

"I guess."

"Don't guess, dear. Tell me what you know."

I liked Elaine, but sometimes she made me feel as though I'd been sent to the principal's office and she would get the truth out of me, no matter what.

"I told you that I had the sense that the volunteers I spoke with, the two young girls, were hiding something. Will you please come with me and see what you can get out of them? And see if you pick up on anything else? I think I'm missing something." I paused, feeling as though I should come up with something more solid to answer Elaine's question. "I guess I just want a second opinion."

"I can do that. I just wanted you to firm up your thinking. Let me grab my keys."

Elaine left a note on the table in case Stephen came back to find her gone. She picked up her purse and we headed outside. Blue sky extended as far as we could see with little wind and low humidity. At a balmy 72 degrees the weather was more reminiscent of early spring than late autumn.

"After last night, I've been a little nervous about continuing this investigation," I told Elaine as we walked to her car. "But Detective Awful is not going to give up on Linc—not unless we find out who actually killed Sarah."

"Why do you care so much, dear?"

Before I could answer, a silver pickup careened around the corner with its wheels squealing.

Chapter 17

No one has time for doors that don't unlock easily.
Houses settle, locking mechanisms wear. There are lots
of reasons for a lock in your home to become difficult to
work. But there's no reason not to fix it right away. Call
a handyman or locksmith if you don't have the skill to
take care of it yourself. An easily working lock will save
you time, frustration, and be safer for everyone.

From the Notebook of Maggie McDonald,
Simplicity Itself Organizing Services

Friday, November 7, 11:00 a.m.

I grabbed hold of Elaine's arm and pulled her back toward the house.
The truck continued down the street and disappeared from view,
but we could hear its tires squealing as it drove way too fast for the
narrow lanes in a residential neighborhood.

"That's the truck that chased us last night," I told her, reaching
into my backpack for my phone and breathing heavily as if I'd just
run a mile or two. "He knows where I am, Elaine. We have to get out
of here."

"I'm surprised that truck is still running, after all the damage it
did to your car," Elaine said, grabbing her own phone from the front
pocket of her purse. "Do those trucks have reinforced side beams and
bumpers? Maybe I need to get one."

I shook my head as I dialed Paolo's number. "I have no idea. All
I know is that the driver is crazy and probably a murderer. I need to
tell Paolo we saw him."

I stared at my phone. "The line's busy . . ." My voice trailed off as I realized I had no idea what to do next.

"Are you okay, Maggie? Do you want to go back inside? You had quite the shock last night, little sleep, and now this." I didn't answer, so Elaine continued: "Try the number again. Could you have misdialed? Why would a police line ring busy?"

I frowned. "I was tired before, but now I'm steamed. That silver truck guy must have been the one on the phone. He was watching me at Stanford, listening. He lured me here with that garbled phone call. He might have killed us. Or one of the dogs. Or a mom and a baby out for a walk."

"I'm thinking that if he's working so hard to stop you from investigating, or doing whatever it is that you're doing, then we'd better press on. He's not targeting the police in Orchard View or Stanford or the county crime team. He's after *you*, Maggie, which means you must be on to something. Something he wants to keep a secret."

"So, you still want to go to the garden?"

"Absolutely."

We climbed into Elaine's car. I buckled my seat belt and felt my heart pounding from the adrenaline rush of the silver truck's appearance. I could no longer pretend that what I was doing was safe. Whatever information we were close to uncovering was worth killing for. I didn't know how all the violent events of the last week were connected, but I was sure that they were. I just needed to prove it, and prove that Linc was as much a victim as Sarah.

I dialed Paolo's number again. I kept getting the "press three to reach dispatch" message. I didn't want to talk to dispatch and several minutes had passed since we'd seen the truck. It would be useless to call Paolo now. I sighed and returned the phone to my backpack.

I took a deep breath. Was I being reckless to pursue this case? Was I endangering my family? I shook my head, trying to clear it. I thought of the alternative. I could leave the investigation to Detective Awful, but what good would that do? The chief had apparently told the district attorney he'd assign someone else to the case. But that hadn't happened yet. And whoever took Awful's place would need some time to get up to speed. We could all be dead by then.

I thought of my dreams for my family and my business. Did I want to live in a town where someone could murder a school librarian and get away with it? Sarah and Linc had been planning a future together. Their dreams had ended. I was afraid to continue, but I was even more terrified to live in a world where a person this evil could thrive.

I looked at Elaine, who had paused in the process of inserting her key in the ignition. "Are you still game?" I asked.

"To boldly go . . ." said Elaine as if she knew what I'd been thinking. "We can do this."

We spent the entire drive across town searching for the silver pickup with the scraped-up sides and crumpled front end.

I wondered how Jason was doing and hoped we'd get an update soon. Stephen must be frantic. I was sympathetic to both of them, but a small, unattractive part of me was frustrated because Stephen hadn't had time to do background checks on my suspects.

I bit my lip and scolded myself for my self-centered thinking.

"That was a heavy sigh," Elaine said. "What's up?"

"Elaine, you've lived here forever, right?"

"Since the days of the dinosaurs, dear."

"I didn't mean that, but you were with the school district for a long time."

"Is there a point to this or are you reviewing my history so you can write my eulogy after Mr. Silver Truck tries to run us over and I leap in front of you, sacrificing myself to save you so your sons don't grow up motherless?"

I snorted. "That's some imagination, Elaine. Why do you get to be the heroine?"

"Because I'm writing the narrative. Now, what do you really want to know?"

"Is there a database of students for the district? I mean, I know there is, but how far back does it go? I wondered if we could cross-reference the names of the kids on the garden's volunteer roster and see if any of them were troublemakers when they were in school."

"I think a list like that would be against about a dozen laws and there's no way we could have access to it without breaking several more. If you're looking for a way to get information on your suspects while you're waiting for Stephen or Jason, I think your best bet is Boots. She'll know the background of each of those kids, probably going back to when they lost their first tooth."

"But would she tell me any of it? She scares me a little. Especially when she's protecting her kids."

Elaine sniffed in disgust. "You've eluded a murderer twice now, right? I think you could take Boots if it comes to a fight. Suck it up."

"What did you say?"

"Did I offend you? Did you think I didn't know any vulgar expressions? I was a middle-school principal, dear, not a hermit."

I was out of my depth trying to argue with Elaine and I needed to change the subject in a hurry.

"Can we stop at Linc's house first? I'm thinking we should stop waiting for the county electrical report and hire our own electrician to give an unbiased report on how Sarah was electrocuted and how or why she walked right into such a dangerous situation."

Elaine pulled up in front of Linc's house and we climbed up the steps to the porch. The lockbox was gone. I pulled out my key and tried to unlock the door. It didn't work right away, so I pulled up on the knob and tried again. I tried a few more tricks, none of which worked.

"Let's try the back door," I said. "I've had more luck with that lock."

We were about to step down from the porch when I pulled Elaine back into the shadows near the door. I heard an engine revving and by now I recognized the sound of the black Range Rover.

"Get the license-plate number," I said, pulling my camera out of my pocket to take another time-stamped picture.

"California plate ending in three-six-seven," said Elaine as the Rover raced off. "I couldn't get any more. What are we doing?"

I texted the picture and the numbers to Paolo to let him know we'd spotted the vehicle again in Linc's neighborhood. I explained the situation to Elaine, admitting that while I was curious about what the black vehicle was doing here, it seemed less important when compared to being stalked, chased, and shot at by the driver of the silver truck.

My phone rang before I could stash it back in my pocket. It was Paolo.

"I've got you on speaker, Paolo. Elaine is here with me. We're at Linc's. We just saw the black Range Rover and the silver pickup was racing through Stephen's neighborhood when Elaine and I were there about twenty minutes ago." I stopped to take a breath and realized I'd rattled off all the information as if I was in a speed-talking competition. "Sorry, Paolo. I'm a little wired. Did you get all that?"

"I did. You're in danger, Maggie. And you're putting Elaine in danger too. We know nothing about the drivers of those vehicles except that one seems to want you dead, the other is threatening, and they both seem to know way too much about where you will be and when you will be there. Can you get inside Linc's house?"

I started to answer, but Paolo interrupted. "Never mind. Get in the house, even if you have to break a window. Then lock the doors and stay put until I call you back with instructions or I send a uniformed officer to take you home."

Paolo took a deep breath and let it out. "I know you don't want to hear this again, Maggie. I know you've heard it enough from Gordon Apfel. But you absolutely must stop your ad hoc investigation before you get killed."

"Paolo, I'm sorry. You're right. Elaine and I will follow your instructions to the letter."

I ended the call and looked sheepishly at Elaine.

"Don't you dare feel guilty about getting me into this," she said. "I jumped in with both feet. The only thing we can do now is follow Paolo's orders and get inside as soon as possible."

"I think my key will work better on the back door. If it doesn't, we can knock out one of the windowpanes."

As we passed the basement door on the side of the house, we both heard a crash that made us jump. Elaine grabbed my arm.

"That's not good," she said in a whisper. "Someone's in there already. Call 9-1-1."

I pulled out my phone and dialed. I told the 911 dispatcher we'd heard someone rummaging around in a house that was supposed to be empty. She told me to get to somewhere safe and she'd send a patrol car as soon as possible.

I thanked her and hung up.

"Let's see if the back door's unlocked," Elaine whispered.

"No way. That's how the ditsy blondes in horror movies get chopped up with a meat cleaver. They go into the house when everyone knows that's where the bad guy is." Tears of frustration and anger filled my eyes. I struggled to slow my rapid breathing and heart rate and get my thoughts in order.

"Great. We're not safe inside and we're not safe outside," Elaine said. She bit her lip and had her hand on her throat. Her gaze shifted from the back door to the path that lead around the house to the front yard. She shifted from one foot to another and took on the frantic look of a trapped animal.

"Just check the doorknob," I whispered. "Then we'll know whether someone broke in or let themselves in with a key." When I didn't offer to test the door myself, Elaine shook her head and stepped carefully up the steps, tried to turn the knob, and came back down when it wouldn't move.

"It's still locked."

I sat on the bottom step and hugged my backpack to my chest as if it might protect me from an attack. "Go? Stay? Call the police again?"

Elaine sat down next to me, then stood up with her feet planted shoulder-width apart and her hands on her hips. She looked for all the world like a superhero and I could almost see a cape fluttering out behind her.

"This is ridiculous. I will not be cowed by an overgrown brat in an overpowered car. And whoever is in the basement—if it even is a *who*; it could just as easily be a raccoon or a rat or a squirrel—they probably assumed we went away. We're safe enough for now, don't you think?"

"The police will be here soon," I said with more confidence than I felt. "We'll hear anyone coming up the basement stairs. They creak under the slightest pressure. If we hear that, we're out of here, right?"

Elaine nodded.

I rummaged in my backpack looking for something I could use as a weapon. My hand closed on the folder I'd made for Linc and Sarah's project. I pulled it out, opened it up, and temporarily forgot about the trouble we were in.

"Look, Elaine, these are the pictures I took of the house when Linc hired me. I take 'before' shots of every project." I handed her half the stack. "I've been meaning to go through them and see if they offer any clues about what's going on here."

"Like if there's a Maltese falcon on the newel post?" Elaine said, flipping through the pictures.

I laughed quietly, trying not to alert the intruder to our presence. "Right. Help me look through them. Set aside any pictures of Linc's workroom. You'll know it when you see it. Lots of jumbles of wires and electrical test equipment."

I compared the "before" pictures to my memory of when we found Sarah. In the early photos, a whiteboard covered with formulas and calculations rested on the windowsill, blocking the light. The day we'd found Sarah, the whiteboard was missing and the window was open. I pointed out the change to Elaine, explaining how the room had looked on Monday morning.

"I wonder if someone could have left the window open, knowing a big storm was forecast and that Linc or Sarah would have to close it," I said. News of the storm had been on the radio, TV, and on everyone's lips. We all had hoped it would mark the start of our winter rainy season and the end of our lengthy drought.

"Do you know if they tested the water that was on the floor?" Elaine asked.

"No, why?"

"If it was rainwater, it could have been an accident, right? The window was open. Wind could have driven the rain inside and Sarah raced to close it before the rain did any damage."

"But if it were tap water that would mean someone put it there."

"Not necessarily," said Elaine. "What if Sarah had been carrying a glass of water, slipped, and the glass fell?"

"I didn't see a glass in the room. But that doesn't mean one hadn't rolled under a table."

"We need to get that water analysis."

"If the water was even collected," I said. "Jason said Detective Awful is known for cutting corners. But we can ask Paolo about it, maybe, if he doesn't think we're continuing to investigate."

I flipped through the rest of the pictures quickly until I came to the last few I'd taken of Sarah and Linc clowning around on the front porch.

"Look at these. They were so happy. It should hurt to look at them, but it doesn't. After everything that's happened, it's nice to remember her this way."

Elaine looked at them over my shoulder. "Linc might like to have some of these. They're adorable. But why didn't you just do digital photos?"

"These were originally digital. But Linc and Sarah were both much more comfortable working with hard copies of everything. I encourage my clients to go digital as much as possible, but I'm flexible. Whatever makes the project easier for my clients."

I laid out some of the best photos, trying to choose a few to enlarge for Linc. But then I picked up one of them again and peered at it. I found my reading glasses, put them on, and looked more closely.

"What are you looking at?" Elaine asked. I handed her the photo and pulled my camera from my pocket. I pushed buttons searching for the original image.

"Look in the background, behind Linc and Sarah. Out in the street. Is that the Range Rover? I'm trying to find the original so I can enlarge that part of the screen."

I found a photo that looked similar and compared it with the hard copy.

"That's the one," Elaine said. "How big can you get that section?"

I enlarged the photo as much as I could, but the license plate wasn't legible.

"Do you think the crime lab could apply more contrast and get a better read on the number?" Elaine asked. "They do it on TV all the time."

"I'm not sure. I know it's not like on TV where the whole license plate might be just a few pixels, but they blow it up and suddenly you can read the whole thing. Can I look at that photo again?"

I took the photo from Elaine and squinted, pointing to the license plate. "We know these last three numbers are three-six-seven, right? That's what you saw this morning. Does the first digit look the same as that three?"

Elaine held up the photo and looked at it from several different angles. "I just can't tell. Why not send it to Paolo to forward to the lab? If they can't decipher it, fine. But if there's a chance they could . . ."

I tapped out a message on my phone and sent the picture to Paolo, telling him it was taken nearly a month before Sarah's death and seemed to show the same Range Rover that had been hanging around Linc's house and the garden.

A few minutes later, Paolo called back. "Thanks for sending that photo, Maggie. I passed it along. We were able to enhance part of the plate that was in the other photos you took. We had to make a few guesses, but we ran all the possibilities–none of them are Range Rovers.

The mostly likely set belonged to a cream-colored Lexus that was stolen in Los Angeles six months ago."

"If that's the right plate, that proves the Range Rover's driver is in possession of stolen plates, right?" I said. "That proves he's a bad guy, even if he's not connected to Sarah's death. Can you pull him in for questioning based on the stolen plates?"

"Pull him in?" Paolo repeated, laughing. "You watch too much television, Maggie. We've already got law-enforcement teams all over the Bay Area on the lookout for the Range Rover, and we've given them our best guess at the plate. Once we locate it, we can figure out the next step. It's easy enough to follow someone until they neglect to use their turn signal, go over the speed limit, anticipate a red light turning green, or do one of those rolling stops. No one is a perfect driver all the time."

I heard the short *bloop* of a siren on the street. "I've got to go, Paolo. The patrol car is here."

The officers were polite, efficient, and took their time thoroughly searching Linc's house. They found nothing and suggested that we may have heard a rat or squirrel that had made a home in the house. They gave us their cards and asked us to call them again if we heard or saw anything worrisome.

After they'd gone, Elaine and I debated what to do next. Paolo had originally asked us to close ourselves up in the house to protect us from the guy in the Range Rover. However, Santana had been afraid when I showed her the Range Rover picture. I wanted to warn her that we'd seen the vehicle again. I texted Paolo to let him know we were headed over to the garden.

I showed Elaine the way through the hedge, which was thankfully free of spiderwebs today. We walked on the gravel path, enjoying the scents from the herb gardens and the chirps of birds that were feeding on insects and seeds.

Just as the shed came in view, we heard loud, unintelligible shouting that made us slow and then stop. A bulky guy ran from the shed toward the parking area. He wore jeans and a navy hooded sweatshirt, the winter uniform of nearly every student in the area. Next, we heard the sound of a powerful engine starting up, followed by the squeal of tires. Both sounds were consistent with those I now associated with the Range Rover.

"Maybe we should come back later," Elaine said in a whisper.

I shook my head. "No, listen. There's water running. No one would leave water running unattended in this drought . . . not unless they wanted to incur the wrath of the water district and the neighborhood."

I tiptoed past the front of the garden shed and around the corner where the water tap dripped at the hose connector. "Time for a new washer, there," I said, pointing out the drip to Elaine.

"You'd think Boots would be on top of things like that."

I followed the hose past a circle of shrubs that badly needed trimming. And then I stopped. Stopped so suddenly that Elaine banged into me from behind, forcing me to lurch forward until I caught myself. I covered my mouth and turned to Elaine.

"Am I really seeing this?"

Elaine didn't answer. I watched the blood drain from her face and grabbed her elbow as we both sank down on one of the splintery benches spaced throughout the garden.

In front of us, wearing her polka-dotted Wellingtons, was Boots, stretched across the path with one foot tangled in the dripping hose. She lay facedown with her head resting on an antique wrought-iron boot scraper as if it were a pillow and she'd felt the need for a sudden nap. Only the fact that blood oozed out from under her skull, pooling and mixing with the growing puddle of water from the hose, told us that if Boots were napping, she might never wake up again.

Chapter 18

It's much easier for most people to keep items organized
if they know exactly where those items belong.
Especially tools that are used by more than one member
of a team or family. I have a dustpan and broom labeled
with the words *I live under the kitchen sink.*

Young children and many adults may do better with
labels that incorporate pictures or photos in addition to
or instead of words.

*From the Notebook of Maggie McDonald,
Simplicity Itself Organizing Services*

Friday, November 7, 11:30 a.m.

Holding Boots's left wrist in my hand, I could feel no pulse. Not
being an expert pulse-taker, I checked her other wrist and her
neck before standing, looking at Elaine and shaking my head.

"Blast it!" said Elaine. She stood and kicked at the leg of the rick-
ety bench, which threatened to collapse under her assault. She let out
a brief sob and then looked at me. "This is ghastly. Unbelievable.
Oh, Boots."

There was nothing I could say. Nothing I wanted to say aloud,
anyway. I pulled out my phone and speed-dialed Paolo.

Moments later, we heard sirens out front. I was on my way to meet
the emergency teams and direct them to Boots, when a moan erupted
from the shed.

"Hello? Is anyone there?" I called out. I was answered with another unintelligible moan. "Ketifa? Santana? It's Maggie McDonald. Are you hurt? Are you safe?"

The moan turned to a sob. I eased the door open and peered into the shed, unable to see anything after the bright sunlight outdoors.

"It's Maggie. I'm coming in."

Ketifa crouched in the far corner of the shed, clutching the bird-seed bucket in her arms.

I sank to the floor next to her, put my arm around her, and tried to take the bucket from her hands. She gripped it as if her life depended on it.

"Are you okay? Is it the baby? What happened?" I pushed her hair back and wiped away her tears as though she were a small child. She had a huge swelling bruise on her cheek, along with a deep cut on her forehead that would need several stitches.

"I just heard the sirens," I told her. "The police are here and an ambulance crew is coming for Boots. They may be able to take a look at you. Or I can drive you to urgent care."

"Is she dead?" sniffed Ketifa.

I shook my head. "I don't know." Though I hadn't found a pulse, I supposed there was a chance she was still alive.

"I was supposed to meet her. She was going to go over my résumé. She was going to help me find a job." Ketifa buried her face in her hands. Whatever else she was going to say was lost in a new round of sobbing.

After a moment, she looked up and pulled herself together enough to explain. "I was on my way here when heard shouting. Boots and some guy. I was afraid, so I waited. I didn't want to eavesdrop, but I didn't want to walk into the middle of a fight, either. I'd just decided to talk to Boots another day when this guy ran up behind me. He was wearing a dark hoodie. I think I saw him once with Santana. I thought he was her ex-boyfriend, but she mentioned an uncle she used to live with. She didn't like him."

Ketifa sniffed and I handed her a rumpled tissue from my pocket. "It's clean," I said. "Just crumpled." She wiped her nose and went on.

"He—he shoved me off the path and I tripped over one of those railroad-tie barriers. He yelled at me: 'Tell Santana the bitch is dead and it's all her fault. The same thing will happen to her if she doesn't come back where she belongs.'"

Ketifa began shaking with the memory. I shrugged out of my jacket and draped it over her shoulders.

Outside the shed, we could hear the sounds of the ambulance arriving, the crew shouting instructions to one another, and the wheels of a stretcher bouncing on the gravel path. I heard several voices that must have belonged to EMTs or police officers. Elaine answered, but I couldn't hear what she'd said.

Ketifa's phone pinged and I realized it had been pinging rapidly since I'd entered the shed.

"Do you need to answer that?"

Ketifa shook her head and sobbed again. I patted her back. I wanted to know what was going on outside the shed, but I was certain there was nothing I could do that wasn't already being done by the emergency team or Elaine.

"Ketifa, did you see Boots?"

She nodded. "I walked behind the shed, thinking I'd find Boots and ask her who the guy was. But when I saw her lying there and the blood . . . I felt faint and I wanted to sit down. I was afraid that the guy might come back and—and—" She shook her head. "I don't know what I was doing. I'm such a coward. I should have gone to her. Helped her. Called 9-1-1. Done something. But I just ran in here and hid."

She dropped her head in her lap and cried. Without looking up, she handed me her phone.

It was protected by a pink plastic case with glitter paint spelling out *SANTANA*. So it wasn't Ketifa's phone, but Santana's. There were at least a dozen text messages with more coming in. All were vile threats, should Santana refuse to come home or should she tell anyone what had been happening between them.

"We need to give this to the police," I said. "Do you know where Santana is? Is she safe?"

"She's in Linc's basement. We were both staying there. No one is supposed to know, but we're both homeless. She said she had studying to do, but she must have been hiding from that guy."

I wondered if the crash Elaine and I had heard coming from Linc's basement had been Santana. But the police had checked out the whole house. I told Ketifa that and she snorted.

"The police couldn't find Santana if she was right under their noses. When you've bounced around the foster system for a while you become good at becoming invisible. Santana has lots of practice getting in and out of that house without being seen."

"Did she have a key? I thought Tess and I had the only ones."

"She didn't need a key. Those locks are ancient. Super-easy to pick. Besides, Santana has been climbing up the oak tree and in the window of the professor's office. With all that electrical equipment in there, it gets pretty warm, so he leaves the window open most of the time."

I looked pointedly at Ketifa's pregnant belly. "But you couldn't go that way. How did you get in?"

"Do you know how easy it is to find a hidden key? Everyone hides them in the same places. The professor's key was resting on the top of the doorframe. I just reached up, got the key, unlocked the door, and put it back so no one would know it was missing." She shook her head. "You're too nice, Mrs. McDonald. You suburban moms don't know anything."

I was about to protest, because she'd said the words with such disdain, but then I realized she was absolutely right. I'd grown up with plenty to eat, always feeling safe and loved, no matter what I did. What must it be like to grow up in an atmosphere that was the polar opposite of that? Where no matter what you did, you knew you'd never feel safe, never be sure you'd have enough to eat, and never experience unconditional love? I shuddered and hoped no one I loved would ever know what that was like.

"Ketifa, do you know what kind of car Santana's uncle or boyfriend drove? Was it a black Range Rover? Something that looked like an army jeep, only bigger?"

Ketifa nodded.

"I've seen that car here in the parking lot," I said. "And outside Linc's house. Do you think he knows where Santana has been staying?"

Before she could answer, the EMTs passed by the shed with Boots loaded on a stretcher. Their faces were grim.

Elaine followed them and stopped as she passed the shed. "The police said I could go," she said. "They're going to stay awhile to process the scene."

I felt my face fall. I'd previously thought that phrase was only an expression, but it was like every muscle in my face let go at once, having completely given up on maintaining any kind of cheerful look. Ketifa sobbed and buried her head in her long skirt.

"No, no. Wait." Elaine said. "She's not dead. The EMTs called in a neurosurgeon at Stanford to evaluate her as soon as they get her into the emergency room. They told me they've seen a lot worse."

"But there was so much blood," Ketifa said.

"But they're processing the scene!" I added.

"The police told me that with a head wound the bleeding isn't necessarily a bad thing. It means the blood might not be building up inside the skull and putting pressure on the brain. They'll know more tomorrow, I'm sure."

Elaine turned to me. "They also explained that they are processing the scene because Boots looked like she'd suffered a violent attack. I told them about the guy we saw running to the parking lot. They'll do everything now while the evidence is fresh. That way, if it turns out to be . . . well, never mind about that just now." Elaine looked alarmed by what she'd been about to say. Though she had stopped abruptly, I had no trouble filling in the blank, and I didn't think Ketifa would, either. Elaine had been about to say that if Boots died, they'd want to have collected all the evidence they could from what would then be the homicide scene.

Oh, please God, no, I thought. We didn't need a second murder. Boots might not be my favorite person, but I didn't want her dead. I didn't want to ever see another murder in Orchard View.

"Does he need to talk to us?" I asked.

Elaine shook her head. "They're understaffed today and working hard to gather up the evidence before dark. Unless you or Santana know more than what I already told them, I think we're good to go. I gave them your names, like I said, and they gave me these cards for you."

I traded glances with Ketifa. Her shoulders drooped. I nodded, then turned to Elaine.

"Ketifa does have some information and evidence she should probably pass along to the police."

Ketifa pressed against the ground in order to stand up. I reached out a hand to help her. Young and nimble as she was, she'd reached the awkward stage of pregnancy and her balance was off.

"I never asked you, Ketifa—were you hurt when he pushed you? The baby? We still need to get your head looked at, but if you've got cramps or discomfort, we should go straight to the emergency room."

Ketifa gasped and grabbed her belly. "I didn't think of that. Do you think he's okay?"

"Probably," I said. "Those little guys are pretty well protected in there. But if you've got any pain or worries we need to get you checked out."

Ketifa sighed. "But Santana. And the police."

"Your health and the health of your baby come first," I said. "Any pain? Cramps? Discomfort? Bleeding?"

She shook her head.

"Then let's go talk to the police. You can give them a quick run-through and your contact information, and then we're off to the ER for stitches and a pregnancy status report."

The officers, a young woman with a dark ponytail and an older male sergeant with a grizzled beard, looked up as we approached. They introduced themselves, then glanced at Santana's pink phone and asked Ketifa if she knew where Santana was and whether she was safe. When Ketifa said she didn't know, I didn't correct her. She was an adult and this was her story to tell.

They popped the phone in an evidence bag as it continued to ping with what I guessed were more threats. Ketifa told them everything she'd told me about the man in the hoodie, who she thought he was, and the kind of car he drove.

"If you see your friend Santana, please ask her to call us," the younger cop said. "It sounds like she could use some help. She shouldn't have to fight this guy on her own."

Ketifa nodded, but I wondered if she'd pass along the card she'd been given.

I thought we were done and had turned to go when Ketifa added one new piece of information. "Santana says he has a handgun. He carries a knife and has a shotgun in his car."

I whipped my head around then. "Officer, the Range Rover he drives is one that your department is already looking for. Paolo Bianchi knows about it. If the driver is armed, you might want to make sure everyone knows."

The young officer's eyes grew large and she took a few steps away and started talking into her shoulder mic in the police codes that I found so mystifying. But at least I knew she was taking the information seriously.

* * *

After the police were finished with us, Elaine, Ketifa, and I walked slowly back across the garden and Linc's yard toward Elaine's car.

"Can we give you a lift home, Ketifa?" Elaine asked. "Or are we taking you straight to the emergency room?"

Ketifa shook her head and took on the guarded look of a trapped animal. I took her hand. "It's okay, Ketifa, you can trust Elaine."

"Would you come with me to check on Santana? I'm afraid—if he's found her—"

I wanted to hear a lot more from Ketifa and Santana about why they were crashing in Linc's house, how they'd avoided detection, what they might know about Sarah's death, and who the guy in the dark hoodie actually was. But before they'd say anything to me or to Elaine, they would have to trust us.

"Of course," I said. "Elaine, the girls are in a tight spot and have been . . . um . . . camping out at Linc's house."

Elaine looked from me to Ketifa and back. "Okay," she said. "Lead on, Ketifa. Show us your digs."

We followed Ketifa up the steps and waited while she stood on tiptoe to retrieve the key, unlock the door, and return the key to its hiding place. She crossed the kitchen and went directly toward the basement stairs. When she reached the landing at the turn of the stairs, with Elaine and I following like baby ducklings after their mother, Ketifa stopped and called out.

"Santana? Are you here? You can come out. Mrs. McDonald and her friend are here, but we can trust them."

She descended the rest of the stairs and stood in the middle of the empty basement. "Santana, some stuff has happened that you need to know about to stay safe. That friend of yours? The guy with the Rover? He hurt Boots. Maybe killed her. He's looking for you and he's really angry. Out of control."

Ketifa shrugged her shoulders and turned back to climb the stairs. "I think she would have come out if she was here."

"Should we check the other floors?" I asked. "Would she come out for us if we told her you wanted to talk to her? I want to make this quick so we can get you to the hospital. You really need to get that cut sewn up. And you don't need to be climbing all those stairs."

Ketifa frowned. "If you're calling for her, tell her about Boots. And to stay hidden if she won't come out. That guy really scares me. Maybe we can come back later?"

Elaine and I agreed, and we checked every level of the house delivering Ketifa's message. We didn't find Santana.

"Should we call the police?" I asked. "In case Mr. Range Rover has found her?" If I'd been on my own, I would have called them in a heartbeat. But I was working hard to get Ketifa to trust me, and I wanted to consult her.

"No," said Ketifa, nearly shouting the word. "I'm sure she's found a safe place. The police are not the answer."

She was adamant and unswerving. I looked at Elaine, who raised her eyebrows in an expression I wasn't able to read.

"Okay," I said. "I'll come back and check on her later. Should we leave her a note?"

Ketifa made a sound of disgust. "And do what? Pin it to the front door so that guy can find it? I don't think so."

Chapter 19

When you've got a tricky topic to tackle with your teen,
I recommend starting the conversation in the car.

With everyone's eyes focused on the road ahead, a
young adult can avoid eye contact and will often feel
less like they are on the spot. As a result, they may be
better able to listen to what you have to say.

From the Notebook of Maggie McDonald,
Simplicity Itself Organizing Services

Friday, November 7, 4:15 p.m.

Elaine asked me to drop her off at her house before taking Ketifa to
El Camino Hospital, which was smaller than Stanford and likely
to have a shorter wait. It was also only a few blocks from Elaine's.

I took her up on her offer to borrow her car when she told me her
daughter was traveling in Europe and had stored a car in Elaine's
garage.

"Are you sure?" I asked. "I don't have a good track record with
cars at the moment."

Elaine raised an eyebrow. "You have insurance, don't you?"

I nodded, taking her comment seriously.

"I was kidding, Maggie. I know you'll take good care of it. The
bad guys won't recognize my car, so you're much safer driving it
than you were with your own car. Don't worry."

Maybe because Ketifa was pregnant or because we'd arrived at a
slack time, we were in and out of the emergency room in just over an

hour. Six stitches and a very large bruise had marked Ketifa's face, but the baby was fine and showing no sign of popping out early. She was checked for concussion and while she passed all the tests, the ER doctor suggested someone keep an eye on her for twenty-four hours.

One of the hospital employees came out to talk to me while Ketifa was being examined.

I assumed she wanted to know how Ketifa's bill would be paid and I said I would take care of whatever expenses she had incurred.

"That won't be necessary. She has insurance. What she needs most is someone to stay with her for the next twenty-four hours. I can't tell you anything specific about her condition without her permission, but I can tell you we expect she'll be fine. Having someone available to check on her is just a precaution. We'd want someone who'd be willing and able to bring her back here quickly if necessary."

I nodded. "I can do that. She's our houseguest." It was mostly true. I'd planned on inviting Ketifa and Santana to stay with us for at least a few days, if not longer. There was very little furniture left in Linc's house. It was no place for a pregnant woman, and Ketifa had demonstrated that it wasn't secure.

As soon as we were out of sight of the emergency room, Ketifa stopped and whispered to me: "Thanks for telling them I was staying with you, Mrs. McDonald. But I'll be fine. Can you take me back to Dr. Sinclair's house?"

"Please, Ketifa, call me Maggie. And if you're willing, I really would like you to come home with me. Dr. Sinclair was staying with us, but I texted him while we were waiting and he's going to stay at Sarah's house. His dog was injured and he doesn't want him to climb all the stairs to our third-floor guest room. I talked to my husband and he's already expecting you. As soon as I drop you off, I'm planning to try to find Santana. It's going to be cold tonight and she needs someplace safer and warmer than the basement floor of an unheated house. You do too." Ketifa looked skittish and ready to turn down my offer. "Think of your baby. The best thing you can do for him or her is to look after yourself. You've had a dreadful day. We all have. You need to eat, rest, and feel safe."

Ketifa shivered. The wind had come up and the temperature had dropped. Clouds skittered across the darkening sky. We were due for another storm.

I took my coat off and draped it over her shoulders again. "Let's talk in the car with the heat on." Plump drops of rain pelted us as we ran to the car.

I turned on the car and the heat and let it warm up while Ketifa and I fastened our seat belts. Ketifa put her hands to the vents, looked at me, and smiled.

"It's warm already. It feels good."

I turned the heater knob to maximum.

"Okay." I said, "While you get warmed up, prepare yourself for the sell job on my house. Here's the upside." I ticked off the points on my fingers. "We want you to come. We're expecting you. It's warm. You'll have your own room and a bathroom you'll share with Santana, if we can find her. The sooner I drop you off, the sooner I can look for Santana. You won't need to cook. My husband has already made some soup and fresh bread. We can fix you up with warm, dry clothes too." I took a deep breath and studied her face. She still looked skeptical.

"And here's the downside: It's a crazy household. We've got a dog and two cats and we're looking after Dr. Sinclair's kitten, who's been living in what will be your room. If you're violently allergic to animal fur, we'll find you another space. I've got two teenaged boys, both still in school. While they're home, they're loud. And those dry clothes I promised? They won't fit well or be the height of fashion. I can only promise warm and dry. Any questions?"

Ketifa bit her lip and looked at me as if trying to read between the lines to uncover any malice or danger in my offer. I realized there was much more to this young woman's backstory than I'd probably ever understand—or that she'd ever be willing to share with me.

"You promise you'll look for Santana?" she asked as the rain turned to hail and wind gusts rocked the car.

"Right after I introduce you to my nutty family. I promise."

"And I can leave whenever I want?"

"Or stay as long as you need to."

"Okay."

"Good. Let's go." I smiled, patted her hand, and headed home, where I hoped Max had a fire going in addition to the warm soup and fresh bread. Tonight was no night for anyone to be out alone in the dark.

After I'd driven a few blocks, I remembered I had a ton of unanswered questions for Ketifa.

"Ketifa?" I began. "Look, you don't have to answer if you don't want to, but I've got a bunch of questions. Starting with what you were doing with Santana's phone. And is there any way we can reach her?"

Ketifa shook her head. "Santana started getting calls and texts from that guy this morning. They were horrible. Just horrible. She was scared and angry and frustrated and then completely overwhelmed. We were talking in the shed while I transplanted some seedlings. Finally, she just threw her phone against the wall and stomped out. I picked it up so I could give it back to her. She needs it to get her class assignments."

"Was Boots really angry about Linc and Sarah's plan to sell their house?"

Ketifa leaned away from me with her hand on the car door.

"I mean, I don't think she was angry enough to kill anyone. I'm not saying that. I'm just wondering what was going on. Tess and I worked with Linc—Dr. Sinclair—for several weeks to get the house cleared out. He never mentioned an arrangement with Boots or the Plotters. Did Boots think he knew about it and was pretending not to? Or did she think that his mother had never told him about the will?"

"Boots? She was glad Linc was fixing up the house and planning to marry Sarah. But when she realized they had plans to sell the house, she was furious. Like, stomping her feet and pacing and tearing-out-her-hair furious. She had a copy of Mrs. Sinclair's will, and she kept waving it around and slapping her palm with it, you know, like she was going to hit Linc over the head until he saw sense." I nodded, trying to signal to Ketifa that I was listening and she should continue. "But she seemed pretty confident she'd get her way. She told the volunteers to come to work as usual and assume the house and land would still pass to the Plotters as Linc's mom intended."

Ketifa went quiet. I peeked at her, afraid I might put her on the spot again if she saw me looking or if I asked her a question. She shook her head and sighed. "Boots wouldn't have killed Dr. Sinclair or Sarah. She has a temper, but she's really sweet underneath. She told us to look out for the professor—you know, because he forgot things when he was busy. We brought him fruits and vegetables and sometimes even started a pot of soup for him that we'd be sure was turned off at the end of the day when we left."

I risked asking a question. "And how did Santana feel about Boots? Did she get along as well with her as she did with Linc?"

Ketifa nodded. "I think so. Boots was working on finding Santana housing. She was squatting in the old shed at the garden. We were hoping to find someplace we could rent together. And Santana hoped Boots would help her get into Stanford. Santana would have done anything for Boots, I think."

I wondered if any one person would be able to do all that the girls hoped Boots would do for them. But superheroes come in all shapes and sizes. If anyone could pull off trying to become a one-woman social-service agency, I'd put my money on Boots. I felt sure she'd eventually find Santana a better place to sleep than a rat-infested shed or an unheated basement.

I pulled into our bumpy driveway and the car lurched to the front door. Ketifa held her belly to protect it and grabbed the door handle to steady herself.

"Sorry about the bumps. It can't be a comfortable ride for you. I'm always afraid I'm going to bite my lip or something."

She laughed politely. I stopped the car at the front door and rushed to help the very pregnant girl from the car. I wondered if there was actually a father in the picture, but I knew it was none of my business.

I took her arm to help her up the steps, but she shook off my hand. "I'm okay, really, Mrs. McDonald. I'm pregnant, not sick."

And independent too, I thought.

I held the door for her anyway. "I'll introduce you to my husband and get you settled in the room that Linc was staying in. You can meet his cat, Jelly. But then I'm going to make sure Santana knows she has a warm place to stay tonight."

Ketifa insisted on doing some chores to help out, but I hoped I'd convinced her to enjoy the shower and maybe take a nap. If she really couldn't relax, I suggested she might set the table.

As I left the room, she stopped me. "Why are you doing this? You don't know me or Santana, and I don't think you like Boots much, either."

I wasn't sure of the answer. I hadn't given it much thought. The girls weren't that much older than my own kids, though. And I wouldn't want the boys or any of their friends to live like Santana and Ketifa had been living. Besides, they were exactly the kind of kids that Sarah had been trying to help with her library programs. Helping them was kind of a tribute to Sarah. But Ketifa didn't need to know that.

"It's not supposed to be this hard, Ketifa," I said. "I just want to help you and your baby." I started to leave the room again, then turned and looked at her. "I'm sad about my friend Sarah and worried about my friend Linc. There isn't much I can do for either one of them, but giving you and Santana a place to stay helps me not to worry about them quite so much."

I dashed down the stairs and turned on the electric kettle. I hoped that Santana might be more willing to listen to me if I offered her hot tea and a snack on a wet and rainy night.

I filled Max in on my plans for the girls while I bustled around the kitchen. He shrugged. "My Aunt Kay always had students staying in the house. In a way, we're just continuing her tradition."

"I hadn't thought of it that way, but you're right. Spooky." I smiled back at Max and gave him a quick hug, wishing we had time for something more—even if it was only a moment to sit on the porch and enjoy a cup of coffee together.

"Max, I need to leave again to find Santana, the other young volunteer at the garden. I'll tell you all about it later."

"Tess will be bringing the boys back soon. If they haven't eaten, I'll invite Tess and Teddy to stay for dinner."

I gave Max a hug and a kiss. "You're a gem."

"I know."

I poured hot water over tea bags in a battered stainless thermos I'd used since before Max and I were married.

Max put the thermos of tea into one of our canvas grocery bags with the sandwich I made. He pulled a package of chocolate-chip cookies from the freezer and snuggled them in beside the thermos. He handed me the bag and pushed me toward the door.

Belle snuffled my hand and tried to follow me, but I wasn't sure where or how I would find Santana, and I didn't know if she was afraid of dogs. I hesitated. Sometimes a friendly dog could be a good ice-breaker. I knelt, scratched Belle's ears, and buried my face in her fur.

"Not this time, Baby Belle. I'll be back soon, though. I promise."

Chapter 20

In earthquake country, it's a good idea to keep your car
stocked with emergency supplies—water, warm clothing,
comfortable shoes, first aid, and nonperishable food.
While these supplies can be essential in a disaster, they
prove helpful in lesser emergencies as well.

From the Notebook of Maggie McDonald,
Simplicity Itself Organizing Services

Friday, November 7, 6:00 p.m.

I parked in the lot as close to the garden shed as I could. Tonight
was no time to be ducking through hedges or slogging across the
lawn.

I'd grabbed a raincoat and shoved my feet into waterproof boots
before leaving the house, and I'd grabbed a warm winter jacket for
Santana, but we'd both want to limit our time out in the wet.

I was nearly certain Santana would be holed up in the shed.
Elaine and I had looked in the house, and while there was a chance
she'd hidden there from us, I thought it was more likely she'd run
off.

Mr. Range Rover had already checked for her at the garden, so
she might assume the shed was the safest place to hide. But not in
this rainstorm. I wasn't sure the roof was watertight, let alone the
walls or the dirt floors.

The old shed and its one window looked almost homelike through
the rain. Muted light streamed from the tiny window and the door
that was partly open. I felt my shoulders relax. The light and open

door both meant someone was inside. Someone who was almost certainly Santana.

I knocked lightly on the door, afraid I might startle the girl. Through the partially open door I could see her tense but then relax when she turned and saw it was me. She took the earbuds from her ears and stood up politely, smiling and inviting me in.

"Mrs. McDonald," she said, brushing off her overalls and looking around the surprisingly dry room. I couldn't tell whether she was checking to see if she'd tidied up or was looking for a seat to offer a visitor.

"Santana, I'm sorry to interrupt you." The girl had obviously been catching up on homework. A battery-operated lantern and an ancient laptop sat on a splintered box. Next to them were a calculus book and a dog-eared copy of *Hamlet*, along with a stuffed backpack that must have weighed nearly thirty-five pounds.

"It's fine." She pulled two five-gallon pails from the workbench and handed me one. She upended the other and sat down. "I'm sorry I have nothing to offer you, unless you'd like some water?"

Someone at some point had taught Santana excellent manners. I thought accepting her hospitality might put her at ease. "Thank you," I said, stepping into the room and seating myself on the perch she'd offered. "Or, if you'd prefer, and if you've got some mugs, I brought hot tea."

She poured water from an old plastic jug into two pastel-colored tumblers of similar age. After wiping them out and drying them, she handed them to me. "I've been staying here to make sure no one bothers the gardens at night," she said. I filled the cups with steaming tea and handed one to Santana. She took it and held it with both hands and breathed in the steam.

"You're not afraid to be here alone? After Sarah's death, I mean. It's not too cold? I'm not sure how long this old place will stay dry with all this rain."

Santana blushed and looked down into her cup. She shook her head.

"I spoke to Ketifa," I said.

She glanced quickly toward Linc's house and her cheeks blushed a deeper shade, but she didn't say anything.

"I didn't think the basement was a great place for a pregnant woman. It's too cold, for one thing."

Santana stayed silent, so I plowed on, hoping I wasn't digging myself into a hole. Her gaze darted around the small room like that of a caged animal searching for an exit. What could I say that would soothe her instead of throwing her into a full-scale panic?

"I offered Ketifa a temporary place at my house. Our attic has two extra bedrooms. I was hoping you might be interested in taking the second one, at least until you can find someplace better. Between my husband and my two boys it's very much a man's house. I'd appreciate the company and I expect Ketifa would feel more comfortable with another young woman there."

Santana let out a breath. Her shoulders relaxed and she met my gaze. She bit her lip and paused, looking at her cobweb-filled surroundings before speaking. I thought she would snap up a chance to leave the shed, but she shook her head.

"I need to stay here on my own," she said. "I used to be in this other place. A place I thought was perfect. I was just starting to feel at home when one of the men who lived there started staring at me and asking me to help him with his car. But somehow it always seemed to have more to do with him rubbing up against me than with getting the car running." She shuddered. "He gave me the creeps. I'd rather share this place with the four-footed rats than stay in the house with him." She hugged herself with her arms. "And, no offense, but I barely know you. Why should I trust you?"

I thought about that for a moment, but I couldn't come up with a good response. She was right. Why should she trust me? Maybe the answer was for her to get to know me better. I asked if she was warm enough and handed her the jacket I brought.

Santana took it from me and spread it over her lap like a blanket. She picked up one of the sleeves and held it in two hands, weaving it between her fingers. Her lamp provided dim light, but I could see that her eyes were rimmed with deep shadows, making her look old and tired.

"Do the rats here bother you?" I moved away from the offer of the room. I'd extend the invitation again a little later.

She smiled a sheepish-little-kid smile. "I sprinkled some of the birdseed outside the shed to keep them busy so they don't come inside." She blushed again and looked away. "I've been showering at night at Professor Sinclair's and eating the food he left. He doesn't notice stuff like that." She looked down at her hands. "But there's not much food left there, now."

"We turned off the heat and hot water earlier this week too," I said. I shivered. "Those must have been some very cold showers."

We sat for a moment in silence, sipping our tea.

"More?" Santana asked and held up the thermos and I was reminded of playing tea party with my niece when she was small.

"Have you heard anything about Boots?" I asked.

Santana's eyes filled with tears. She looked away, twisted the jacket sleeve and moaned softly.

"It was my fault," she said in a voice that was almost too quiet for me to hear.

Silence coaxed the story from her.

"It was my fault. If I'd gone with him when he started texting me, he wouldn't have come here to bother Boots and Ketifa. Everyone says Boots tripped over the hose before she hit her head. It was my job to coil up the hoses and make sure the pathways were clear. If I'd done that, she wouldn't be dead. She shouldn't be dead." I was so focused on her feelings, I nearly missed what she'd said about Boots.

"Did you hear something recently?" I asked. "She was still alive when they put her in the ambulance. No one could say for sure, but the EMTs were optimistic that she'd make a full recovery."

She buried her head in her hands, shaking her head. "I never meant to kill anyone. It was an accident."

I patted her hand. "I know it was, Santana. I know. You didn't put the boot scraper there, either. It was bad luck, but I'm guessing you'll never forget to coil up the hoses again."

Santana's shoulders shook and my throat grew tight as I held her. Where was this girl's family? She was a great kid, owning up to her mistakes and taking responsibility for them, trying to make it right.

"And it's Mr. Range Rover's fault that Boots was hurt. His alone. You didn't push her. You didn't scare her. If you'd gone with him, you might be in bad shape yourself, sharing a room in the hospital with Boots. He shoved Ketifa too. I took her to the emergency room. They sutured her forehead, but she'll be fine."

"Her baby?"

"Cozier than we are right now." I patted Santana's back. "The best thing you ever did was leave that guy, Santana. It was very brave.

You did the right thing to stay away from him. He's been stalking you, hasn't he?"

Santana sobbed. Poor kid. She was hanging by an emotional thread. I moved my upturned pail next to hers. "If you want, a little later we can call and get an update on Boots's condition. And when she's awake I'll take you to see her. Ketifa told me the two of you are really close."

She glanced up with a hopeful look. "Can we do that now? Call, I mean?"

Teardrops glistened on the ends of her eyelashes. I nodded and texted Paolo.

His return text arrived quickly: *Boots still alive. Close monitoring for 24 hours. Many stitches. Lots of bruising. Good chance of full recovery.*

I relayed the message to Santana. She wiped her eyes.

"Really? She's going to be okay?"

"I won't lie to you, Santana. It sounds like she's still in rough shape, but they are doing everything they can and keeping a close watch on her. I see no reason to think she won't pull through. You know Boots. She's too stubborn. Have you ever seen her give up? On anything?"

Santana shook her head and tried to smile. Tried and failed. Her brow knitted and her lip quivered. Something still troubled her.

On a hunch, I asked softly, "Are you worried about Sarah's death? Afraid you were responsible?"

Santana nodded and tears streamed down her cheeks. "Sarah was so nice. On a super-cold day last winter she brought us hot chocolate and brownies and a bunch of extra sweatshirts and stuff." She looked up again, smiling and brushing away her tears. "The clothes were all too big and some had paint and others were torn, but they were warm and we were freezing. She told us to come up to the house if it started raining or we got cold. She didn't have to do that, you know? A lot of the people who have plots here don't even notice us. They'd look through us like we're not there, even when we say hello. I really liked Sarah. But I didn't know she spent time in the professor's workroom. I'd only ever seen Linc there, ya know?"

I nodded without speaking. I didn't want to say anything to break whatever spell I'd cast that had prompted Santana to give me the details about what she thought had happened.

"The things I did . . . they were wrong, I guess. But I didn't . . . they didn't. Did they?"

I assumed she was worried that something she'd done had contributed to Sarah's death.

She went on talking: "Boots was so upset about the house. The land was supposed to go to *her*—Professor Sinclair could live in it as long as he liked and Boots couldn't do anything about it, but the will said that if he moved out, the house would belong to the Plotters. Not Boots, not really, but to her Plotters. And she really is the Plotters, you know? She got all of us to help maintain the gardens, and she used her own money on the renovations that were done ten years ago. She was always writing grant applications and begging the city for more money. But the whole time she was doing that, she knew it would pay off when the professor moved out. When he started dating Sarah, Boots and Sarah became really close. I think Boots genuinely liked her—at least until Sarah and Professor Sinclair started talking about selling the house."

Santana was running out of steam, and I still wasn't clear what had happened. She wiped her eyes with the sleeve of the jacket.

"Why do you think she was so upset?" I asked.

"Boots *is* the garden. She poured everything into it. She has lots of other charities and her foster-care work, but she's all about the garden. She could give up any of her other work, I think, but without the garden, she'd lose . . . herself."

"But she'd still have the garden if the house were sold, wouldn't she?"

Santana stood and folded up the coat. She shook her head. "You don't get it. She *is* the garden," she repeated. "Its future means everything to her. She's spent decades planning improvements. Boots is great to us and she would do anything for us, but I think she's a little nuts too. And any one of us would do anything for her. She didn't even have to ask."

In the silence that followed I heard tiny, scurrying footsteps outside and Santana's old hard-drive laptop revved and spun, performing some automatic function.

"Santana, I know you're upset. But what is it, exactly, that you're afraid you did?"

"Boots had a plan and she was lining up lawyers, but she was afraid when Professor Sinclair hired Mrs. Olmos, the Realtor. Everyone knows how efficient Mrs. Olmos is and Boots was frantic. It was like the first time I ever saw her confidence crack. She was so afraid that Mrs. Olmos would come in, fix up the house, have her party, line up buyers and backup buyers, and the house would be sold before Boots could take care of whatever paperwork she'd need to put a stop to the process."

Santana picked up her tea and took a long drink. "Boots tried to talk to Sarah, but Sarah said to talk to Professor Sinclair. And . . . you know him. Trying to pin him down to talk to was, like, impossible."

I rummaged around in my tote and pulled out a small package of tissues. I'd been carrying them around so long they'd begun disintegrating into powder around the edges.

She took one, wiped her eyes with it, and then balled it up in her fist.

"So what did you do?" I prompted.

"Um . . . little things, mostly. I loosened a bunch of the lightbulbs and some of the connectors on the electrical box so that the lights would flicker. I started talking about the ghost of old Mrs. Sinclair and how she must be restless and dangerous, angry because her son was selling the house since she'd wanted it to go to the Plotters." She shrugged. "I figured folks would be afraid to buy a house full of ghosts or maybe they'd want extra inspections that would slow down the process."

"Did it work?"

Santana shook her head. "The only person who believed the story about the ghosts was Ketifa. So I tried other things, like flipping circuit breakers and fraying wires so they'd create a short. I figured it might be hard to sell a house with faulty wiring, so Mrs. Olmos and the professor would have to do a major renovation before they started looking for a buyer."

"Weren't you afraid you'd start a fire?"

"That was part of the reason I was sleeping in the basement or in the shed. I could keep an eye on the house in case anything went wrong."

She took another sip of her tea and looked at her watch.

"Go on," I said softly. I was afraid she'd realize how long she'd been talking to a relative stranger and shut down.

"But it turned out the professor had no trouble spotting where I'd done my fiddling. He'd fix the problem and move on. I'm not sure he even noticed what he was doing, to tell you the truth. You know that look he has when his mind is in his lab, but his body is somewhere else?"

I chuckled. It was an apt description of Linc and not nearly as trite as the head-in-the-clouds description I'd always used for the same behavior.

"After a while, it got to be a sort of a game. I'd started thinking of new ways to fool him and I almost forgot about why I'd begun doing it. His lab is awesome. I couldn't believe anyone could have a lab like that, let alone one at the university and another one at home. He was tutoring me too. He's so nice. And so smart."

I let the silence linger until Santana looked up from tearing the bunched-up tissue into bits.

"What do you think happened the night Sarah died?" I asked.

She bit her lip and shook her head. "I'm not sure. Boots said a power surge fried her computer that night. She doesn't live too far from here. The power went on and off all night, all over town. I'm thinking maybe Sarah touched one of those machines right in the middle of one of the power surges. Could that have done it? Could that have killed her?"

Santana looked up at me with her eyes glistening again.

"I'm not sure," I said. "Most houses have ground-fault interrupters to stop that sort of thing. And the professor, as you guessed, knew about your experiments with the electricity and made sure everything was safe before he went to bed at night. I don't think anything you did or didn't do killed Sarah."

Her shoulders relaxed and I was grateful my words had comforted her. I didn't understand electrical currents well enough to be sure my answer was correct. But Santana had spooked when I'd mentioned the police and I didn't want to suggest contacting them again.

A gust of wind blew rain against the shed wall and the little building shook. The hunted-rabbit look returned to Santana's face. Remembering her story of the lecherous man who'd sent her from a warm and dry housing situation to a rat-infested shed, I put my hand on her shoulder.

"Santana, it's getting late, cold, and wet." I pointed to a dark space near the door where water was seeping in. "I think this whole situation will look a lot better once we get you some dry clothes, a hot meal, and a good night's sleep in a warm bed where you don't have to worry about anyone coming after you. Won't you consider letting me take you home? You can leave anytime you want, but staying with us will give you some breathing room to sort things out. And maybe visit Boots too."

I remembered that Ketifa had seemed to relax when I told her the downside of the arrangement. Maybe admitting it wasn't perfect had convinced her I wasn't trying to scam her. It was worth a try on Santana too.

"Look, Santana. What I'm offering you isn't perfect. I've got a dog, two cats, and a kitten we're looking after for the professor. I've got two noisy teenaged boys. And the house isn't close to the college or anywhere else. We've had a few problems with our cars and we're short on transportation, but we're working that out as fast as we can. If it's within my power, I'll help you get wherever you need to go."

"Ketifa's there already?"

"Would you like to talk to her, to check?" I held out my phone.

Santana reached for it, then dropped her hand, stood up, and put on the jacket. She shoved her hands in the pockets, squared her shoulders, and said, "No. I trust you. Your offer sounds like something Sarah would do."

I blushed and was flattered, but I didn't want to embarrass Santana by telling her that. "Let's get you out of here, then." I pointed my key fob in the direction of the car. "Maybe we can get the doors unlocked from here. Ready?"

Santana nodded. She grabbed her backpack, switched off the light, and locked the door. Then we dashed through the puddles to the car.

Chapter 21

There's nothing as comforting as homemade soup and
warm bread. Whenever I make either, I make extra and
freeze the rest to reheat on cold, rainy evenings.

From the Notebook of Maggie McDonald,
Simplicity Itself Organizing Services

Friday November 7, 7:00 p.m.

As we drove home, I repeated the words I'd spoken to Ketifa earlier. "You don't have to answer any questions you don't want
to, Santana, but I'm curious about some things." She didn't protest,
so I pressed on: "Were you there when Boots was hurt?"

"We heard the Range Rover coming and Boots told me to go.
There's that big plot with the sunflowers just behind the shed and I
hid back there. Buck, that's my uncle's . . . er—I'll explain that another time. Anyway, Buck confronted Boots, wanted her to tell him
how to find me. Boots wouldn't, so he pushed her. She fell over the
hose and hit her head on the boot scraper. Then Buck kicked her,
hard."

"So that's why you thought she was dead?"

Santana nodded. "I was going to go to call 9-1-1, but Ketifa had
my phone. Then I was afraid if the police came, they'd find out about
the hose and say I killed her. I was afraid they'd make me go back to
Buck too. I was scared, so I ran."

I knew the police would need to talk to Santana. But not tonight.
Tonight she needed food, warmth, comfort, and her friend Ketifa. I
passed her my phone when we stopped at a red light.

"Ketifa's been very worried about you. Would you like to call her? You can find the home number if you can't remember hers."

Santana tapped quickly on the phone with her thumbs. Max must have answered. With impeccable manners, she identified herself, explained that I was bringing her home, and that she was using my phone.

"Tell him we're about five minutes out," I said. She relayed the message, asked to speak with Ketifa, and the two girls talked the rest of the way home.

Tess and Teddy dropped the boys off and came in to meet Ketifa and Santana. We ate all the soup and both of the loaves of bread that Max had reheated, but he dodged our compliments, saying that as hungry as we all were, we'd have pronounced ketchup-drenched cardboard a gourmet experience.

We wrapped things up early. I helped the girls settle in, making sure that they had everything they needed and were comfortable hosting a relentlessly frisky kitten.

Afterwards, I said good night to both boys, thankful to tuck them in safely under our own roof. Belle was sticking close to me as I made my way around the house. I wasn't sure whether she was double-checking my work as a mom and a hostess, or if she wanted to make sure I didn't leave her behind if I went out again. I stooped and hugged her. "I'm sorry I couldn't take you with me today, Belle, but tomorrow should be much less crazy."

We took the front staircase down to the living room, where Max sat on the couch between our two cats, Holmes and Watson. Two glasses of golden chardonnay sat on the coffee table in front of him.

"Is there room there for me?"

"It depends upon who you ask," Max said. "But I think Holmes here would be willing to move."

I snuggled up next to Max and put Holmes on my lap. Belle sighed heavily and plopped her head on my foot so she'd know whenever I moved. Max grabbed the wineglasses and handed me one. We touched glasses.

"So," Max said. "What are we appreciating this evening?" It was a practice we'd started early in our marriage, making sure that we took the time to recognize good moments and share them at the end of the day—especially on really bad days.

"That it's nearly over?" I said.

Max laughed. "I think we can do better than that. We're all safe and warm and out of the rain. It looks like Boots is going to recover. Oh, and I can't believe I forgot to tell you this—Stephen called and said that Jason's fever has broken. The antibiotics seem to be winning the war against the infection, and he may be able to come home tomorrow afternoon."

"I'm so glad." I'd nearly forgotten about Jason in the midst of everything else that was going on, but from what Elaine had said, he'd been close to death and Stephen had been deathly afraid. While I felt tremendous joy knowing that he was healing, I also felt like a terrible friend for not checking up on him sooner.

"Is it against the rules to talk about less wonderful things?" Max asked.

"We made the rules. We can change them. What's up?"

"I spent much of the afternoon on the phone with the police, the insurance company, and local car dealers."

"What a mess. Thanks for doing that."

"Both cars are totaled and will be needed for evidence. It will take time for the dust to settle, and I'm not completely clear on what we'll get for the cars or when we'll get it. Paolo sent me pictures of your car." Max's pulled me closer to him. He kissed my head. "I can't believe you and Linc came out of that with no injuries. I-I made a decision without asking you. You were pretty happy with your car and it did such a good job protecting you that I ordered the same one again. I hope that's okay. If not, I'll drive it and you can pick out something else. They had a green one. Hunter green. They're delivering it tomorrow morning."

"You're kidding."

"I'm sorry. I knew I should have checked. They might take it back—"

"No, you goose. I can't believe you took care of it that quickly. The color is perfect, of course. And I loved that car. I wondered how on earth we were going to get wheels under us within a week, let alone this quickly." I kissed him firmly and thoroughly. "Thank you."

"So, are you cured of chasing bad guys, now that one of them has chased you back?"

"I think maybe, just maybe, I've had enough. If we'd known how many murderers we'd run into here, would we have been so anxious to move?"

"Admit it, though. You love this house."

"I love you."

Belle leaped up from where she was sleeping and scrambled around the coffee table to the window seat overlooking the side of the house. She scratched at the window, barking and snarling. The cats dashed upstairs so fast they skidded at the turn on the landing.

Max jumped up, turned out the light, and told me to stay put.

"Call 9-1-1," he said, but I'd already dialed and was waiting for dispatch to answer. Max stood to the left of the fireplace and peered around the curtain. "Do we know anyone with a black Range Rover?"

I told Max to get away from the window. He ducked down and pulled Belle down with him. The fur on her spine stuck straight up and she growled as if she was impersonating a Rottweiler.

"He's armed," I said as I continued to wait for someone to answer my call. "He's got some connection to Santana and he's bad news. Very bad news."

Dispatch answered and I said as calmly as possible that we had an armed and dangerous intruder on our property and needed help right away.

"I'm sorry, ma'am, can you repeat that more slowly?"

I told her the address and asked her to hurry. "He's on the porch, rattling the doorknob. I have to go. My kids are upstairs."

Crouching in front of the sofa, I crawled through the dining room, made sure the kitchen door was locked, and then ran upstairs. The boys were in the hallway holding the cats. Santana and Ketifa stood on the attic stairway clutching their blankets around their shoulders.

"What's going on, Mom?" David asked.

"The police are on their way," I said.

"Is it Buck?" Santana asked.

Ketifa gasped.

"Who's Buck?" asked Brian.

They were all standing in the light of the overhead lamp in the hallway and would be easily visible through the big window on the staircase. I turned off the light and motioned them all to move to the other end of the hall.

"I think it is Buck. It looks like his car. Boys, Buck is someone who has been bothering Santana. He's also the man that hurt Ketifa. Did anyone hear him come up the driveway?"

All four of the kids looked at each other and shook their heads.

"We were asleep," said Ketifa. Santana nodded.

"I was listening to music," Brian said.

"Maybe the rain and the wind drowned out the sound," said David. "It was really loud in my room."

"Dad and I were talking. He must have come up with the lights off. Belle heard him, but we didn't notice until she started barking. Stay here, all of you. I'm going to look out the bathroom window."

I'd never before appreciated having a big window in the bathroom. I peeked through the curtains.

"Jane! I know you're in there," Buck bellowed. "Come out. You don't want to know what I'll do to you if you don't."

Brian scooted into the bathroom and handed me his phone. "It's set to record—just hold it up."

"Jane Evans! Your mama and daddy want you home. Either come back to me or I'll tell CPS you ran away. They'll send you right straight back to Arkansas."

Jane? I turned and looked at Santana, who had buried her head in Ketifa's shoulder.

"I have a gun, Jane. I'll start shooting if you're not down here in sixty seconds. Do you want these people to get hurt? I'll come in if you don't come out."

Santana straightened up, threw off the blanket, and started to stand. David put his hand on her shoulder and pushed her down.

"No way you're going out there," he said.

"David's right. The police will be here any minute. Just stay put. We aren't in any danger as long as we stay away from the windows. These walls are thick," I said.

Belle and Max appeared at the top of the back stairs.

"Paolo just texted me," Max said. "He and two patrol cars are out front with their lights off. They're walking up the driveway, hoping to take him by surprise."

We heard the shouts of the police officers telling Buck to drop his gun and lay flat on the ground. Max ran to the window in our front bedroom, accompanied by Belle. He waved us all in.

"It's safe now, if you want to watch," he said.

One of the officers had brought his patrol car up from the road. It took all three of the officers to get Buck, screaming and cursing, into the backseat, but as soon as he was settled, the car took him away.

Paolo and the other officer talked for a moment. Then the officer walked back down the driveway to his own car and Paolo walked toward the house.

I sighed and looked at all the kids.

"Paolo will want to talk to Santana. Do any of you think you can go back to bed?" I asked. They all shook their heads, looking like a line of wide-eyed bobbleheads. "Hot chocolate and cinnamon toast? Bed in thirty minutes?"

Brian looked at Ketifa. "Just say *yes*. It's the only deal we'll get. She'll set a timer. See if she doesn't."

Ketifa smiled. "I could learn a lot from your mom," she said, patting her belly. And we all trooped down the stairs to meet Paolo in the kitchen.

The next morning, Max and I were up earlier than the rest of the household. We sipped coffee on the back steps and watched Belle chase the rabbits she'd never been able to catch. It was chilly on the porch, but we'd grabbed jackets. With the coffee and the company, I was toasty warm.

"Who is Jane?" Max asked.

"Santana, obviously. But I have no idea what the story is. She must have told Paolo at least some of it last night. We're supposed to take her in to answer more questions when she wakes up."

"Do you think I should call Forrest? Will she need a lawyer? It sounds as though, at best, there's a complicated family situation going on."

I nodded. "It couldn't hurt. Would he know how to handle a situation like this?"

"I'm not sure. What kind of situation is it?"

I laughed and said, "I have no idea."

It wasn't funny, though. Even without Buck in the picture, both Santana and Ketifa had problems I couldn't imagine, and Boots, the only person they really trusted, wasn't available to them. I liked to think that my own kids would never be in a similar situation, but I guessed it could happen to anyone. If things had gone wrong with the car chase, or if Max had been in his car when it crashed into the tree, what would have happened to our kids? We had wills. And I had plenty of family—parents and brothers—who would take the boys in. But would they survive that? Probably. However, I understood as I never had before how homelessness can creep up on almost anyone.

I shook my head as if it were an Etch A Sketch and I could erase my morbid thoughts.

"Max, if you were going to electrocute someone, how would you do it?"

He nearly spit out his coffee. "What? Are you kidding?"

"No," I said. "As far as I know, no one has looked at the electricity in Linc's house. Sarah was electrocuted. But how? Santana thinks it's her fault, because she'd been fiddling with the lights to make them blink on and off at odd times."

Max looked at me as though my brains had drained out my ears overnight.

"She was trying to simulate a haunted house, to delay the sale," I added.

"Hmm. Not that I've ever electrocuted anyone or plan on doing so, but let me think. Linc's house is old. Was it up to code?"

"I think so, mostly. Linc said that he'd upgraded it after his mom died. There was more work he'd need to do if he stayed there, but that was more about having all his equipment on at once than it was about safety. Knowing how safety conscious they were in the lab, I think he'd maximize the safety of the electrical system."

"So you'd have to do something to override the fuses or breakers—whatever the house had. And you'd need to disable any ground fault interrupters. But once you did that, the highest voltage connection in a house is the dryer—two hundred and forty volts. I'm not sure how you'd do it, but if we're talking about Linc's lab, I'd wire one of the outlets up there into the dryer connection. And I'd throw some water on the floor. Water and electricity don't mix."

"There was water on the floor," I said. "But I don't know whether it was from the rain or whether the murderer put it there. I need to call Paolo." I kissed Max. "Thanks, hon. I think you may have found the answer. If you're right, the murderer may have left fingerprints on the dryer, the wall outlets, or the breaker box. Fingerprints that Apfel may never have looked for." I kissed him again. "You're the best," I said. "This information may be all we need to nab Sarah's killer."

I pulled out my phone and dialed. When Paolo answered, I

jumped in with no preamble or polite greeting. "Paolo, who collected the evidence at Sarah's?"

"What? I'm not sure. Apfel ran the scene, though he may have called in some of the Orchard View officers with more experience. He sent me off to Sarah's cottage. Why?"

"It wouldn't have been the criminalists from the county lab?"

"Not usually. The DA's office oversees the crime lab for all the law-enforcement agencies in the county. The criminalists can't be everywhere, so unless it's a particularly tricky scene, the crime-lab experts wait for the evidence to come to them."

"Do you know if they opened up the electrical outlets in Linc's workroom and looked for fingerprints? Did they look for prints or evidence around the dryer outlet and the surrounding wall or on the dryer itself?" I told Paolo what Max had said about how a home electrical system might be rigged to give someone a nasty shock.

"Apfel's gone. The files are a mess. I'll call the electrical guy and see what he did or if Apfel even called him. Every time I asked what progress he'd made, he dodged the question. He was so focused on Linc that he wasn't looking for other suspects. Apfel was sure he could get Linc to confess, so he didn't look for much evidence, either. What an idiot. I'll talk to the lab too, and see if we can get them out to Linc's to take a look. This long after Sarah's death, we'll need their expertise. I'm guessing with all those boxes in Linc's workroom, Apfel would have been too lazy to move them, let alone go into the basement. When he worked for Orchard View PD initially, it was before evidence-handling training was common practice, so he could have really messed things up in there."

"Thanks, Paolo. What's the word on our gentleman caller from last night?"

"You know I can't tell you that. Are you bringing Santana down here later? Call before you come to make sure I'm at the station."

I told Paolo we were going to call Forrest and have him talk to Santana. "I know you can't tell me anything, but her situation sounds really complicated, and I want to make sure she doesn't say anything that makes things any worse."

"Good idea," said Paolo. "She won't need a lawyer while she's talking to me, but she'll need one soon enough."

I gasped. "It's that bad?"

"I shouldn't ever tell you anything. Santana's fine. I'll do everything I can to keep her that way, okay? I'm not a bad guy, remember?"

"Sorry, I know that. Thanks. I'll call you before we come down."

When Santana and I reached the station a few hours later, Forrest was there to meet us with an associate who specialized in family law. I'd told Santana that we hoped they'd be able to get her on solid legal footing regarding her family situation so that she couldn't be threatened or bullied into doing anything she didn't want to do.

I'd discussed some of her legal issues with Max, and we agreed to foot the bill for the time being, using some of the money from his Aunt Kay's estate. But Forrest and his associate had agreed to work with Santana pro bono.

I waited in the lobby for at least an hour, until Paolo came out to tell me Forrest would bring Santana back to the house when they were finished.

"I just got a call from the team at Linc's house," he said.

"Already? That was fast."

"They wanted to get out there before the evidence deteriorated any further. You were right. Apfel never called them. He was just going through the motions and pocketing the paycheck."

"Isn't that fraud? Or a breach of ethics? Or something? He's not just lazy, he's a crook."

"Right now, I'm just happy he's gone. I'll let internal affairs worry about the rest. But that's not what I wanted to tell you. The results won't be official for quite a while, but the team found fingerprints exactly where you suggested we check. A quick look showed that they're neither Linc's nor Sarah's, nor those of any of the contractors Linc used to upgrade the electrical system after his mom died. We compared them to Linc's colleagues at Stanford, and it looks like they are a match for Keenan Barnaby. He's being questioned now about Sarah's murder and the lab explosion."

"Barnaby? Keenan Barnaby? Not Walt Quintana? Barnaby's the younger one. Quintana's older. Are you sure you've got the right man?"

"I thought you'd be thrilled that Linc's been cleared," Paolo said, looking disappointed at my reaction.

"Of course I'm happy," I said. "I am *thrilled*, in fact. I'm just so confused about Barnaby and Quintana. Belle and I both liked Barnaby better than Quintana. Shows what we know."

"He's almost certainly a sociopath," Paolo said. "And a gifted manipulator. He saw you had a dog and played on your emotions."

"He was at Stanford the night of the explosion," I told Paolo. "Acting just a little off. I saw him there around maybe two-thirty or three."

"Let me send a text to the captain," said Paolo, pulling out his phone. "That may help the team interviewing him ramp up the pressure to get him to confess." He finished punching in the message and frowned. "Maggie, I know you must be completely sick of all of us down at the station, but I'll need another statement from you about when you saw him and what he said."

"I don't mind. Let me check the log on my phone. I may be able to pinpoint the time more closely. I phoned Stephen just after I spoke to Keenan." I scrolled through my phone, continuing to talk as I did so. "I'm trying to remember his exact words. All I remember really are impressions. He seemed . . . disconnected. The fact that so many of the labs and probably much of people's work was destroyed didn't seem to bother him. Even the kids watching seemed to have more empathy with those whose lives would be disrupted. But Keenan just seemed happy that his own lab hadn't blown up. Looking back at it now, it seems really creepy."

Paolo continued staring at his phone, then looked up and beamed. "This is great news, Maggie," he said, tapping the screen on his phone. "Jason's old mentor, Findley O'Brian, has been called out of retirement and will take over Apfel's hours until Jason is fully recovered."

I threw my arms around Paolo and hugged him, letting go as soon as I remembered how uncomfortable it made him. "That's wonderful news. We have to celebrate. And you have to tell me all the details. Can you come for dinner? Or can I bring you dinner here? Can we get coffee?"

Paolo shook his head. "I've got a pile of paperwork that will keep me busy for at least a week, assuming everyone in Orchard View behaves himself and I don't catch any new cases. All the celebration I need is a good night's sleep and a lull in the murders, explosions, and car chases. I joined this department thinking that because this was Silicon Valley, the work would be all cybercrime, all the time. I aspired to computer forensics. Not death, destruction, and bombs."

"What *were* you thinking?"

Chapter 22

At the end of any big project, assignment, or job, allow plenty of extra time to tidy up the details that inevitably remain after you consider the job "done."

From the Notebook of Maggie McDonald,
Simplicity Itself Organizing Services

Saturday, November 22, 5:00 p.m.

A little more than two weeks later, Tess and I, with a little help from everyone we knew, welcomed a record number of guests to her holiday tea. The Sinclair home was trimmed with holiday garlands and a photographer had taken beauty shots of every room for a sales brochure. The notoriety the house had earned following Sarah's death, Linc's arrest, and the announcement of Linc's innocence had exploded into a macabre interest. Rumors that must have stemmed from Santana's effort to prove the Victorian was haunted meant everyone in Orchard View and the surrounding towns wanted a look inside.

As if determined to shed its undeserved goth reputation, the house showed like a dream. Fairy lights sparkled inside and out. Garlands festooned the mantles and banisters. Tess had placed realistic-looking flickering electric candles on every surface. Servers dressed in turn-of-the-century costumes passed trays of petit fours and canapés, and the high school's madrigal singers helped set the mood, followed by a string quartet clad in formal Victorian evening wear.

Linc hadn't had the energy to finish tidying up his workroom, but Santana had agreed to help him with it after the tea. With special lighting, a blackboard covered in chalked calculations, a skeleton on a stand, and several trays of beakers filled with glowing red and green liquid, Tess had transformed the cluttered workroom into a vision that conjured images of the dark laboratory of Mr. Hyde in the home of kindly Dr. Jekyll. It played wonderfully into the house's recent history and the period atmosphere.

The crowd was thinning and I was gathering crumpled napkins and empty teacups when Tess blew into the room from the kitchen. Her hair had escaped her Gibson-girl bun.

"Maggie, I'm all out. Do you have any more business cards or flyers?"

I patted my pockets and shook my head. "If the box in the kitchen is empty, then I'm out too."

"I can't believe how well it's gone. I'm going to be super-busy for the next three months, at least." Tess grabbed one of the chairs from the nearest table. "We should think about doing another one of these events in the spring." She moved to lift the chair onto a cart the rental company had provided, but then changed her mind and sprawled onto it, sighing.

Linc, acting as busboy, brought out a gray dish tub from the kitchen and began loading it with teacups and saucers. When he reached our table, he pulled out a chair and sat down.

"Did I hear you say you thought this afternoon was a success?" he asked Tess.

"Stupendous, overwhelming, soared beyond expectations." Tess spoke effusively, waving her arms in the air to dramatize her enthusiasm.

"Does that mean you wouldn't be horrified if I told you I wanted to stay in the house?"

Tess's mouth dropped open and her eyes threatened to pop out of her head like those of an astonished character in a children's cartoon.

"Surprised, yes. Horrified, no. But where did this come from?" she asked.

"Does this have to do with Boots and the Plotters?" I said.

Linc shook his head and toyed with the handle of an empty teacup. "Not at all, Maggie, that's a whole separate issue that I've got a plan for. No, I've been staying at Sarah's so that Newton wouldn't have to climb the stairs while he was healing, but he's nearly fully recovered. And we want to come home. Sarah and I were happy here and I can picture her in every room. I know that Santana tried to convince people it was haunted, and in a way, it really is. In a good way."

"But . . . she died here," Tess said.

"She lived here too. We fell in love here. And it's my home more than Sarah's cottage is, though I may bring some of her furniture over and a few of her things." He looked around the room as if picturing Sarah's artwork and books in the room. "But living at Sarah's house without her is awful. We'd planned to live there and spent most of our time there, but that means I feel her absence there more than I do here. In this house, I hear her laughing at my dreadful housekeeping skills and reminding me to pack my lunch or walk Newton." He brushed tears from his eyes, but he smiled. "It's a good thing. In this neighborhood, I'm close to work and I know where everything is. And the neighbors know about Sarah. I won't have to keep explaining my story. Everyone already knows it.

"I'm going to hang onto Sarah's cottage for a while in case I change my mind. The grief counselor I'm going to says not to do anything too big for at least a year. I'm hoping to lease it at a below-market rate to the new school librarian for six months and renegotiate a rental agreement after that."

"So April found someone—" I was going to say "someone to take Sarah's place," but I couldn't complete my sentence. No one could take Sarah's place.

"They found a former high-school librarian who worked with at-risk youth," Linc said. "April says she's full of ideas about how to augment Sarah's programs and how to fund them."

The front door blew open, followed by a metallic clatter. Jason hobbled in on crutches with Stephen following behind. I leaped up to grab a chair for Jason, but he'd grown so adept with the crutches he barely needed help. Stephen caught my eye and smiled. "He's so dang independent—makes everyone around him feel useless."

Jason sat down and deftly whirled his crutches, then leaned them against the table. If I'd tried a move like that, there would be broken teacups on the floor and a knot growing on someone's forehead.

"All healed?" Linc asked. "No more infection?"

"Healing fast and getting better every day. I told the chief I want to come back in January—three mornings a week to start and building up from there."

"What happened with Detective Awful?" I asked. Tess and I had been working long hours to get Linc's house ready for the tea, and I'd scarcely had a chance to check up with anyone else.

Jason leaned over and planted a loud kiss on my cheek before answering my question. "Internal affairs never tells anyone anything. We know they're investigating his negligence in handling the crime scene and evidence in the investigation of Sarah's death, but we don't know any of the details. The most important thing, though, is that he'll never be back. Findley's great. It's fun to be working with him again. Apparently the chief had called Findley originally to fill in for me, but Fin was off on a cruise to Alaska with his wife to celebrate Mrs. O'Brian's retirement. Findley had been first up in the reserve rotation, not Apfel. It was a simple matter to cut Apfel loose."

I thought through the rest of the questions that remained unanswered. "And what about Boots? Is she really going to be okay?"

Linc leaned forward and answered. "Boots is recovering well. She's still in a rehab facility while they strengthen her motor functions, but Santana and I went to visit her yesterday and she's hoping to go back home early next week."

I felt a twinge of guilt. I'd promised Santana I'd take her to visit Boots in the hospital, but I'd forgotten about it in the rush to pull off the tea. Santana hadn't reminded me about it, either. I was glad Linc had picked up the slack.

"Boots has renewed her status as a foster mom and is planning to take charge of Santana," Linc continued. I raised my eyebrows and tilted my head. Santana and Ketifa had been living at our house and helping with the preparations at Linc's, but neither one had mentioned any of this to me. Then I remembered Ketifa saying that Santana idolized Linc and he'd been tutoring her in electronics, engineering, and physics. In any case, from what Linc was saying, everything was under control. But then I thought of another snag.

"Is Santana still eligible for services?" I asked. "She was talking about applying to Stanford. Don't foster kids age out of care at eighteen?" I was sure I'd heard from someone that Santana was nineteen.

Jason nodded and smiled. "Our Santana was a little loose with the truth, but Findley put on his granddaddy-like charm and convinced her to tell us everything. Paolo confirmed the details. Her real name is Jane Evans and she's only sixteen. Starting in January, she'll take classes at both the high school and the junior college. In two years she should be able to transfer into Stanford as a junior."

"Her grades are that good?" I wondered how an essentially homeless young teen kept up with her schooling.

Linc chimed in. "She asked me to help her fill in the gaps in her education, but she's seriously brilliant and more focused than most of the undergraduates I teach. Based on the little she's told me, she comes from a very conservative family in Arkansas. Her parents must be pretty bright, because they were homeschooling her and her fundamentals in most subjects are solid. She'd finished the religious homeschool curriculum her parents were using and wanted to go to college. Her parents discouraged her, but she was aching for more and was studying calculus and engineering on her own with some help from a program at her local library. Her parents found out, feared for her spiritual welfare, and sent her to live with her aunt and uncle in Menlo Park. But that didn't work out, either and she ran away. Boots and I have been talking to her family and smoothing some things out. The legal aspects of her situation are complicated, but Forrest Doucett is helping with that."

Linc waved across the room, and I turned. Boots herself walked in through the kitchen door. She held a cane but didn't appear to be using it.

"I've been trying to catch everyone up on Santana and Ketifa," Linc said as Boots approached. He hopped up to help her to a spot at the table.

"Now, Ketifa, I know about," I said. "She's been going to her doctor's appointments and eating well, and the baby is due shortly before Christmas." She'd been helping me out with some of the paperwork for my business and organizing files for Max.

"Linc says Santana will be moving in with you," I said to Boots. "I'll miss her."

Boots tapped her cane twice on the floor. "Indeed." But then she smiled and her demeanor warmed. She grabbed a cookie from the few remaining on the plate in the center of the table, looked at it, and popped it into her mouth.

"The girls have been very happy at your house, Maggie, and I can't thank you enough. Santana's going to move in with me so we can help each other out. If Forrest can shuffle the paperwork fast enough, I'm hoping to adopt her. She's terrified her dreadful uncle is going to force her to go back home. Adopting her would put that fear to rest. It's complicated. She may have to emancipate herself from her parents first. Forrest is figuring out all that for us. Including what charges might be brought against her uncle." Boots tapped her cane on the floor again and it echoed in the nearly empty room.

"And Ketifa?" I asked. Max and I had talked about the possibility that we might soon be hearing an infant crying for a midnight feeding and find ourselves parenting a child who was mother to another child. We weren't sure of the legality of the situation, but Max had promised to send out a few feelers on the subject when he met Forrest for lunch the following week.

But, if Forrest was already working with Santana and Boots, that might not be necessary.

Boots spoke up then. "Ketifa's situation is completely different. She's married, for one thing, and an adult. Her husband is missing in action in Afghanistan."

"Seriously?" I said. "She's never mentioned it. She told us he was missing, but never elaborated. I guess I assumed he was just out of the picture and had left her to raise the baby on her own. Poor Ketifa."

"I've been helping there," Stephen said. "Putting her in touch with the right people at the VA to confirm her husband's status, get her some counseling, and make sure she and her baby receive all their benefits."

"She's welcome to stay with us as long as she likes," I said.

Stephen grabbed a cookie. "We think she's still entitled to an apartment at Moffett Field," he said, referring to the federal airfield in Mountain View. "She and her husband lived off the base, where rental costs have soared. She got news of the rent increase the day before the Army notified her that her husband was missing. None of that put her in any position to figure out the paperwork required to solve either problem. She was staying with friends before she started hiding in Linc's basement.

"We're working hard to learn more about her husband's situation and fix her up with shared housing with another Army mom. Her old landlord liked her and saved her belongings from the apartment. He was relieved to know she was safe."

"That's good news," I said. "But what happens now?"

"Knowing she can stay with you and Max has given her great peace of mind," Stephen said.

"She's been a huge help," I said. "She can stay as long as she likes. I want to offer her a job when she's ready too."

"Time will tell," Stephen said. "And Ketifa herself, of course. She's been mourning her husband and worrying that she shouldn't be grieving because he's officially missing, rather than deceased. She doesn't talk about it because it's difficult to explain. Dealing with an MIA situation is complicated, but the VA's helping now."

I sighed heavily and leaned back in my chair. When I looked up, I found everyone focused on me as if I were about to say something brilliant. I sat up and waved them off with my hand. "I'm sorry. I just can't believe everything these girls have been through. Being sixteen like Santana and nineteen like Ketifa is not supposed to be this difficult."

A profound silence followed, interrupted by the sound of breaking glass in the kitchen. Tess and Linc jumped up and ran to help out.

"Has Keenan been arraigned?" I asked. "Does the district attorney have enough evidence to take the case against Keenan to trial?"

Jason grinned. "He's confessed to Sarah's murder, planting the bomb at Stanford, and assaulting Linc with his truck. He's denied chasing you down. He says someone stole his truck."

I leaned forward to ask a question, but Jason held up his hand and continued: "He never reported a theft and we've got him on a Stanford security video climbing into the truck the day after the car chase. We're checking red-light camera footage too."

"Has he said why he did it? Any of it?" I asked. "I've never been able to figure out what he stood to gain from Linc's death."

Jason buried his face in his hands and sighed. "Maybe you have to be an academic to understand it or maybe you just need to be crazy. Keenan told us he was tired of working in a lab that was off in the portable annex. He wanted to be in the thick of things, where the other researchers joined each other for lunch and coffee breaks and invited each other to parties. Keenan felt like an afterthought off in the annex and wanted Linc's office. He set the bomb up because he was getting frustrated. If the explosion killed Linc, fine. But if it didn't, it would mean that the university would have to build a whole new building that would fit the entire department."

Linc must have walked back into the room while we were talking, because I heard him sigh heavily behind me.

"It's not an academic thing to murder someone as a career move," Linc said with a catch in his throat. "That's insane. In fact, all Keenan would have had to do to get my office was to ask to trade with me. I loved being in the annex. It was quiet and out of the way. No one popped in for a visit. Half the reason I do so much work at night is because I can get more done without interruptions."

He pushed the hair back from his forehead, causing it to stick up in the middle. "A few years ago the administration got wind of the fact that the Nobel committee had been interested in some of my work. They moved my lab because they didn't think it was right to house a potential Nobel laureate in a temporary building." A sound that was halfway between a sob and a laugh escaped. "And Sarah died because of that?" Linc's eyes grew damp and his lower lip trembled.

"Sorry," he said. "It's still really hard." He wiped his eyes and continued. "Back when she was alive, I would often tell her that all the Nobel attention was a distraction and one of the worst things that could have happened to my career. But Sarah was the one who encouraged me to enjoy it and not to think of it as a curse."

Linc grabbed the tub of dirty dishes from the table and turned toward the kitchen.

"Linc, wait," I said. "I don't want to cause you pain, but have you given any thought to a memorial service? Did Sarah have any other family? I'd be happy to help."

"Thanks, Maggie," he said, brushing his hand over his eyes. "Sarah was alone like me. All her family died years ago." He cleared his throat. "She said she wanted to be cremated. I thought I might rent out one of those whale-watching boats and scatter her ashes in Monterey Bay. That's what we did on our first date. Whale watching, not ash scattering." Tears slid unchecked down his cheeks. "I thought maybe revisiting a happy place and memory might be good."

I smiled and wiped tears that threatened to spill from my own eyes. "That sounds perfect."

Linc looked at the people gathered at the table. "You'd all be welcome. I'd love to have your support, and I think Sarah would like it. It'd be a chance to say good-bye." A murmur of assent started quietly and grew as it moved around the table of Sarah's friends.

Linc nodded firmly and retreated quickly to the kitchen.

"It's going to take us all a long time to be able to remember her without suffering that kind of pain. It will come, though, won't it? For Linc and for the rest of us?" I said.

Boots bit her lip and nodded, but said nothing.

"Does anyone know if there's any tea left?" Stephen asked, standing and searching the tables, lifting the teapots as if gauging their weight and contents. He must have found some, as he quickly returned with two cups and handed one to Jason.

"Meaning no disrespect to Sarah or Linc, but may I change the subject? I still have some questions," Stephen said. No one stopped him, and he continued after taking a sip of his tea. "What about Santana?" he asked. "Does she have any lingering guilt related to Sarah's death or Boots's injuries? Didn't she think she was responsible for both at some point?"

Boots pounded her cane again. I was now certain she carried it not for support but for the commanding presence it gave her. "She was guilty of making some poor conclusions based on adolescent logic. Both the medical examiner and the county's utility expert reported that a storm-related electrical charge, coupled with the amped-up power Keenan rigged, was responsible for Sarah's death. They speculate she picked exactly the wrong moment to unplug those electrical units in Linc's workroom. The chemotherapy drugs she was taking for her breast cancer had weakened her heart and a lightning strike did the rest."

It took me a moment to let that sink in. My assumption about the letter I found in Sarah's desk had been accurate. She'd not only had cancer, but had started treatment without telling anyone. I'd be furious if Max did something like that without telling me. I hoped that Linc would recover from that news. Anger and grief so often went hand in hand.

Linc came back to the table wearing an apron and carrying another gray bin to load dishes. His eyes were red, but he stoically stopped to talk more before busing the tables.

"Forrest and Boots are helping me with another memorial for Sarah. Once the dust settles, Forrest is going to write up an agreement that will turn most of the back portion of the yard here over to the Plotters," he said, patting Boots on the shoulder. "We want to talk to an architect about converting the second floor of the carriage house that overlooks the gardens into a small apartment for security staff. This house is pretty big for just me, so we're going to see if there is an attractive way to convert the inside to shared housing or small apartments. I'd take one and rent the rest. Possibly at reduced market rates for foster kids who have aged out of the system. Like I said, I'm not making any decisions for a year, but working on the plans has been a positive step forward."

"So, what happened with the confusion over your mom's will?" I asked.

"We were both right about that," Boots said. "The only problem was that the will Mrs. Sinclair showed me was an earlier will. She later changed it without telling me—which she had every right to do."

Max had come in without my noticing and placed his hands on my shoulders in an echo of Linc's stance behind Boots. He reached forward and grabbed a clean teacup from the table, lifting it in a toast. "To new futures and happy endings."

"To Linc," I added. "You're going to need patience and persistence with the town council to push that plan through."

Linc shook his head. "I've got Boots to run interference."

Boots sat up straight, squared her shoulders, and smiled as if she were a little kid with a mischievous plan. She pounded her cane on the floor. "Damn straight."

Then she turned to me and scowled. "And as for you, missy: I hear you were snooping about the garden to see if I was running a teenaged crime ring."

I opened my mouth to speak, but no words came out. I flushed and stammered.

Boots burst out laughing and patted me on the shoulder. "It's okay, Maggie. I kind of liked being a crime lord, even if it was only in your imagination." She turned and winked at Linc. "Maybe we should consider it as a sideline if we find it's difficult to get funding for all our plans."

I was relieved Boots had forgiven me, but my embarrassment lingered. Now that I knew her better, the idea of her veering into lawlessness was ridiculous. To cover my confusion, I stood and began collecting dishes.

Linc sneezed explosively. He pulled a large red bandanna from his pocket, blew his nose loudly, then wiped his eyes.

"Allergies," he explained. "It's Sarah's cat, Jelly."

"We can take her for you," I said. "If she's making you sick, I mean. We all love her, including Belle, who decided that kitten is her puppy. While you were staying with us, she kept trying to carry Jelly around in her mouth."

Linc stuffed the bandanna back in his pocket. "No way," he said. "I'm getting allergy shots and have a full regimen of antihistamines and steroid drops. She's the last living reminder of Sarah, and she's staying with Newt and me."

I felt like applauding, but instead clapped Linc on the back. Everyone pitched in and we made fast work of the cleanup. Stephen and Jason moved to the front porch, hoping to watch the floats line up for the town's annual Festival of Lights parade.

When we were done, all I wanted to do was go home, curl up in front of the fire on the sofa with Max, and spend time with whichever teenagers were home for the evening. The high school band was performing in the parade, but David had insisted we stay home. He planned to go out for pizza with friends afterwards. One or both of us had attended all his performances earlier in the season, so we'd agreed with David's suggestion to skip this one.

In the car on the way home, Max tuned the radio to a station that was playing Tchaikovsky's *Nutcracker Suite*. "I love this time of year," I said. "When the holiday music still seems fresh and festive."

"Unlike late December, when it makes you grit your teeth and think of everything you have left to do," Max said, giving my arm a little nudge and laughing.

"Tess's party went well and we both handed out every business card we had. Now I just have to sit back and wait for the phone to ring."

"About that," said Max. "Connie called to say things are pretty slow in Stockton at this time of year. She wondered if you needed any help setting up Simplicity Itself here."

"That'd be wonderful," I said, yawning through my words. Connie had been my assistant in Stockton, and we'd worked out a deal for her to manage and eventually buy out the business there.

"Now all we have to do is figure out how to entertain twenty-four family members for Thanksgiving and Christmas. Piece of cake," said Max.

If I'd had any more energy, I'd probably have snarled at Max. Instead I asked, "Do you know any deserted islands where we could escape?"

"Seriously, Maggie. I think you need to focus on getting more help. Not overcommitting your time. I've been really worried about you. You're doing too much."

"But I need to return the favors I called in to make the holiday tea a success."

"Friends don't keep score."

"But friends helping friends is what life is all about. It makes the world go 'round."

"I thought that was love."

I rolled my eyes but smiled at him.

"Maggie," Max said, waiting until I looked him in the eye. "The flip side of the friends-helping-friends thing is remembering to ask for help when you need it. Before a small problem becomes a crisis."

"I've learned my lesson, honey. I promise."

"Of course, dear," Max said. But then he snorted, ruining the formal and dignified tone of his statement. "So, where does that leave your interest in murder investigations? They're becoming a habit with you."

"What are the odds of another murder happening in Orchard View? The town has recorded six violent deaths in the last twenty years, and three of them took place in the past four months. Orchard View should be safe for at least a decade, don't you think? Statistically speaking, I mean."

Max covered my hand with his and didn't answer as the car lurched over the potholes in our driveway. We'd made it back safely. Home again.

Be sure not to miss the first book in Mary Feliz's
Maggie McDonald Mystery series

ADDRESS TO DIE FOR

**For professional organizer Maggie McDonald, moving her
family into a new home should be the perfect organizational
challenge. But murder was definitely not on the to-do list . . .**

Maggie McDonald has a penchant for order that isn't confined to
her clients' closets, kitchens, and sock drawers. As she lays out her
plan to transfer her family to the hundred-year-old house her
husband, Max, has inherited in the hills above Silicon Valley, she
has every expectation for their new life to fall neatly into place. But
as the family bounces up the driveway of their new home, she's
shocked to discover the house's dilapidated condition. When her
husband finds the caretaker face-down in their new basement, it's
the detectives who end up moving in. What a mess! While the
investigation unravels and the family camps out in a barn, a killer
remains at large—exactly the sort of loose end Maggie can't help
but clean up . . .

Keep reading for a special look!

A Lyrical Underground e-book on sale now.

Chapter 1

When moving or traveling, pack last the things you'll
need first.

From the Notebook of Maggie McDonald
Simplicity Itself Organizing Services

Thursday, August 28, Morning

"Awesome! I bet it has bats!" My fourteen-year-old son, David, exploded from the car and mounted the steps of the old house three at a time. He peered through the grubby porch windows.

"Is it haunted?" Brian, my twelve-year-old, leaned into my side as we stood in the front yard. I eyed the dust motes cavorting in a light beam that had escaped the shrubs and overgrown trees surrounding the 100-year-old California Craftsman house. I put a reassuring hand on Brian's curly mop of hair. "I doubt it, honey." I hoped it was true.

I swallowed hard and watched my husband, Max, ease his long legs out of his Prius. Like my minivan, Max's car was overloaded. We'd packed both cars with everything too fragile to transport in the moving van. In among the breakables, our two kids, one golden retriever and two cats, we'd tucked picnic food, cleaning supplies, and sleeping bags.

Today was Thursday. The plan was simple. The movers would arrive tomorrow. Since Monday was Labor Day we'd have four days to get settled. The kids would start school on Tuesday, and Max would begin his first full day at the new job the same day. I was giving myself a month to focus solely on house and family. After that, I was determined to restart my career as a professional organizer.

Two minutes into the plan, it was unraveling.

"Max, didn't Aunt Kay's lawyer say the house was in turn-key condition? Is this the same house we looked at in February?" I stared at the weedy front yard, dusty porch, and drooping gutters. I wondered what we'd gotten ourselves into and what had happened to the spotless house and garden I'd last seen five months earlier.

Max's feet crunched dead leaves that covered ruts in the gravel drive. Belle, our two-year-old golden retriever, bounded to him.

"Hmm." Max tilted his head and squinted at the house. "His exact words were 'shines like a showpiece.'" He scratched his head. "A handyman was supposed to be coming a couple of times a week to fix things. The house looked perfect when I saw it in April."

Max picked up a dead branch from the walkway and swiped at a weedy flowerbed, beheading some wild carrots. "Needs a little work, doesn't it?" He took my hand and squeezed it gently.

"A little work? I'm not sure it's safe." I looked at the house again in professional terms, calculating how big a team I'd need to whip it into shape. At first glance, I could tell it wouldn't be easy. A film of silt covered everything, but that was normal for a dry August day in Northern California—nothing a hose, broom, and some window cleaner couldn't fix. But I counted three broken windows.

David poked his battered sneaker at a gaping hole in the floor of the porch—a hole that begged to break the leg of an absentminded new homeowner. I wanted to gather the kids, jump in the car, and hightail it back to our plain vanilla split-level in California's Central Valley. I was scared. Afraid of spiders, bats, and the huge to-do list this ancient house presented. I was even more terrified that Max and I had made a terrible decision and were in way over our heads.

Max put his hand on my shoulder—his calming gesture. "Maybe it's better on the inside and the problems are superficial. It was fine a few months ago. How bad could it have gotten? Let's wait, take a breath, and check things out before we panic."

That was Max. Always confident that things would work out. My approach was the opposite of his. I tried to anticipate problems and organize my way out of them.

I took a deep breath and pulled my shoulder-length hair into a ponytail. I should have checked the house out more recently myself. We'd peeked in the windows in February before we had the keys, and Max had done a walk-through in April. Both times, the house looked fine. After that, wrapping up Max's work, my business, and everything else had consumed every spare minute. Pressed for time, we assumed our earlier examinations of the property would suffice. It looked as if we'd been wrong, but there was nothing we could do about it now.

Today, my job was to move my family into this house and get started on our new life in Orchard View, a small town in the hills above Silicon Valley. Efficient organization is my passion and my profession, and I was eager to get started.

I clutched my binder filled with the phone numbers I'd need to set up the phone, Internet, cable, electricity, and gas. It held the kids' birth certificates and school records and my growing list of the things we needed to accomplish in the next few days. It was my security blanket.

"Honey, wait," I called to David, who tugged at the windows and searched for a way in. "Dad's got the key. Let's go in together."

Max patted the pockets of his rumpled jeans like a caricature of the absentminded professor he'd been until a few weeks ago. He held up the key, tied to a grubby cardboard tag with gray twine. The steps creaked as he joined David on the porch. Sidestepping the hole in the floorboards with a dance move worthy of Fred Astaire, he brandished the key and flung open the door, bowing low and waving his arm to invite us in. This house—Max's great-aunt Kay's home—featured large in stories from his childhood. He'd grown up here and loved every inch of the house, the grounds, and the surrounding countryside.

I squeezed past Max and peered up at the oak-beamed ceiling and the fireplace that dominated one end of the expansive front room. I hoped the skittering noises I heard were dry leaves and not mice. From Max's stories and from our earlier sneak peeks, I'd imagined the house with polished wood paneling and comfortable, welcoming rooms that were free of rodents and insects. I shivered. I hate spiders. One encounter with a web makes my face itch for a week—or a couple of minutes, at least.

I crossed my arms, gripping my elbows with my palms. This was the first room we'd seen. What lurked beyond? If the visible parts of the house were this neglected, what did that say about the parts we couldn't see, like the electricity and the plumbing? I needed a house inspector. I needed to find a hardware store. I needed my head examined.

"Max . . . honey? Didn't the title company require an inspection?"

"The lawyer said he'd be out of the office the rest of the week, but I'll call him. We'll straighten this out."

I took a deep breath to center myself and stall my runaway thoughts. We had to make this work. There was no going back. Max had left his job at the university in Stockton to take an upper-level management position in software engineering at Influx in Santa Clara. He'd worked part-time from home since wrapping up his teaching responsibilities in May.

This move was a dream Max and I had shared for ages: Getting away from Stockton. Leaving the university community where I'd lived all my life and Max had lived since his freshman year in college. Where my parents were part of the fabric of the university and everyone knew me and still thought of me as a child. Max wanted proof that his knowledge base wasn't ivory-tower nonsense and was valuable in the global technology marketplace.

Max grew up in Orchard View, a small town straddling the freeway between San Jose and San Francisco. He'd always wanted to go back. For years, his only relative had been his reclusive great aunt Kay. She'd died in her sleep just shy of her 100th birthday in February, and left the house and the rest of her estate to Max. At Silicon Valley property rates, the house, barn, and two acres of land backing up to an open space preserve were worth more than fifteen million dollars. Without Aunt Kay's generous savings we wouldn't have been able to afford the taxes, let alone the house.

As soon as Aunt Kay's house was officially ours, we'd put our Stockton house on the market. Max resigned his job at the university and I stopped taking on new clients. Once launched, the plan took on a life of its own. Our belongings were sardined into a moving van that would groan up the hill tomorrow.

I rubbed what I hoped was an imaginary spiderweb from my nose, turned to Max, and gave him the best smile I could muster.

"Are you going to introduce us to your dream house?" I said. The only time I'd been inside for any length of time had been years ago, before we were married. I'd been preoccupied with wedding plans and meeting Aunt Kay and barely spared the house a glance. After that, knowing how busy we were with kids and work, Aunt Kay had come to visit us. Before we knew it, years had passed and she'd moved to assisted living. A Stanford professor had rented for a while, but the house had stood empty for several years since then.

"I know this isn't what we expected, Maggie," Max said. "But it's got good bones."

"Even good bones get broken," I muttered under my breath. I tried to drum up something more positive to say to Max. Tried and failed. I sneezed. The house was stuffy, dusty, and smelled as though a squirrel, rat, or bird had died somewhere. I crossed the room, unlocked a window, and struggled to push up the sash. Max helped open the rest of the many windows and a pleasant breeze wafted into the room. Chalk one up for old houses. In the absence of air-conditioning they relied on thick walls, graceful porches, and cross-ventilation that worked whether we had electricity or not.

"Mom, Mom, Mom," called Brian, rubbing at the tiles on the fireplace, his hands and face covered in greasy soot. "There are knights!" Nearly a teenager, he was still 85 percent small boy.

"Nights?"

"Knights! With lances! On horses! Fighting!"

Max dashed across the room, knelt next to Brian, and rubbed at the copper tiles himself. Sure enough, armored knights on horseback charged full-tilt across the top of the fireplace.

"I'd forgotten about these guys," Max said. "Aren't they great? In the firelight, it can look like they're moving."

Brian beamed at Max and Max grinned back. I knew that if there were knights on the fireplace, the house undoubtedly had other hidden treasures, and I'd need a lance and armor of my own to get anyone out of here tonight.

Belle barked in the back of the house. Her insistent, needing-to-go-out bark. I remembered the cats in their carriers in the car had similar needs.

"Brian, can you find a room upstairs where we can get the cats settled?"

Brian leapt up from the floor and wiped his hands on his jeans, smearing black handprints the length of his thighs. With feet huge like a growing puppy's, he clomped up the stairs to join his older brother. David, running from room to room over our heads, sounded as though he'd invited a herd of elephants to help him explore.

"This is going to be my room," David called down the stairs. "It's got its own fireplace. How much you wanna bet it's got bats?"

I looked at Max, still gazing at the knights. I could tell that he wanted to show me the world that encompassed his childhood dreams, but we had a ton of work to do.

"Max, can you check on the electricity? And see if we've got hot water or any water at all? I need to let Belle out and I want to clean at least one room to sleep in."

"Yes, m'lady," said Max, still inhabiting the world of Camelot. "I'll see if I can round up the knights-errant and arm them with brooms, mops, and paper towels."

"I brought some of that stuff in the car," I said. "I think it's close to the top layer. Don't bring anything else inside until we've got a clean place to put it down."

Finding my way through the gloom to the back of the house, I opened windows as I went. I felt overwhelmed. Fixing up this house would be the largest project I'd ever undertaken, and the condition of the house had shaken my confidence in my ability to get it all done. My Stockton organizing business had been busy, but my projects were small—bringing order to the offices of absentminded professors. They were nothing like this house with its dignified historical significance and rapidly expanding list of renovations.

The dining room had nice windows, a built-in sideboard and china cabinets, and a long oval table surrounded by a dozen chairs. To my right was a swinging door that I expected led to the kitchen. I pushed the door, which opened halfway and stopped. My forehead wrinkled and my mind scurried in wild directions as I imagined what I might find on the other side of the door.

Get a grip, Maggie! You've watched too many episodes of *Masterpiece Mystery*. I peered around the door, relieved to find an innocent pile of old newspapers. I'd heard they were good for cleaning windows, so we were set if we ran out of paper towels. I was working hard to stay positive. As soon as I'd scooted the newspapers out of the way, the door swung open into a narrow pantry connecting the dining room to the kitchen. Each wall was lined with cupboards and a long counter. I'd dreamed of having a room like this for projects and homework and storage. No one designed houses like this anymore.

The kitchen was well lit with windows over the sink and across the south wall, opening the room up to the vista of a sloping lawn, an old red barn, a creek, and golden rolling hills. The gnarled trunks of coastal oaks dotted the hillside. The view was drop-dead gorgeous. Soothing. A red-tailed hawk soared and glided on thermals. A breeze started at the house and moved downhill across the grass, rippling it like someone shaking out a silken roll of fabric. No wonder Max loved this place.

Belle barked sharply. I unlocked the back door and pulled at the knob. The door didn't budge. I braced my feet and pulled, praying that the knob wouldn't come off in my hand and send me sailing across the room. The door screeched open as a jagged piece of flashing caught on the metal threshold. I added *Get back door to fit* to my growing mental list. But I pushed the list away for a moment and stood on the covered back porch, imagining bringing my coffee out here in the mornings and sitting with a blanket on a rocking chair while watching Belle explore. I had no rocking chair, blanket, coffee, or even a mug, but I enjoyed my delusional moment.

Belle raced through the tall grass, invisible except for her tail. I turned and went back into the house, enjoying the sound the wooden screen door made as it banged against its frame. It was an old-fashioned sound, straight out of *The Waltons*.

I pushed an early twentieth-century two-button switch on the wall and waited. Nothing. I pushed it twice more, whispering: "Please." It was a hope, prayer, or incantation, but I wasn't sure which.

"Max . . . honey? Any luck with the electricity?" I tried not to panic. The electricity was probably fine. This light was the first I'd tried to switch on. It might have a burned-out bulb or be linked to a fuse that had blown.

I'd grown up as the daughter of professors in a house near the university campus. If we wanted electricity and didn't have it, we called maintenance. I knew how to change a lightbulb, but my electrical expertise dwindled to nothing after that.

Plumbing wasn't my strong suit, either. I turned the cold-water knob over the white farmhouse sink. Nothing. My shoulders drooped. I stepped away, rubbed the small of my back, and jumped as the faucet jerked with a bang. Swampy gurgles that sounded as though the house had severe intestinal issues erupted from the tap, and dark-brown water poured into the sink. Just when I was starting to think there was something about the innards of old houses that I didn't want to know, Max stuck his head through the pantry doorway. He carried a ladder and a bucket filled with lightbulbs.

"Oh, good," he said. "Leave the water running for a few moments until it clears. It's a bit rusty, but the plumbing seems solid. I'm taking the ladder up to David. He's going to check for burned-out bulbs and replace them."

"Good work. What's Brian up to?"

"He's getting the cats and their litter box organized."

I followed Max up the stairs and was delighted to find a built-in window seat and cupboard on the landing. Above the seat, the top of the windows held stained glass. Late-morning sun shining through the glass wisteria vines spilled lavender and green splotches of light on the stairs. The house was doing its best to charm each one of us.

As we turned the corner at the top of the stairs, Brian crested the top of a second staircase, lugging a cat carrier in each hand. Back stairs? Just like *Downton Abbey*! I took one of the cat carriers as Brian held it out. Holmes, our grumpiest cat, growled his disgust with the lurching trip from the car.

"We'll get you settled as soon as we can, Holmes," I said, trying to comfort the four-year-old orange tabby. "Brian found you a great hidey-hole."

"I did!" Brian said. "I swept out the closet and put Dad's old sweatshirt on a shelf in there."

I knew that Holmes's partner, Watson, would be the first to explore. A small female, Watson had large splotches of white in her orange coat, including one on her face that made her look as though she'd had a comic encounter with a dish of whipped cream.

It would take time, but if we kept the cats contained to one room for a few days, I was sure they'd settle in. I hoped the same would be true for the rest of us.

Max carried the ladder and bucket down the hall. "David? I've got the ladder so you can get started on the bulbs."

"In here, Dad," David called from the bathroom at the end of the hall, his voice echoing off the tiles. "Look at this toilet! The tank is way up there and you pull this chain to make it flush. Gravity! How cool is that?"

David perched on the curved edge of a voluminous claw-foot tub. He stepped from tub, to sink, to toilet, and jumped down.

"This house is great, Mom," David said, beaming. "There's a desk that turns into a bed—the bed comes out of the wall—in the next room."

David would be starting high school next week. He'd been reluctant to leave his Stockton friends and seemed wary of starting the next chapter of his school career without them. His enthusiasm for the new house was a welcome change from his sadness over leaving the old one.

Holmes howled and the normally quiet Watson joined in. I put a hand on David's shoulder to stem the flow of questions, surprised anew at how fast he was growing. He was almost as tall as I was. I straightened my posture and turned to Brian.

"Did you get their litter box set up?"

Brian nodded.

"Food? Water?"

"Yup."

"And the closet is secure?" I didn't want the cats escaping and freaking out before they'd had a chance to learn they were home.

Brian nodded and rolled his eyes like the young teen he was becoming. "All checked out and ready to go, Mom."

"Perfect, go for it, then."

He disappeared into the bedroom with the two complaining cats and shut the door behind him.

Max's new work phone rang with the doom-filled Darth Vader's theme. Apparently we had cell service.

"Hey, Jim," Max answered the phone. "Yup, just arrived, thanks. Really? You're kidding, right?" Max looked at me, covered the phone, and mouthed, "Be right back." He walked down the hall with his head down.

Uh-oh. Something was wrong.

I turned to David. "Can you open that window? It's still a bit whiffy in here."

The window screeched and stuck, but David muscled it up.

"Can you flick that light switch?" he said. "This should be working."

I pushed the old-fashioned two-button switch. Nothing. I hoped the problem was as simple as a few blown fuses.

From the bathroom, I could hear tension in Max's voice as he paced in the hall and talked to his new boss on the phone. "Okay, Jim, I see. Let me talk to Maggie and I'll call you back . . . yes, tomorrow . . . that's right . . ." Max looked up at me, grimaced with a *What can ya do?* look, and ended the call.

I lifted my eyebrows.

"I'll fill you in later," Max said. "I need to check out the fuses and see if we can get some lights on in here before it gets dark."

I headed down the back staircase, delighted to find that it ended in the kitchen. I assumed the narrow, utilitarian stairs had been planned as a way for children and staff to go about their business without disturbing the serenity of the living room. To me they seemed as much fun as full of possibility as a secret passage to Narnia. I was a self-proclaimed gluttonous reader, prone to quoting from both children's and adult literature without warning.

My next step was lunch. It was time to grab the cooler from the car and dust off the back porch to set up our sandwiches and drinks. Belle joined me on the walk to the car. She butted her nose into the back of my knee. I scratched behind her ears.

I grabbed the cooler from the backseat with my right hand, tucked a nested set of pet dishes under my arm, and grabbed a bucket of cleaning supplies with my left hand. Loaded up, I headed back to the house.

"Maggie!" Max called from somewhere inside the house. I picked up the bucket and struggled to open the kitchen door, giving it my shoulder and some muscle.

"I've got lunch," I called to Max, thinking he must be in the next room. "There's a cold beer with your name on it."

"Maggie!" Max said, clomping up the basement stairs. He flung open the door at the top of the stairs and a dreadful smell wafted up. I gagged as Max yelled "Call 9-1-1!"

Mary Feliz, author of the Maggie McDonald Mystery series, has lived in five states and two countries but calls Silicon Valley home. Traveling to other areas of the United States, she's frequently reminded that what seems normal in the high-tech heartland can seem decidedly odd to the rest of the country. A big fan of irony, serendipity, diversity, and quirky intelligence tempered with gentle humor, Mary strives to bring these elements into her writing, although her characters tend to take things to a whole new level. She's a member of Sisters in Crime, Mystery Writers of America, and National Association of Professional Organizers. Mary is a Smith College graduate with a degree in Sociology. She lives in Northern California with her husband, near the homes of their two adult offspring. Visit Mary online at MaryFeliz.com, or follow her on Twitter @MaryFelizAuthor.

45061357R00146

Made in the USA
San Bernardino, CA
30 January 2017